HIDDEN IDENTITY

Ralph Alcock

AuthorHouse™ UK Ltd.
500 Avebury Boulevard
Central Milton Keynes, MK9 2BE
www.authorhouse.co.uk
Phone: 08001974150

This book is a work of fiction. People, places, events, and situations are the product of the author's imagination. Any resemblance to actual persons, living or dead, or historical events, is purely coincidental.

© 2010 Ralph Alcock. All rights reserved.

No part of this book may be reproduced, stored in a retrieval system, or transmitted by any means without the written permission of the author.

First published by AuthorHouse 4/14/2010

ISBN: 978-1-4490-5509-7 (sc)

Printed in the United States of America
Bloomington, Indiana

This book is printed on acid-free paper.

For my sons; Rory, Antony and James

Thank you Jane and Trudie

Chapter 1

Instructions

Merriden, Western Australia. April, 1975.

This was an unusually cold and damp day with a strong southerly wind carrying low winter temperatures to the pale-yellow stubbled wheat fields in Western Australia. A steel-gray sky was smeared with streaks of low dark cloud, and a steady soft rain had transformed the choking red dust of summer to a wet, slick and shiny surface. Several large earth-moving machines were at work, skating on this slippery rink with an ease and grace that belied their size. They were being used to remove the old dam wall that had been built some forty years earlier. The Environment Agency had decided riparian rights must be restored which meant demolishing several small farm dams to allow streams to follow their natural paths.

The earth movers extended their hydraulic muscles and retracted their giant steel arms with precision and timing, gouging earth into fist-like buckets and spewing their contents into the waiting trucks. As they powered across the slick surface, they created waves of soft mud and their powerful spinning wheels flung long arcing plumes of red dirt in the air, some of which splattered onto the metalwork and cabs of adjacent machines. The cab windscreens became rendered with red glaze as wiper blades blinked slowly and monotonously across the glass.

The driver of a large yellow CAT digger caught the foreman waving frantically at him from the corner of his eye as he was just about to nudge his vehicle forward to scoop another layer of mud and clay from the base of the old dam they were slowly dismantling. He waved to acknowledge the signal to cut his engine and pulled on the red fuel cut-off knob, holding it out until the giant diesel spluttered and died from lack of fuel. The foreman ran towards him, shouting excitedly and waving his arms in the direction of the dam wall.

The driver slid back the cab window.

"What's up Wally? Why the panic?"

"There's a body buried down there! It's in the clay you just uncovered!" Wally waved excitedly in the direction of the dam wall. The driver flicked open the cab door and jumped down, ignoring the three metal steps. He landed with a squelching sound into the soft mud and clay. He followed the foreman round to the digger's scoop bucket. The clay sucked at their heels. They clutched at each other like novice skaters grasping for support while the incessant rain pooled in the depressions their boots created.

A section of the old dam wall had fallen away revealing an upper torso. The rest of the body was trapped in the mud. The visible part of the body was upright with one of its arms thrust deep into the adjacent dam wall as if not daring to let go.

"Jesus Christ!" shouted the driver. "What the …" He stared wide-eyed through the driving rain. "It looks bloody weird, standing up like that."

"It frightened the shit out of me," stuttered Wally. "I'm still shaking. It just appeared when you lifted that last bucket." The two men stood transfixed at the sight of the statue-like body, red mud weeping from its shoulders and slipping down the sleeve of the upper arm. They both jumped nervously when a chunk of half-dried clay suddenly cracked open and slid off the corpse, revealing more of the jacket and shirt on the body.

"What the hell's happening! This thing's giving me the creeps," breathed Wally. The driver nodded, his eyes still fixed on the body in a frightened stare.

Two other workers drove towards them in a jeep, skidding to a halt near the two startled men and their grim discovery.

They both stood up in their seats and shouted.

"What's going on over there?"

"There's a fucking body stuck in the clay," screamed Wally, his voice uncharacteristically high-pitched and shrill. He breathed hard and forced himself to gulp air into his tight chest. "You fellas drive into town," he shouted as loudly as he could. "Get the police out here—and a get a bloody move on!" But for his panic, his normally gruff voice would have been lost to the wind and the rain.

* * *

The London Train. Friday 12th May, 1975.

I turned away from reading the crumpled piece of beige paper and stared out of the window of the train as it passed high above the River Trent. I had read, and re-read, the polite and tantalizing request that had come by special delivery. It was more of an instruction than a request; an instruction I felt I couldn't possibly ignore. I slid the silky paper with its embossed heading from the lined envelope, even though I could now recite its contents from memory. And besides, I liked the way it slipped effortlessly from the envelope, even though it was now creased in several places and stained with my fingerprints.

The letter was from a firm of solicitors in London.

5th May, 1975

Dear Mr. Jackson,

I have been instructed by my client to request that you visit my office to receive details that will be of considerable interest to you and which are of a financial nature. I am not, however, at liberty to divulge their content by letter.

You are requested to visit my office at 3:00pm on Friday, May 12th in order that I can discuss these matters with you at length.

Please contact my office if you are unable to make this scheduled appointment. I hope that you will allow me to be of service to your family.

Yours sincerely,

Mr. G. A. Leonard. (Wilcox, Vietch and Leonard)

Just as much as the tantalizing suggestion of financial gain, it was the last line that intrigued me. I hadn't many family members to speak of and certainly none of them could afford to use such a reputable (and presumably expensive) firm of London solicitors such as Wilcox,

Vietch and Leonard. I slipped the letter back into its tissue-lined sheath and returned the envelope to the inside jacket pocket. I instinctively patted the outside of my jacket for reassurance. I had begun to develop a habit of checking and re-checking my possessions as if convinced they might inadvertently slip out of my pockets or be pilfered by a light gossamer hand. I kept reaching into my jacket just to finger the edge of the envelope, despite the fact I could feel its presence through the cloth of my jacket.

I wondered, of course, who or what was associated with the letter. I speculated endlessly in my mind on who it could be and had fanciful speculations on what it might mean, like an eager child going to bed on Christmas Eve. The letter served as very tangible evidence in support of my expectations, a bit like the weight of an orange lodged in the toe of a Christmas stocking.

I peered round at the other passengers, looking for some hint that would trigger a connection in my memory and remind me of some person or event that might in someway be connected with the letter. It only served to remind me of what a stoic and reserved lot we are when traveling on public transport. Only a group of school children, boasting loudly and sniggering at some joke, seemed blissfully unaware of the rules of travel behaviour that the rest of us passengers insisted in maintaining. Their long legs straddled the aisle, heads bobbed up over their seats, bags were tossed carelessly into the corner of their space, feet kicked restlessly at the seats, and arms stretched in wide arcs across the window. I watched their carefree antics with a degree of amusement, perhaps even envy. Theirs was a journey marked by the simple passage of time; for me, it was one of distance and expediency.

I did find myself smiling vacantly into the eyes of a slim girl sitting opposite. They were blue and bright, hooded by eyelashes thick with black mascara. I remember blushing involuntarily and lowering my head to break the immediate embarrassment of her gaze; one of those rules to be included in the compendium of travel etiquette.

Two girls in poorly fitting blue and white uniforms had succeeded in maneuvering a trolley along the aisle. It was sparingly adorned with plastic wrapped sandwiches, soft drink cans and bags of crisps.

"Black or white?" asked one of the attendants, as if there were some exotic and selective difference between the offerings. The scalding hot brown liquid was poured, absent-mindedly, into a plastic cup, capped with a plastic lid, and served with two micro-urns of long-life dairy cream. I struggled with the plastic lid on the coffee that had become seemingly vulcanized to the rest of the cup. The jolting of the train only exacerbated my premonition of hot coffee being launched over my crotch. With a final daring pull, I succeeded in removing the lid, spilling only a few rivulets of liquid over my fingers and onto the table. I tugged at the lid of the dairy creamer with my teeth, pulling with my left hand to separate the micro-urn from its covering. I sloshed the lot into my coffee and sat with poised arms to absorb the train's vibrations. With some satisfaction, I lowered my head to the cup and slurped a frothy morsel of scolding liquid. My eyes lifted over the rim of my cup to notice my slim companion sipping her coffee as she leaned rather elegantly against the folds of the ill-designed seats.

"Mine's hot," I declared. She gave a half smile – or was it a smirk – and squinted through her mascared lashes. They shuttered out the light, dimming the intensity of her eyes. I suddenly felt uncomfortable, as if I had transgressed by daring to engage in conversation.

The crackle of the tannoy was immediately followed by an announcement that breakfast was being served in the dining car. I wanted breakfast anyway. I placed my near full cup of coffee on the floor and strode off in the direction of the dining car - just managing to mutter "breakfast" to my rather sultry companion.

I knew that British Rail's full breakfast was one of the true remaining bargains. I slipped into the oversized first-class dining seat and felt the warmth of its soft cushioning wrap around my back and thighs. Even the headrest seemed comfortably placed. The air was filled with the mouthwatering whiff of bacon, the delicate hint of tea and the distinctive aroma of coffee all tinged with an acrid tang from the curls of smoke that rose from between stained fingers.

The white, starched tablecloth was in stark contrast to the mottled, once-white and ill-fitting shirt worn by the waiter. It was an 'it'll do' uniform worn by a 'he'll do' employee. Still, I was very pleased with myself. An interesting letter in my pocket, a very comfortable seat, and the prospect of a more than adequate breakfast. My fingers flicked again at the edge of the envelope tucked into the inner pocket of my jacket. It gave me the reassurance I craved.

The dining car was fairly full with its usual contingent of professionals, young and old. Some were brash and loud. One in particular was making himself known by first rebuking the poor waiter for not serving him quickly enough, and then calling for the head steward when it looked as if the waiter might prefer to play to another section of the dining car. This entertainment provided a delightful interlude that nicely filled the time between the supply of coffee in an elegant miniature coffee pot and the arrival of my breakfast order. The breakfast trays whisked by and I had all but given up hope until one was slipped unceremoniously onto my table. The particularly loud executive was now complaining to the head waiter about the lack of service, and the undeniable fact that he had paid for a first class ticket and that he expected to receive service commensurate with his level of investment. This line of reasoning was lost on the steward; but I couldn't help but feel that it was directed at those like me, who had paid for a second class seat and who now enjoyed the relative luxury of the first class dining car.

I picked steadily at my breakfast, my thoughts never far away from the contents of the letter I had received. I must be mad, I thought, dashing off to London, losing a day's pay, spending money I didn't have on what was probably a fruitless exercise. It was a mistake, I knew that. Some administrative error that had me confused with someone else, someone of the same name; how many Joe Jacksons are there I wondered, thousands? Yes, thousands. But I couldn't just ignore it, could I? It had gnawed at me ever since the contents of the letter had registered in my brain. I had gone from initial astonishment when I first read the letter, to incredulity. I had developed an insatiable longing to know what it all meant and where it might lead. I had racked my brain so many times thinking about the content of the letter that it hurt; but it was a pain I couldn't get enough of. It was a pain that held possibilities.

The train was rapidly approaching King's Cross Station. Open fields gave way to concrete lined housing estates, and they, in turn, yielded to old and blackened red-brick factories with their classic pitched roofs and glassed sections. Some of the factories had chimneys; tall, erect and redundant. They stood like monuments to an age of coal and dirt. I could still see pulleys and dangling belts in some of the factories that had once driven rows of lathes. I imagined the workers with grease-stained bib overalls leaning over the revolving steel shafts, standing on wooden platforms, their boots partially covered by a metallic bed of shiny spiral swarf.

I moved quickly back through the train to retrieve my coat and bag. I grabbed my things and stepped off the train just as it came to a halt. I wanted to beat the rush to the taxi stand if I could. The queue was small and a succession of black, imperial machines ensured that the waiting time would be short. My destination was to a small set of offices just behind the National Gallery, near Trafalgar Square. The taxi driver swung his machine to a stop with a screech of the brakes, leaning back with his hand outside the driver's window to release the rear door catch.

"Where to?" he asked, as he flicked off the 'hire' sign and raced off toward the exit ramp just as I was stepping into the cab. I stumbled over my bag and pitched myself onto the ribbed leather seat.

"Wilcox, Vietch and Leonard..."

"Solicitors they are," interjected the driver.

"Yes," I said, leaning uncomfortably forward to make myself heard through the window grating, grateful that he at least knew of them.

"Back of Trafalgar they are."

"That's the firm," I meekly replied and sat back in the seat, suddenly exhausted by the journey and the strain of this conversation.

After ten minutes or so the taxi swung into a narrow street and screeched to a sudden halt.

"This is the place, Gov. Good little café that, if you need food. I goes there meself." He nodded in the direction of a tiny café on the other side of the street. He snapped the note I gave him in his fingers and flipped it from side to side. Satisfied as to its authenticity, he spread the change coins in his palm and picked them out one by one waiting for me to call a halt to the procedure. I left a few coins in his hand and reached for the door catch.

"Thanks," I said, glancing at the café's faded red door as I climbed out on to the street. There was a brass rectangular name plate on the door listing the solicitors and their partners etched one beneath the other. I pushed the buzzer next to the brass plate. The door's electronic latch released and maintained a steady buzz as I pushed open the heavy door. I peered down the corridor and edged my way forward to an office with a reception desk. I announced myself to the secretary.

"Do come in," she instructed. "Do you have an appointment?" She sat very erect and had dark hair pulled tightly into a bun at the back of her head. She reminded me of my school music teacher – an instructor, a very serious-minded instructor. And there were other similarities: the perfume, which might have been hairspray; the voice, with its polished diction and affected articulation and the look, imperious and commanding.

"Yes," I replied, "I'm here to meet Mr. Leonard." She ran the polished nail of her forefinger down her desk diary.

"Ah yes, you must be Mr. Jackson. Mr. Leonard is expecting you."

She buzzed through to the inner sanctum.

Chapter 2
UNCLE CHARLIE

The secretary ushered me down a corridor to an office on the left. She rapped on the heavy mottled glass and without waiting for an answer, opened the door and directed me to enter. The office was dimly lit. Window blinds were drawn and the only light came from an ornate desk lamp. It was heavily diffused by a dark green lamp-shade, its muted light casting a viridian hue on the ornate inkwell and pen set, which was carefully positioned at the front of the desk. I blinked several times in trying to adjust my eyes to the lighting. Pleasantries were few, only a thin, bony hand stretching towards me from the shadows gave any sense of there being another person in the room.

"Take a seat," commanded a voice from the other side of the large desk. I positioned myself on one of the neatly arranged high-backed leather chairs that faced the desk. It was very uncomfortable, lacking in any ergonomic considerations, and had a very tall and narrow back like a poor imitation of a Rennie MacKintosh design. The voice behind the desk introduced its owner as Mr. Geoffrey Leonard of Wilcox, Veitch and Leonard, who were, I was informed by Mr. Leonard, a well-respected firm of solicitors. The top of Mr. Leonard's silvered hair shone with a green tinge, but half his face was in shadow, and I had to concentrate to follow the conversation. I noticed the prominent vein pulsing on the side of his forehead. It stood out when he inclined his head towards the top of the desk. The light underlined his vein and cast a rippled shadow along its edge. He coughed as if gathering attention. Perhaps he noticed me staring at his forehead.

"A close family connection has been taken seriously ill..."

My brain was frantically scanning my immediate family, bringing each to mind in turn.

"He wishes you to visit him in the United States. He has instructed me to give you the necessary funds for your trip to Washington." Mr. Leonard paused from his monotone deliverance and I seized my opportunity.

"But I don't have a relative living in the United States..."

"Quite right, quite right," interjected Mr. Leonard, "however, the gentleman is a very close friend of the family, I assure you. His name is Mr. George Archer. I believe you last met him some time ago at your mother's funeral."

I listened with intense interest. It was then ten years since my mother had died. Her death had been so sudden. It had seemed like a terrible rumour that wouldn't go away. It remained just that, an unpleasant rumour, until, three days later when her mahogany coffin was lowered into the ground.

I had been asked to throw the first shovel of dirt on to the coffin. I remembered standing with the spade in my hand and looking first at the shiny surface of the shovel, bright, gleaming and new; and then at the dirt in front of me, dark, damp and sinister; and then at the coffin with its shapely lid and elegant brass handles. I must have stood looking at each of them in turn for some time. I remember one of the funeral attendants gently easing the spade from my grasp. I simply couldn't stand the thought of burying my mother, covering her with dirt and all it contained. It seemed such a claustrophobic end; entombed and buried, and left to slowly decay and rot. I wished she'd been cremated. That way there would be no rotting flesh, no maggoty body; only ash, good clean ash. And the funeral pyre would have been a celebratory send-off letting her spirit soar into the ether. And her remains would have been always there, in one place, in an urn, not spread over half the graveyard by parasitic worms. I made a mental note to make sure I stipulated being cremated when I made my will.

In those first few years after her death, I had those occasional moments of absent-mindedness that seem inexplicable. I would sometimes come home and fling the door wide open, calling out just as I had done when she was alive, my voice echoing in the empty hallway. At other times I found myself whistling along the path to the front door and would then remember, with a suddenness that seemed to bring me to the brink of tears, that she had died. I had helped bury her.

Mr. Leonard had, in invoking thoughts of my mother, reactivated those dormant cells of my memory that had embedded themselves in the protection afforded by the slippage of time. They were now brought to the surface; fresh, raw and exposed, determined to remind me of the bitter experience that I had so carefully secreted. I had forgotten, of course, that the key to these memories was not mine to control, not entirely. I felt a lump gather in my throat.

Yes, I remembered George Archer. A tall, slim, man; a few years younger than my mother. He had appeared at her funeral unexpectedly. He brought an expensive wreath and took care of all the funeral expenses, as I found out sometime later. I remember him introducing himself as a friend of my mother, but I couldn't recollect meeting him previously. I did recall finding him one day wandering all over the house. I followed him for a while, not meaning to initially, but I found myself following in his trail as he went from room to room, apparently taking time to absorb the atmosphere of the place, and seemingly oblivious to my presence. I hadn't tried to intervene. I had liked the man in some strange way, despite the brevity of our meeting. Perhaps it was because he seemed so genuinely upset about my mother's death? But that was all several years ago. Why should I now go rushing off to the bedside of some stranger with an apparent morbid penchant for delivering expensive wreaths and mourning the dead?

"Mr. Archer was also a close friend of your Uncle Charles," continued Mr. Leonard, as if reading my train of thought, "they had business interests in Australia and were, I believe, friends in their early years." Recollections eased their way into my mind. It was like thumbing through old brown, faded, and sepia-coloured, photographs.

Uncle Charlie, I had never heard him referred to as "Charles", had been somewhat of a mystery man. I remembered mother receiving letters from Charlie when I was a schoolboy. Sometimes, Charlie sent picture postcards of Australia, and occasionally a letter with money pinned to the corner.

Charlie and Maggie, my mother, had been very close as children. When Charlie was just a raw youngster of twelve years old, he had come home from school to find their mother lying on the cold hard kitchen floor, her body twitching and convulsing. She was suffering a massive cerebral hemorrhage. She had clutched at the helpless Charlie, unable to cry out with the searing, anguishing pain that fluxed through her left side. Her left arm kept stiffening and pointing toward the ceiling. Charlie was convinced she was pointing toward heaven. He knew she was about to die. With a sudden violent twitch, her whole body stiffened. Her left leg and arm gave one final spasm as she collapsed into death. Tears streamed down Charlie's face. The sight of blood oozing from his mother's mouth and from behind her eyeballs caused him to become violently sick. He retched over his dead mother's body.

Charlie and Maggie were left to fend for themselves. Charlie regarded his older sister as a surrogate mother, a role that Maggie filled to perfection. Charlie was always in trouble. He skipped school whenever he could and shirked work if he found it at all disagreeable, which, as it turned out, it usually seemed to be. But he was fun to be with and fun to listen to. He always seemed to have a flood of tales, which were, in his early years, about evading teachers, splashing tar on gate posts and door handles, or spilling water on steps in winter. Then he started to get into more serious exploits. He roared around the countryside on a motorbike, and operated an informal taxi service for those who got slightly more intoxicated than he usually was. He was easy prey for the loitering laggards who were only too keen to admit a new member to their informal club and encourage wild exploits from their latest recruit, which would be retold and embellished for the pub fraternity.

Charlie seemed to revel in his reputation as a maverick, not only embracing the wildest of suggestions thrown in his direction, but also enhancing his reputation by scowling and muttering at local policemen in an intimidating manner, and intentionally cursing and spitting on the ground in front of youngsters so that they would run home part in fear and part in admiration of wild Charlie.

My own mother, Maggie, found it difficult to establish a relationship outside the family. She married because she was expected to. She looked for someone with Charlie's charm, but only found disappointments in her quest. I think she eventually found contentment in her marriage to my father. His easy going ways made him unobtrusive and quiet; so different from her own volatile, easily angered and frustrated father. She had married comfort, the sort of comfort you find in a favourite armchair. Always there, always in place. Solid and respectable, even a trifle dull. She had always found him easy to live with, and it got even easier with time.

Charlie left home the year she was married. He was seventeen years old when he set sail for Australia. He didn't say a word to anyone. It was a year later before Charlie contacted the family. He sent a letter to my mother, to be passed on to the rest of the family, with a long list of his exploits as if they excused, in some way, his sudden departure.

Charlie worked his way on a tramp steamer, calling at ports in Portugal, North Africa, and eventually reaching Durban, in South Africa. The steamer needed fairly extensive repairs in Durban. The skipper informed Charlie it would be about eight weeks before she was ready. He offered Charlie the option of looking for another vessel. Charlie, however, decided to use this as an opportunity to see something of the country.

He took a job the next day helping on roads and dams with a construction firm. He enjoyed the work and toyed with idea of staying in South Africa. He'd learnt quite a bit about the construction methods in the short time he was there. But his heart was set on Australia, so when he heard that the steamer was ready to sail, he rejoined the ship and set off on the final leg of his journey, finally reaching Freemantle in Western Australia.

Charlie was a bit of a hothead. He was quick to lose his temper. For a young man from England alone in a new country, this characteristic was unfortunate. Freemantle was a tough port and Aussies regarded as fair game a fresh faced 'limey' who was easily goaded into a fight. After several skirmishes, one of which resulted in his spending overnight in the Freemantle goal, Charlie was encouraged to move away from the bright lights and look for work in a less populated part of the country. He found what he was looking for in a classified section of the *West Australian* newspaper. A wheat and sheep farm near York was looking for a hand to work with stock. Charlie wired to the post office and waited for a reply. To his surprise, the return message asked him to come out on the next train from Perth. He would be met at the station in Northam.

The train had a single carriage for passengers, right next to the guard's van. The rest of the train carried goods and livestock, mostly cattle. Watery dung oozed from the bottom of the cattle cars, spilling on to the gravel beside the track. Charlie found the smell quite intense but not unduly unpleasant. The passenger carriage had wooden bench seats and an overhead luggage rack for small cases. Larger luggage was slung onto the roof of the carriage. Charlie had a sailor's sack stuffed with his clothes, a small wooden box containing his personal items and two pairs of work boots. He heaved the sack toward the guard on the carriage roof.

"You getting off at Northam?" Charlie nodded and climbed aboard, leaving the guard to arrange the baggage and secure it with rope to the eyelets fixed around the roof.

The train moved out from the Perth Station at such an incredibly slow pace that Charlie had to stare out of the window to convince himself it was actually moving. Eventually it picked up a little speed as it climbed out of Perth. It was a long steady climb that found them passing a series of smallholdings with small acreages, mostly of fruit trees and grapevines. They eventually reached a plateau where the land leveled out and the train snaked along the river Avon, passing through a thick area of bush, eucalyptus trees, large white gum trees, and black stumps with green, fern-like, leaves. After half-an-hour or so, the train left the small fruit farms and the inhospitable bush and scrub. They were now up on the plain that formed the wheat belt. Charlie was transfixed by the vast sweeping fields, which were marked out by flimsy-looking barbed wire fences strung between their huge corner posts, and dotted with rusty towered windmills. An occasional thin lines of trees snaked along the edges of a river bed. The train passed a road grader, its angled blade skimming the red dirt into a swath on the verge and creating a shower of sparks as it bounced off the embedded rocks. The driver of the grader waved at the train as if regarding it as a passing friend. Charlie instinctively waved back and watched as the grader slowly slid from view.

The train's whistle shrieked loudly as it approached Northam station. The station consisted simply of a single wooden platform and a small wooden shack with a stove pipe sticking up through the roof. Charlie, and a couple of other passengers, stepped onto the platform while the guard scrambled onto the roof looking for their bags.

"That's mine," shouted Charlie, "that canvas bag..." It was hurled towards him with a flamboyant toss.

"Steady," shouted Charlie, "it's got valuables in there."

The guard grinned. "Looks more like a grain sack!" he shouted as he slid expertly down his ladder leading to the guard's van.

Charlie watched the train slowly inch away from the platform. He liked the smell, the noise, and the shear mechanical power of these big steam trains. He let the steam from the engine engulf him as the cast iron wheels screeched for purchase on the rails and the carriages nudged back and forward at one another like kids in the school assembly hall. The rolling stock settled as the train picked up speed pulling along its caboose. The guard stood at the rear and waved from the back of his van leaving Charlie standing alone on the platform.

A horse and buggy had been standing quietly on the other side of the tracks, waiting for the train to clear. The driver flicked the reins and swung the buggy close to the end of the platform.

A big half-blood Aborigine shouted across to Charlie.

"You Charlie?"

Charlie nodded. "Yes, that's me."

"I'm Frank. Bring your gear Charlie and climb aboard." Charlie threw his bag into the back of the board buggy and climbed onto the bench seat next to Frank. With nothing more than a grunt of recognition, Frank flicked the reins and they set off south from Northam station.

"Won't be long," said Charlie after some time of traveling in silence. "It isn't far from here, about half an hour, I reckon."

The road was rough and rutted. The spring rains had washed deep gullies on the verge and bumpy corrugations on the road. The seat on the buggy was pitched constantly; Charlie needed to hang on firmly. He sat stiffly at first, but soon learned to ride the bumps and move with the bucking seat, instead of against it. Frank didn't say much. At first Charlie tried some small talk and then quickly realized how difficult and futile this was. The severe jolting from the buggy ride distorted his words and left him breathless. Charlie concentrated on keeping his seat. Frank would offer the occasional few words, which were made largely incomprehensible by the severe jolting. He grinned broadly in Charlie's direction after each attempt at conversation, swaying once again with the seat and spitting black tobacco on the buggy floor.

The buggy traveled for some distance along the edge of the river Avon, finally branching off on to an area of cleared land. Charlie could see buildings on the horizon. A cluster of buildings on the left revealed a small homestead, outhouses and barns. The building on the right was about a mile away. It looked broken down and disused.

"We'll go and meet the Boss first," said Frank, "then I'll run you over to the staff quarters." He nodded in the general direction of the disused buildings. Charlie thought Frank was joking and laughed nervously.

The Boss was a small stocky Aussie. He had a red, wind-tanned face, thinning hair and tiny blue eyes. It was as if his eyes had been painted by an artist of limited skills, giving him the look of a blind person. Charlie found it hard to look into the pale blue of the Boss's eyes, but they fixed on him as if they could find nothing else in their focal range. Charlie felt very uncomfortable under this relentless rude stare. The eyes finally moved in Frank's direction.

"He looks a bit raw," said the Boss, as if Charlie wasn't a human worth talking to. "Make sure he works, or he walks." With that, he turned and headed off to his ranch-style house.

"That's the Boss," said Frank, somewhat redundantly. "Don't cross him, not if you want to get paid."

Frank had been sincere about the staff quarters. The old building with its corrugated iron roof, wooden floors and open windows became unbearably hot in the heat of the day. Frank bunked in one room; Charlie had the other. When it became excessively hot, especially at night, they soaked grain sacks in well water and hung them over the open doors and windows. It gave some cooling effect to the night breezes.

The next morning, Charlie woke to find that Frank had already gone to the house for breakfast. It was just dawn. Charlie set off in the half-light to walk the mile or so. The early morning sun shot rays of orange and red through the leaves and boughs of the trees making the graded path a dappled kaleidoscope of colour. The track wound through a small thicket and the howling dingoes encouraged Charlie to quicken his pace. They seemed to move closer, yapping and howling, first on the edge of the woods, and then actually padding down the track behind him. Charlie lobbed a few stones in their direction. This only seemed to encourage the dingoes. The chorus of howls grew louder. He could hear them panting behind him. The house was now only a hundred yards away. Charlie's bravado was lost in fear. He took flight and sprinted for the house. He flung himself against the door, snapping the sneck as he did so. His bursting lungs heaved as he stumbled in to the kitchen and on to the slab floor. The Boss and Frank were still having breakfast; they hardly looked up from their meal.

The Boss wiped the remnants of his breakfast from his mouth with the back of his sleeve.

"Charlie, you're late. Don't let it happen a second time."

Charlie stayed with them for about three years. The work was tough and the hours long, particularly at cropping and harvest time. Frank showed him a trick or two with a rifle and also taught him how to ride Western-style, with long stirrups and a full-horned saddle. Charlie enjoyed handling sheep the best. One of Frank's dogs took to sleeping in his room and soon became his own work dog. Together, they became quite expert in handling the huge flocks on the property. Feed always became scarce towards the end of the hot summer months and Charlie spent much of his time herding the sheep from one wheat field to another, letting them find some measure of sustenance from the dry, cellulose straws.

Water was a problem. The river Avon, which was a torrent in the winter months, became a mere trickle in the summer. The river water was also heavy in salt and consequently unfit for both humans and livestock. The boss had installed a series of windmills that pumped from aquifers into stock tanks.

Charlie was amazed at the effect the sudden downpours had in transforming the arid landscape. The rains were steady and at times intense. The dry ground sucked up all the initial rains filling the sap of dormant grasses and plants creating a wispy green blanket almost overnight. Heavier rains gouged angrily at the soil surface, creating deep fissures and channels of muddy water as the rains ransacked field after field. Frank and Charlie stood on the porch of their bunk house, deafened by the incessant beating of the rain on the corrugated tin roof. They looked vacantly out at the rain through the sheets of water streaming off the porch roof.

"Some rain," offered Frank, as the wind dropped and the rain eased a little. "That's water we could do with. It's filling all them water butts." He nodded in the direction of the barrels at the foot of each down spout. "We need water in the summer – we gets too much now. It just washes away all that top soil."

Charlie nodded sagely as if he fully understood the problem.

"See that creek," said Frank, "it'll be busting its banks in a day or so. All the water from this valley runs into that little creek." He pointed to the ridges on either side of the valley.

"Look over there," said Frank, pointing to the soil being washed off the sloping fields in muddy slips, creating deep crevices at the edges of the fields and oozing mud lakes across the farm road. "That's good soil washing down the road."

Charlie opened two bottles of Swan lager and handed one to Frank.

"Sounds like a big problem," said Charlie. Frank took a long pull on his bottle of Swans. "Boss is always going on about it, specially at this time of year," replied Frank.

"What about those banks on the grade, don't they help?" asked Charlie.

"Contour banks," replied Frank, "yeah, they help. We should have put more in on the steep slopes. They move the water off the slope so it don't eat into the soil as bad."

"I suppose it helps with water for sheep and cattle in the dry season?" commented Charlie.

"Some," replied Frank, "but the water never hangs around long enough. The river gets to a trickle and the water gets salty. Hundreds of cattle and sheep will die in this area in a bad year. And we get plenty of them."

"What we need," said Charlie, "is a giant stock tank." He took another long swig on his beer and laughed at his own remark.

Frank smiled. "We've got some big ones," he replied, "but nothing that would last more than a week or two."

"Hey," said Charlie, "what about a dam … down stream." He suddenly leapt to his feet and pointed down the valley. "You know Frank, if we could build a dam where the creek cuts through that narrow opening … see where I mean?"

"We'd flood half this area," replied Frank.

"Exactly," shouted Charlie excitedly. "We could control the level with a spillway. I saw it done near Durban in South Africa. I worked for a few weeks helping build one there."

"You serious about this?" asked Frank.

"Yea, why not. It could be the salvation of this place. But before we go off to the Boss, let's go down early and look at the area. It needs clay to line and seal the dam, otherwise it's no good."

Frank grunted. "Huh, ok with me. Clay shouldn't be a problem. That bottom land is real heavy ground."

The next morning, Charlie and Frank walked along the creek each carrying spades and Frank also had a pick axe. "This looks like a good spot. We could build a dam between these two rock faces." He gestured towards the banks that rose on either side of the creek. "Let's have a look for some clay."

The clay wasn't hard to find. They dug five or six test holes revealing layers of blue and white clay about three feet from the surface of the bank. The clay seemed uniformly spread. It looked, and felt like a layer of cheese, streaked with blue, red and gray. It was clay. The squelching clay stuck to their boots with limpet like strength, pulling at them with such strong suction that their boots often became anchored to the oozing mix of mud and clay.

"It's worth talking to Boss about," suggested Charlie.

"You might just be on to something," commented Frank. "Let's get the Boss down here. Once he's convinced, he'll go for it, I'm pretty sure."

It took quite awhile to explain it all to the Boss. He was dismissive at first, telling them to stop wasting his time and get back to work. But it was obvious to Frank that the Boss wasn't hurrying them out of the door with a string of expletives to hasten their departure as he usually would if he felt anyone was wasting his time. Charlie, on the other hand, had given up all hope as soon as the Boss uttered the first "bull shit" in response to Charlie's enthusiastic description of the proposed dam. But Charlie didn't understand the Boss as well as Frank did; and he certainly couldn't read the lack of negativity from the Boss as representing a positive response. Questions began to flow from the Boss' mouth.

"Where did it come from?"

"Had it worked?"

"How big would it need to be?"

"How much land would it take?"

The Boss listened intently now to Charlie's answers, before probing with a further barrage of questions.

"Where will the dam be built?"

"What materials will be used?"

"How will it be built? Tell me exactly what you will need."

The Boss's interest soon turned to a more practical assessment of their needs.

"We'll need a heavy roller—old Morrissey has a cast iron job...I'll see him in town tomorrow."

"We'll also need a digger," added Charlie, "the railway at Northam has graders and earth levelers, maybe they'll have a digger."

"Right," said the Boss, slapping the palm of his hand on the table, "let's do it!" He began to chuckle. "I love a gamble, it's what life is all about." His face contorted into a thin smile and his pale eyes narrowed. "And as for you two, it'll be a hell of a gamble—so don't let me down."

Frank grinned and winked at Charlie. "Okay with me Boss, I'll make sure Charlie gets it done."

Charlie nodded meekly, suddenly feeling frightened by the awesome responsibility he'd assumed.

The Boss shook hands with them both, holding Charlie's hand in a firm grip while his pale eyes fixed on Charlie's. "Let's get to it boys," said the Boss.

Work started the following week. Charlie borrowed a level from the railway yard to set out contour lines on the slopes of the catchment. He marked out a one percent slope line. He wanted a gentle gradient to ensure the torrential rains wouldn't erode the soil banks. Under Charlie's watchful eye, Frank expertly maneuvered a team of horses pulling a disc plough, creating a soil mound over the surveyed lines. After several passes, they agreed that the bank was sufficiently high. A light roller was pulled along the top and sides of each contour bank to firm the soil. The final act was to seed grass along the banks, with an extra handful strewn at the base of the bank to ensure good grass cover. This was one of Frank's ideas. He thought a good grass cover would help in stopping the collecting torrents from eroding the soil in the contour banks.

Building the dam was the next major task. The Boss agreed with Charlie and Frank about the location of the dam. There were also plenty of rocks around for the dam foundations. Rock picking was an on-going exercise in most of the wheat fields and huge piles stood like rough pyramids in the centre of many of them. The Boss hired a crew of Aborigines to help. They spent two weeks loading rocks and transporting them to the dam site. Tons of rocks were dumped to form the base of the dam. The work was monotonous and exhausting. Charlie had reoccurring fears that he had bitten off more than he could chew. He contemplated, with increasing frequency, hiking out to Northam and jumping a train to Perth. It was the steadying influence of Frank that encouraged him. The old Abo worked with seemingly no awareness of time; the sun's rise and fall were the only indicators he needed. Frank also kept an eye on the other Aborigines to make sure that they didn't have a free minute that wasn't due. They were good with horses but disastrously rough with machinery. As a consequence, several days were lost because of broken axles, cracked blades, and overturned equipment. Frank acted like a knowledgeable foreman. He goaded, instructed, helped, persuaded and cajoled until, miraculously, they seemed to blend as a team.

And what a team! Earth and rocks moved with swiftness and precision. The base of the dam expanded and was eventually covered with soil from the wetland area, exposing the thick, white cheesy clay beneath. The dam took shape and grew as they heaped and rolled dirt onto the growing earthen mound. The final step was to coat the dam with a six-inch layer of clay, effectively sealing it from the eroding forces of wind and water. The far end of the dam had a deep gorge that was used to form a natural overflow, a spillway to limit the height of water behind the dam. They reassured one another that it was an excellent site and superbly constructed dam, not that they had anything other than Charlie's word as a basis for comparison. Charlie, Frank and the Boss stood and proudly surveyed the result. "Fine dam," said Boss, gazing at the dam. "Frank, there's extra in the pay-packet for you and the boys. Did a great job." Frank beamed. He knew that this was praise indeed from such a taciturn man. "Charlie, same goes for you. Better work though," he added, still gazing at the dam.

Charlie could hardly wait for the autumn rains to come. Boss and Frank were equally excited, but kept their nervous anticipation to themselves. When the first thunderous rain storm hit the Avon Valley area the following March, the three men stood on top of the dam for an hour, soaked to their skins, watching and waiting. Water only trickled in at first, but then began to flow in torrents, down the contour banks and into the dam. By the end of the winter period, the level of water had risen to twelve feet below the spillway. The lake it created was becoming much larger than they had envisaged; its waters reached out like massive tentacles, grasping at the sloping sides of the dam. Boss was, by now, developing elaborate plans for stocking the dam with fish, and even considered siphoning off some of the water for his stock tanks in nearby fields.

Word traveled quickly; Charlie became something of a local celebrity. The newspaper interviewed him and printed several photographs of the dam. Boss gave full credit to Charlie, making it perfectly clear that it was Charlie's plan. Other articles followed. The *West Australian* gave half a page to a feature article, including a photograph of Charlie and Boss standing on top of the dam. The *Farmer's Journal* followed suit with a similar story and accompanying photograph. Charlie enjoyed the adulation. He even sent a couple of the press cuttings to his sister.

A few months later, Charlie received a wired telegram from Kalgoorlie, a large mining town about four hundred miles inland from Perth. Kalgoorlie was one of the first of the large mining towns in Western Australia. Gold was the lure. In eighty years or so, Kalgoorlie had grown from a few shacks to become the largest inland town in Western Australia, thanks in large part to arrival of water piped in from the coast. An amazing feat of engineering.

Charlie's telegram was from a Mr. George Archer, inviting him to Kalgoorlie to discuss a proposition '*of considerable business potential.*' Charlie was, as it happened, looking for some good excuse for leaving the farm. Now that the dam was completed, the Boss had relegated him to mundane chores. The press attention and the glowing praise had left their mark on Charlie. He was becoming very dissatisfied with his current station in life and this telegram was just the excuse he was looking for. There was, for Charlie, more to life than fencing one dreary paddock after another, more to see than flyblown sheep, red dust and bundles of wheat.

Charlie caught the coach from Northam to Kalgoorlie the following week. The vehicle was fitted with an oversized radiator to counter the summer heat and equipped with large 'roo bars' above the front bumper. Charlie was leaning against them as the bus driver approached.

"Keeps those bloody roos from wrecking the bus," he explained. Leather water bags, wet and shiny, dangled from the roo bars like a series of sad, drooping eyes. They hissed and became murky with steam as they wept on to the hot radiator.

There were only three passengers. Charlie stowed his gear in a hinged trunk fastened to the floor at the rear of the coach and took a seat behind the driver. The coach kicked up a dust plume that spewed from the rear of the vehicle like a vapour trail. It was a long, hot journey. They stopped at every small town to stretch their legs while the driver kicked the tyres, replenished the water bags and fed the hissing radiator. They reached Kalgoorlie at dusk. Charlie thought it strange to see such a bright and lively town after traveling so many miles through the bush. The lights and noise were like a magnet to Charlie. The first thing he did on arriving was to take a tour of the noisiest streets and bars. They were teeming with miners, road builders, house builders and farm workers, each being distinguished by the working clothes and overalls they still wore. There were some office workers too, with their striped shirts, stiff collars and coloured braces. The many bars constantly spewed forth a myriad of revelers, each backed by the noisy excesses of the drinking establishments. Most had a piano tinkling in bizarre competition with the laughter and shouts from noisy miners.

Charlie checked in to the largest of the main street hotels before spending more of the evening strolling around the town. He drank a couple of ice-cold beers that numbed his tongue and washed the dust of the journey from his throat. Charlie found Hay Street interesting. Girls sat outside small corrugated iron huts, encouraging miners to spend some time, and money, in their company. Charlie was amused by the doctor's health certificates; signed, dated, and displayed at the entrance of every brothel. The girls sat on small verandas talking casually, as if the street were their front room. Most looked tired and sad, trapped, as they were, in the business of selling pleasure; exchanging whatever looks they had left for the currency of the day. The younger ones were very appealing and Charlie spent some time on their verandas, discussing the finer points of their trade. Despite his mild attempts at bargaining, the price of admission remained too expensive.

Just before nine the next morning, Charlie paced nervously in the busy hotel lobby, looking for someone who might be a mining engineer. He had in his mind someone in his fifties, small and fairly stout with a full beard – he'd seen a number resembling that description in the bars the previous evening. He ignored at first the figure waving at him from across the crowded lobby. Charlie glanced again at the man now striding purposefully in his direction, his boots clicking off the sprung wooden floor boards. He was similar in build to Charlie but a bit more erect with his head held high as if supported by a stiff collar. He had a copy of the *West Australian* in his hand. He glanced at the grainy photograph in the paper and waved it excitedly at Charlie.

"You must be Charlie, delighted to meet you – I'm George, George Archer." He extended his hand. Charlie was so taken aback it took him a few seconds to register that pleasantries has been offered.

" Oh … morning," stumbled Charlie, as he raised his hand to return the greeting, "yes … er … very pleased to meet you Mr. Archer."

"George, call me George, please," he instructed. "We're not in England. If we are going to work together then it's on a first name basis. Are you comfortable with that?" George Archer prided himself on being a good judge of character and in letting his instincts make a reliable assessment based on first impressions. He wasn't sure he liked what he saw. It annoyed him slightly because he reckoned without Charlie his business ambitions would be hard to realise. His immediate reaction was that Charlie could be someone he might not be comfortable with, possibly someone he wouldn't fully trust. He liked open and honest features, not the somewhat hesitant manner and furtive look he saw in Charlie. He reminded George Archer of a couple of miners he had known who looked after themselves rather than their colleagues. Maybe his first impressions were wrong, he thought. He certainly hoped so.

"I hoped you would come," he continued, "… and that I'd be able to recognise you; this photograph isn't very good." He again waved the *West Australian* newspaper at Charlie. "It was more a process of elimination. I assumed you were fairly close to my age and from the photograph

I could at least see you had a slim build." George Archer smiled, as if pleased at his powers of deduction.

"Let's have a chat over some breakfast." He nodded in the direction of the dining room and strode off to secure a table, with Charlie in tow. The waiter took the order from George Archer. "Ham, eggs and coffee, that alright?" he asked. "Sounds good to me, thanks," replied Charlie. Coffee arrived almost before they had time to straighten their chairs and unfold their napkins. They both took sips from the thick mugs.

"Disgusting, but it's warm and it wakes you up." Charlie gave an acknowledging smile. Without pausing for any further pleasantries, George Archer began to set out just why he had made the offer to Charlie.

"Charlie, I'm delighted you accepted my invitation. Thank you for coming out all this way."

"To tell the truth, I was looking to move on. Now the work on the dam has finished …"

"…And that's the very reason I have asked you to meet with me. You've got some skills and a well-earned reputation that I think we can build on."

"You mean in building the farm dam," replied Charlie.

"Exactly. That dam you constructed has resulted in considerable interest and I think we can work together to build this up into a profitable business. I'll be straight with you; I'm currently working as a mining engineer for the gold mines. The price of gold has crashed and the owners are closing the weaker seams and that means less work for people like me. If there are no new excavations and fewer shafts to maintain, the need for somebody with my skills will be considerably reduced…" George Archer broke off as breakfast was served. "Dig in, nothing worse than a cold breakfast." Charlie needed little encouragement. George Archer took another sip of his coffee and continued.

"Farmers need a reliable supply of water – and your dam has worked for one farm – it could also work for many others."

"I'm not sure," said Charlie, cautiously, "we were lucky, there was a good amount of bottom clay and valley walls we used as sides for the dam. It won't always be that easy."

"Not to just repeat what you built," replied George Archer. "New designs will likely be needed and new approaches for construction. That's where I come in. I can do the designs, your job will be to assist me with the designs and organise the construction of the dams."

" … and I reckon you also need me because of all the publicity?" replied Charlie. George Archer smiled, "I think we understand one another. Still interested?"

"I need to know what's in it for me. What's to stop me going out on my own?"

"Simple," replied George Archer, "in my view you lack skills in two essential areas—training to design dams for different circumstances and the know-how to take this further. But most importantly, you don't have the funds needed to get this going as a business."

Charlie took a long sip of his coffee.

"Alright, but what's to stop you going off on your own. You won't need me after a while?"

George Archer leaned forward across the table. "Look Charlie, this is a gamble for both of us. If this is as successful as I hope it will be, then it will be an opportunity for you. I'm an honourable man Charlie, I have no intention of simply using you. I … we … need to capitalise on your success – it will get the business started."

"And if it doesn't work…?" replied Charlie.

"Then I will have lost time and money, and you Charlie will have just contributed your time. If it does work, and I've every confidence it will, then there will be a business to run."

"Just what's in it for me?" asked Charlie.

"If you contribute to make the business work, then I promise you a share in the business after the first year." George Archer looked directly into Charlie's eyes. "There are two things that would cause me to terminate our arrangement. Firstly, that there isn't enough demand for our work. And secondly, if I think that you aren't doing what's expected."

"And how will I know that?" replied Charlie.

"I'll let you know – I've worked with enough miners in my time out here, mostly good workers, but occasionally you get a shirker. Nothing makes my blood boil like a man not pulling his weight. I'd have the same reaction if I felt you weren't living up to your billing Charlie. That clear?"

"Very. If it works, and I help make it work, then after a year you'll make me a partner," replied Charlie. "Just what does that mean? A fifty-fifty partnership?"

"Not quite," responded George Archer, "I'll give you a twenty-five percent stake." Charlie grunted, as if reconsidering the offer. George Archer went on as if anticipating Charlie's reservations.

"Look Charlie, I'm putting up the capital and quite frankly I'm taking a hell of a gamble. You have one success under your belt, and little else. In return for hard work and commitment I'm offering you a chance I don't think you'll ever get again. This is take it or leave it. It's up to you."

"Alright," replied Charlie, "but I only have your word, I don't know any more about you other than what you've told me this morning."

"I anticipated you might need a bit more reassurance than just my word. I've had a solicitor draw up a letter basically stating what I've told you – that if the business is successful and if you make a full and effective contribution, you'll be entitled to a twenty-five percent stake." George Archer took an envelope from his pocket and passed it to Charlie. "Go ahead, read it." Charlie carefully read every line.

"Still needs you to agree that I am making a good contribution," commented Charlie.

"That's your gamble. We are both taking risks – and I believe mine is the bigger gamble," replied George Archer. "I'm going to leave you to finish your breakfast and I'll meet you back here for lunch. I'll want a decision then." George Archer pushed back his chair and strode off through the lobby leaving Charlie to ruminate over their discussions and pick at his now almost cold breakfast.

George Archer felt a bit more comfortable. His chat with Charlie hadn't raised any further issues, in fact if anything, it had abated some of his earlier concerns. "So much for first impressions," he said to himself, as if trying to be convinced.

Charlie re-read the letter. George Archer was offering him a job as the manager of a surveying and construction company he was about to establish. He promised Charlie a useful wage, a position as the manager and the prospect of a limited partnership after 12 months, if the company flourished.

He was excited at what Archer had offered him. It was certainly an offer he couldn't turn down. And he liked Archer. He seemed very trustworthy, someone who would keep his word, unlike some of the rough diamonds he had known. Could he do it? Could he make a go of this? The farm dam had been a great success; there was no reason to think he couldn't do it, and he'd have Archer's skills and money backing him. He resolved to make this work. He wanted to prove to himself that he could make it in Australia. He'd write to his sister, Maggie, and tell her about this. She'd be delighted for him, he knew. He suddenly felt quite elated. He ordered more coffee and contented himself with reading Archer's letter again. The more he read it, the more he liked the idea. "Me, a manager," he thought. " A business man!" He gave a self-congratulatory chuckle.

George Archer had read of Charlie's success in building the dam near York. The extensive publicity that Charlie received had impressed him. The construction of the dam itself he saw as rather simple exercise. What intrigued him was the widespread interest in conserving water, particularly water that could be used by farmers. Charlie's reputation could be his stepping-stone into the dam construction business. Charlie was now something of a phenomenon to the farming community, an attribute he could work to his advantage.

George Archer was waiting in the lobby when Charlie returned to the hotel for lunch. Charlie shook hands with more enthusiasm than he had done on their first meeting. He could hardly contain his enthusiasm. It had an innocence about it that pleased George Archer.

"Good to see you're still here Charlie, and not put off by our earlier discussions."

"Quite the contrary," remarked Charlie with a broad grin.

"Excellent," replied George Archer, "let's get some lunch."

"The lunch menu has only three items," commented George Archer, as they sat down at the same table they had occupied at breakfast. "The beef and potatoes with carrots and gravy is the one I'd recommend."

"That sounds fine," replied Charlie. "Simple but filling."

"It certainly will be filling," replied George Archer, nodding in the direction of two huge plates of food that were being served at the next table.

The two of them pounded into their food with a gusto that assumed a shared enthusiasm. Charlie in particular was consuming his food with a sense of urgency wanting both to sate his appetite and to get to the point so he could inform George Archer of his decision. Charlie wiped his gravy splattered mouth and waited impatiently for George Archer.

"Well," said George Archer, as he to finished his plate, "have you come to a decision?"

Charlie tried to stay calm, but his enthusiasm betrayed him.

"I certainly have Mr Archer ... I mean George, I'd be delighted to take up your offer."

"Excellent," replied George Archer, extending his hand. This time Charlie responded immediately, grasping George Archer's hand and shaking it vigorously.

George Archer provided Charlie with a cash advance with instructions to buy a new suit, work clothes and boots. He was to report to an office in Kalgoorlie's main street at eight o'clock next morning. Charlie checked in to a smaller and cheaper hotel just off Main Street. This became his home address for the next year or so, but in reality, he was often on the road, supervising the various construction and surveying projects they had undertaken.

The advertisements placed by George Archer had almost immediate results. His new firm secured a number of contracts for farm dams by making great play of the fact that Charlie had "vast experience" and that he was recognised as "the expert in Western Australia." Charlie and George would survey the farm site, draw up plans, and then bring in their equipment from Kalgoorlie. They soon established various holding depots throughout the state, cutting down on the time and effort associated with getting equipment to and from the worksite. Contracts for work were readily obtained. They designed and constructed irrigation ditches in the northern regions of the state around the Ord River and drainage canals for farmers in the southwest region, as well as maintaining a steady supply of contracts for dam construction.

George Archer was true to his word. The partnership he promised was given to Charlie after only one year. I remembered my mother beaming with pride to read that Charlie had been made a junior partner in a successful engineering company.

Chapter 3

THE SOLICITOR

The London office of Wilcox, Vietch and Leonard.

The voice of the silver-haired solicitor seemed to build in intensity as his voice drifted through the stale office air.

"Mr. Archer requests that you visit him as soon as possible. He is very ill and unlikely to outlive the summer." The silver-haired solicitor suddenly stopped in another annoying pause. It was as if he stopped breathing. His small eyes became brighter and his neck redder. I waited for him to choke and even held my own breath in anticipation. Just when I thought I should reach over and slap his back, the solicitor blurted into speech; the words gushed out, pushing stale breath in my direction.

"Mr. Archer ... is the owner of a large freight handling company. He and ... your Uncle Charles were partners in Australia. On his ... death, the company shares he currently owns will become yours. In addition to ... shares, there is a considerable accumulation of capital resulting from the recent sale of some company assets. I am instructed ... to inform you that the capital alone will be in the region of ... five-hundred thousand United States dollars."

This time, his asphyxiating pause came as something of a relief. It gave me time to absorb what I thought I was hearing; to look at my shoes to make sure they were mine. I was only half listening when the silver-haired solicitor grunted and went into another series of painfully extracted sentences.

"Mr. Archer naturally wishes that you visit him prior to his death; in fact, he has made that a condition of the will." My ears were alert now. "Failure to reach Mr. Archer prior ... to his death will mean that you forfeit your rights as a beneficiary. I urge you ... to make every endeavor to visit him as soon as possible. There are no other beneficiaries. Mr. Archer never married ... and there are no children or other relatives that we are aware of." His voice had trailed off into a whisper as if he were revealing some long sought after confidentiality. "You were, no doubt, aware of the close business relationship between Mr. Archer and your late Uncle Charles." I nodded, but in fact my knowledge of Uncle Charles and Mr. Archer was scant, to say the least. The silver-haired solicitor was, once more, gripped in a strangulating pause.

My mother had been devastated by the news of Charlie's death. I was about fourteen years old when the letter arrived. I remember coming home thinking the house must be empty: the door was unlatched. I called from the hallway. There was no reply. I suddenly felt nervous. Something was wrong; I could sense it. I ran into the kitchen, calling as I did so. The kitchen fire was burning low and the room was cold. It seemed colder than the hallway. I shivered. My mother was sitting at one corner of the table staring into the dying embers. In her hands she clutched a blue letter; the envelope lay crumpled on the floor. She didn't stir or give any sign of recognition. I was very scared. I didn't know what to do or say. I stoked up the fire and fetched a blanket from her bedroom. As I draped the blanket around her shoulders, my hand touched her ice-cold cheek. I shuddered both in fright at the unexpected sensation, and in fear of what might happen next. For what must have been over an hour, I just sat watching my mother, occasionally stoking the fire and re-adjusting her blanket. Eventually she stirred, as if coming out of a trance.

"Is that you, Joe?" she asked in a dull listless voice. "It's Charlie..." Her shoulders heaved and shuddered as she said his name. "He's been killed...in an accident...a dam wall gave way...he was crushed and buried. His body wasn't recovered but they marked the spot where he died."

She seemed calmer now. Some colour had returned to her cheeks and her eyes seemed to come back into focus.

After a little while, she got up, smoothed her apron and turned to splash water on her face. She dried herself and then reached into her apron pocket for the crumpled letter. "You'd better read this Joe, it's from Mr. Archer, Charlie's business partner."

The typed letter explained the circumstances of Charlie's death in some detail. It also went to great lengths to assure that everything possible was done to recover the body, which had been buried by several tons of rubble. There had been no hope for survival. Mr. Archer asked for instructions with regard to Charlie's personal possessions. My mother had no intention of replying, and never did;

there was no point. Charlie had gone; she didn't need any other painful reminders of his life.

I noticed something about the silver-haired solicitor. He was different somehow. A small thin hand suddenly shot out from the shadows cast by the desk lamp.

The solicitor had conducted his business and was now standing to issue his formal farewell. The shadow of the light decapitated him and only his white shirt and tie were clearly visible, beaming in the green light. I shook hands with the headless solicitor.

"My secretary has a package of information for you," called the voice from the shadows. "Please collect it on your way out...it's been a pleasure sir." He then added hastily, "I hope I can act on your behalf on your return from the United States?"

"I expect so," I replied. "I'll let you know." With that, I turned, groped for the door and stepped into the brilliantly lit front office. The ever vigilant secretary rose effortlessly from behind her desk. She held out a padded envelope.

"This is your information, Mr. Jackson. I've ordered a taxi for you. It's waiting outside. They are on the firm's account; no need to pay."

I smiled at her efficiency, thanked her for the service and headed for the door.

A black taxi was waiting outside, its engine running.

"They said you need the station," shouted the cabbie, half turning in my direction as he roared off without waiting for me to reply. Rather presumptuous of them, I thought, as I slid back on the shiny leather seat; I might have wanted to celebrate. I wasn't sure what I would be celebrating: the intriguing prospect of meeting this mysterious stranger for the second time, and possibly learning more about my Uncle Charlie; or the thought of being wealthy. But it was Uncle Charlie I kept thinking of. I hoped Mr. Archer would be able to fill in his missing years. It suddenly seemed of paramount importance to learn as much as I could about the life my Uncle had led.

Chapter 4
THE TRIP

I managed to catch the afternoon train and would be back in Glasgow that night. The packet contained a letter from Mr. George Archer asking me to visit him in Washington. I was concerned that it didn't quite fit in any of my jacket pockets. It did fit in the pocket of my overcoat, however that was on the overhead rack, too far away for me to feel its presence under my reassuring hand. I decided to just hold it on my lap, gripping the packet in my left hand and flicking the corner with the thumb of my right hand. Instructions were carefully provided. I was to make travel arrangements to fly to Washington and then cable Mr. Archer as to the flight number and time of arrival. I would be met at the airport and taken to Mr. Archer's home. It was all so precise and so carefully detailed.

I had decided, in the silver-haired solicitor's office, that I would make the journey, not just because it somehow promised a substantial financial inheritance, but because I was intrigued and bloody curious.

The next morning, I got into work earlier than usual so that I could ensure an audience with my boss, the redoubtable Mr. Wilson.

I cleared my throat before knocking on the mottled glass pane in Mr. Wilson's door.

"Yes?" Mr. Wilson's high-pitched reply came piercing through the solid glass-framed door. I cursed at the polished door knob; it always slipped and the catch only half turned. "Yeeas?" shrieked Mr. Wilson. I succeeded in moving the knob far enough to unlatch the door and pushed it open a little too vigorously. The door flew back against a rubber stop and rebounded at me. I caught it by the edge with both hands. "Well man, I'm awful busy, have you nothing better to do than fight we ma door?" His Scottish accent rose at the end of the sentence, it always did when he was agitated. His Western Isles lilt danced through his whining words, his trilled 'rrr's' reverberating off the green plaster walls.

Wilson's office was long and narrow with a large polished desk under the window at the far end of the room.

"I'd like to discuss something with you, Mr. Wilson," I said, still clinging to the edge of the door.

"Well stop swinging on ma door...come in, come in," replied Mr. Wilson, in exasperated tones, beckoning me to occupy one of his infamous armchairs. Two old armchairs were placed on the other side of the desk from Mr. Wilson's wooden swivel seat. They were deceptively soft, and I felt distinctly uncomfortable as I sank low into the cushion. My eyes were only just above the level of the desk. Mr. Wilson looked pleased with himself as he leaned on his desk and peered down at me. "Now what is it that's urgent enough to keep both of us from our work?" I felt like kicking the desk of the sour Scot; we all knew that he spent most of the morning collecting envelopes, string and brown wrapping paper from the other offices. After morning coffee, it was his usual custom to sort his hoard.

"I'd like some time off, er... ten days should be enough."

"We've been to Greece already this year," the sarcasm obvious from the indelicately placed intonations. "What is it that beckons us now, Bulgaria or the beaches of Benidorm?" Mr. Wilson smiled with obvious pleasure at his directed humour.

"Oh no, one holiday a year is enough for me."

"I'm glad to hear it. You've no idea what pleasure it brings to hear of your devoted allegiance to the work ethic!" Mr. Wilson's head pivoted on his narrow neck as if searching for applause from some hidden audience. I waited for Wilson's head movements to subside to smaller oscillations.

"I have to visit a friend of the family; he lives in Washington, in the USA. It's a matter of some urgency... he hasn't long to live and I would need to leave in a couple of days."

Wilson's curiosity was aroused.

"You've never mentioned relatives or family friends living in the United States. What's so special, so important about this individual? You realise I can't make exceptions for one of my staff without getting a barrage of requests from the others. Can't it wait a few weeks, until you've accumulated enough leave time? This really is something that goes against my better judgment. My immediate reaction is to say no, unless of course you can convince me otherwise." He rambled on, trilling his rrr's and swishing his head from side to side as if answering in the negative to every query he raised almost as he spoke. At last he stopped; exhausted it seemed by his verbal communion of the priestly rules he preached. Mr. Wilson seemed to be surprised I was still there. "Will that be all?" he enquired.

"Well no," I replied. "I'd like to take leave without pay." I was pretty sure that the employee manual said something about simply filling in a form for this request. It did, however, require the approval and signature of my immediate supervisor, the rather difficult Mr. Wilson.

"Are you sure you know what you're doing laddie?" demanded Wilson in his strongest brogue. "This is a radical step...radical...leave without pay...it's not something I'd recommend...I'll have to give it some serious thought.... fill out the application form and leave it with Janet. You'd better put down a damn good reason." The succession of trilled rrr's seemed to bounce off one another as if some English comic were mimicking Harry Lauder on stage.

"Yes, Mr. Wilson, I'll have it for you to sign this afternoon."

I knew the awkward bugger would have no alternative but to approve my request, but Wilson delighted in exercising his authority for all it was worth. After staring blankly at each other for several moments, it became obvious that neither of us could think of anything meaningful to say. I simply kept my eyes on Mr. Wilson's and slowly pushed myself out of the pit of a chair and left the pendulous head of Mr. Wilson's wavering on its stork like neck, gussetted as it was by a large adam's apple. I felt myself creeping to the door as if not wanting to disturb the apparent settlement we had achieved. I opened the door in a quite obsequious and stealthy manner, but then I regained some semblance of dignity by pulling the door quickly behind me and obtained some inner pleasure at hearing the glass rattle as the heavy door shook in its liberal frame.

* * *

The departure lounge seemed to be saturated with people. Every available seat was occupied, either with people, or with their bags, coats, rucksacks, nappy-liners, bottles of liquor, packs of cigarettes, boxes of cigars and phials of perfume. Some were sprawled on the floor, looking sleepy and comfortable; others fretted over their kids, their tickets, passports, wallets, sandwiches, and other essential items that seemed to disappear, or be in the wrong pocket, just as the gate attendant called their seats for boarding.

I found myself in the middle of a family section of the plane. Parents with small children were busy marking out their pitch, grabbing blankets and pillows from overhead racks and jamming coats, jackets, and bags into the overhead storage areas. The airline stewardesses stood quietly in the galleys waiting for their passengers to settle. Most eventually did; some had to be coaxed into their assigned seats, others were forcibly stripped of oversized carry on luggage so it could be stored in some unknown corner in the vast maze of luggage compartments. Others demanded magazines, coffee, drinks and air-sick bags. The senior stewardess stopped the mayhem by welcoming everyone aboard over the crackle of the intercom, followed by instructions on appropriate action, should a crisis arise.

I plugged my headset into the armrest and selected a channel playing the soothing music of Vivaldi's *Four Seasons*. The babble of my traveling companions became a distant and dim white noise as I allowed the perceptible motion of the plane and the easy music to lull me into a trance like state that was close to sleep. The perfume of the stewardess, as she leaned across to feed magazines to a man and his wife in adjacent seats, served only to add an intoxicating scent that gave me an erotic charge.

I enjoyed the flight, mainly because it passed without incident and somehow I'd managed to sleep for a good portion of the flight. I could hear the undercarriage being released as the plane banked over to approach the runway. The screeching of the plane's tyres and the reverse thrust from the jet engines quickly abated as we slowed and taxied to the concourse.

I could hear my name being announced over the tannoy.

I was still battling with a US customs official over the legality of the contents of my suitcase.

"But I bought that camera over six months ago," I protested.

"Do you have any proof of purchase sir?" enquired the persistent agent.

God, I thought, everyone of those rucksack carrying types is walking through the 'Nothing to Declare' section with bags stuffed with every kind of contraband, and here I am attempting to persuade a petty customs official that a newish looking camera isn't as new as it seems. I wished I'd scuffed it up a bit, but I doubted if even that would have convinced this eager donjon of the Customs and Excise Service.

"Er..no," I replied. The officer was now writing down the camera's serial number. He handed this information to a courier who promised he'd be back shortly.

"If you don't mind, I'd like you to open your bag for inspection." Of course I minded, but there was nothing I could do but comply with the request.

Meanwhile, the tannoy continued to blare, as if annoyed that I had refused to respond to its call. After several minutes, the courier returned and handed the official a slip of paper.

"Seems it's ok," he said, handing the camera back to me and pushing my suitcase with its now disheveled belongings to one side.

"Have a nice day."

I grunted in displeasure at the stock remark and quickly repacked my clothes and hurried through the automatic doors, hoping to hear the tannoy make once more a bleating announcement bearing my name.

I didn't have to listen. Leaning over the guard rail that separated the new arrivals from the throng was a black and white sign, with large black letters bearing my name, flight number and time of arrival. Holding the sign was a diminutive female, virtually hidden by her message board, except for her legs, arms and a tuft of her hair. It looked like a sugar cube supported by a pair of shapely legs, with manicured finger nails gripping its body. I pushed my cart to the rail.

"Hello, I'm Joe," I called. Behind the large board was a petite girl, in her early thirties, I guessed. She smiled up at me. She was about five feet two inches tall, had short cropped hair with a punk-like tuft spraying from the top of her head. She wore a short white mini-skirt and a sweat shirt that read 'Property of Yale Athletic Department'. I couldn't help but notice that the word 'Yale' was considerably distorted by her full figure and trim waist.

"Hello Joe, how was your flight?" Before I had time to respond, she continued with the introductions.

"I'm Teresa, Teresa Ivers. But you can call me Tracy, everyone does. Bring your things round the barrier and we'll get across to the car-park." I meekly obeyed, following as directed with a mixture of curiosity and intrigue further confounded by tiredness from the journey.

Everyone moved with a sense of urgency; everyone that is except the international passengers. They looked a tired and disheveled lot, trying to find an end to their journey. I followed the petite Tracy into a nearby short-term parking lot. She pointed to a brown Ford.

"That's the car, let's go." Tracy put the Ford in 'drive' and headed out on one of the many roads that circumvented the city. Our destination was a block of apartments close to the infamous Watergate complex. We swung past the Watergate building and onto a road leading to the Georgetown area. Within minutes we arrived at the Moline apartments; a block of luxury flats bounded by neatly-trimmed lawns and a low sandstone wall.

"Which floor does Mr. Archer live on?" I asked.

"You mean George, call him George, he likes to be called George. We're on the third floor. I have a small suite of rooms down the hall from his." I was too tired to attempt to try and work out the exact relationship between Tracy and George Archer. She had been vague, almost evasive, about her role. She wasn't exactly a secretary, she had explained, more of a personal organiser and home help.

"Now that he's bed-ridden, I even rub cream on his bedsores," she said, laughing in a high-pitched cackle. When we arrived at the suite of rooms, Tracy let us in with her key. She showed me into a room that was, apparently, to be mine for the duration of my stay. It was like a hotel room, with a television and drinks cabinet in a section of the room screened off from the bedroom. There were lamps and small writing tables in both sections of the room and the bathroom was stocked with masses of fluffy white towels and a large assortment of toiletries. There was even a new toothbrush and a discreetly sized bottle of mouthwash. I splashed some cologne on my face. It stung my cheeks and made them look pink and flushed.

Tracy knocked at his door and stepped into the room with the agility and perkiness of some mythical nymph. "Hmm, nice smell," she commented. "George is sleeping just now; his nurse says he'll be able to see you early in the morning...it's his best time."

"I think in that case I'll have a shower and grab some sleep," I replied.

"The cook has made you a meal, I'll bring it through." She stepped out for a couple of minutes and reappeared carrying a large tray. "It's an omelet and fries. Press the buzzer when you've finished and the cook will bring coffee, or is it tea?"

"Coffee's fine," I replied. The meal revived me and gave me heart to unpack my case. I left my toilet bag in the bottom of my suitcase. The bar of Palmolive and the half empty bottle of Old Spice wouldn't be needed.

I didn't bother with the coffee. I flopped onto the comfortable bed and within minutes was sound asleep. It was about 9:30 in the morning when I woke. I conducted my ablutionary exercises of shaving and showering with a protracted pleasure. I dressed quickly while watching the TV. A morning news show was in full swing on CBS. The bizarre, the deviant and the gaudy were paraded before the cameras in swift succession, each telling a gossipy little tale to interviewers with identical smiling teeth; perfect teeth. I didn't recognise the names of any of the eminent guests. Their five minute dialogue, punctuated as it was by a three minute station break, didn't give time for their faces to register. Tracy gave a single rap on my door, opened it, and peered in.

"George would like to see you now. You can get breakfast later, if that's OK."

"Fine," I replied.

Chapter 5
GEORGE ARCHER

George Archer was propped up against bolsters and pillows piled high against the head rails of his bed. A catheter led to a urine bag clipped to the folding side rails of the hospital style recliner. There was a faint smell of urine and of body odour, this despite the clinically clean sheets, crisp bed linen and freshly laundered blue and white striped pyjamas worn by Mr. Archer. He looked at me with wide staring eyes. I felt uncomfortable. His eyes followed me as if I was attached to his retinas by an unbending ray of light. I could feel a bead of sweat dropping from my armpit.

"Good morning, Mr. Archer." I moved hesitantly towards him and shook hands with the pale limp limb that was extended towards me.

"Call me George, please." His voice was very weak, but it carried the hint of an English north country accent. His skin looked tight on his skull and his eyes appeared huge and frightened against his emaciated form. But he was easily recognisable as Mr. Archer; the Mr. Archer who had attended my mother's funeral all those years earlier.

George Archer paused, as if gathering strength. Life, that once must have been effortless in such catered surroundings, was now a struggle. It was a reactionary, almost involuntary fight against the inevitability of death. His fingers were slipping from the ledge; the banns of death had been called. My mind raced as if to counter the stillness that surrounded him. It wasn't a quiet or peaceful stillness. George Archer signaled a form of life by occasionally twitching one of his limbs. He suddenly convulsed with a hacking cough and his arm flailed in the direction of the cardboard spittoon on the bedside table. He banged his other hand against the raised bed rail. I was concerned he would hurt himself. His coughing eased as he slowly sank back against the bolstered pillows.

He turned his eyes toward me, holding my gaze with a demanding intensity. He again coughed violently, paused, and then continued.

"I'm afraid you'll have to put up with the effects of my illness. Fortunately, I have good spells—at the moment, I'm feeling the effects of recent radiotherapy."

"I understand," I said, "there's no need to apologise."

"I'm not!" retorted Archer, vigorously, "I just want you to understand the situation. Sit in that chair, I have some explanations to make." I did as I was instructed. The nurse appeared carrying two capsules in a plastic cap in one hand and a glass of water in the other.

"Time for your medicine, Mr. Archer." She thrust the capsules at him in a no nonsense manner. She held the water while he emptied the contents of the plastic cap into his mouth. He gulped down the tablets with practiced ease and held out the half-empty glass.

"We're not to be disturbed. Joe and I have business to discuss. Tell Tracy that we'll be busy for half an hour. I'll ring if I need either of you. Now get out...er, please."

Requests didn't come easy to Mr. Archer, it took almost a change of character to add the final remark. But it had the necessary effect and the nurse left in a seemingly reasonable mood.

"As you can probably see, I haven't much longer to live; maybe one month, maybe two.

I hope it's not much longer than that, time passes unbearably slowly as it is and I dread to contemplate how much longer I'll be forced to live in this hell."

His eyes became suddenly bright and fierce and he shook the sides of the rail in vexation. "I didn't know that life could be squeezed out of a person's body so slowly, so painfully." The whites of his knuckles gleamed as he gripped the bed rails and his sunken face looked pained and drawn. His fingers slowly uncoiled, and he settled back against the elevated pillows.

"Those early days in Australia; you've probably heard something about the business from that fool of a solicitor in London..."

"And from my Mother," I interjected, "she was so fond of her brother and so proud of what he had accomplished. He owed a lot to you, Mr. Archer."

"George! George!" thundered the old man in a sudden fit of rage. Tears filled his eyes and rolled down his hollow cheeks. For several minutes he was incapable of speaking. "I was very fond of her too."

"Let me look at you." He stretched forward with his catheter-laden arms, urging me to come closer. I moved towards him, feeling a bit uncomfortable.

"You have a look of your mother, you've got her pointed chin and her mouth. Yes, your mouth is just like hers."

His voice crackled as he stumbled, painfully, over his words. I wasn't sure what I should do. I could feel that I was being very closely scrutinized by Mr. Archer.

He held up his hand as if signifying a halt. There was a long pause when neither of us spoke; we simply sat staring at one-another. George Archer suddenly gripped the bed rails with both hands and pulled himself towards me.

"Your mother, Maggie, was my sister ... I am your uncle."

He sank back on the pillows, exhausted by the pain of his revelation. I couldn't believe what I was hearing. I stared in disbelief at the old man.

"But Uncle Charlie was killed, I remember the letter..."

If this was a joke, I detested its brutal insensitivity. But it wasn't a joke; this man was very serious; this was I realized, my uncle, Uncle Charlie. I suddenly remembered the intense pain and suffering that the news of his death had caused my mother. Those old memories briefly sparked a hatred in me for this dying pretender. My mind had, as yet, failed to grasp the consequences of one man claiming to be another. I stood up and paced round the room, turning to talk to him as I did so.

"You caused her a lot of pain; you killed a part of my mother, she never got over the news of your death..." I stopped myself in mid-sentence, realising Charlie's death was no longer an issue...but it was...

"Why did you claim to be dead? Why did you write that letter?...I presume you wrote it...and..."

Suddenly, I saw it all too clearly. This man was an imposter. He had taken the place of George Archer; my Uncle Charlie had assumed the identity of Mr. Archer.

The old man sensed that the awful truth of the situation was beginning to sear its way into my reasoning. He held up his thin arm and motioned for me to sit down and be quiet.

"Let me try to explain. Your mother and I were very close. We brought each other up. I fought for her, she protected me, we were inseparable. When I left I promised that I would return someday and take her away to something better, something that I had earned and worked for so that she could be proud of me." He reached for a glass of water and gulped with a ferocity that caused the adams apple in his thin neck to bob violently, as if trying to escape from its housing. He paused for a few moments and then continued. "George and I worked well together for a number of years. Meeting him was the luckiest event of my life. In those early years, our reputation was often based on the publicity from my first dam. I enjoyed it; I reveled in the recognition—it wasn't much, a nod, a handshake from a stranger, but it was mine to be proud of." He was suddenly engulfed in yet another fit of coughing. He grabbed a towel from his bedside dresser, holding it to his mouth to stifle the coughs and catch the phlegm. He motioned to me to pass him another cardboard spittoon. The coughing spasm passed, and he pushed himself back up against the pillows, obviously determined to continue.

"When we branched out into other activities; ditching, road building, land surveying, it was George who got the recognition. Mr Archer this, Mr Archer that ... I became the 'who's this then?' At best I was a sort of junior partner. I began to despise George. He bid on all the contracts, he controlled all the money. As the jobs got bigger, I got even more envious of George. I even started to dream of accidents, hoping one day that George would be killed so that I could prove how successful I could be. I even planned for such an event. George was always keen to have me involved in the business end so that I would understand how to price jobs, set the wages, pay for equipment, and keep the books. I got involved as much as I could. George didn't trust too many people. He kept to himself; we both did. He also kept his important possessions in a small deed box he carried around as we moved from camp to camp. There were no passports in those days, just travel documents giving your date of birth, place of birth, port of entry, and a general description. It would be easy; his travel documents would become my documents.

The banking arrangements were a bigger problem. George had always banked in Kalgoorlie. For a time, we had a lot of work near Perth. I told George it would be more useful to have a second account in Perth; it would be simpler to make deposits and much quicker to make withdrawals. He agreed, and I volunteered to travel into Perth to open the account. George wrote out a letter explaining what we needed, and asked for a transfer of funds to our new account in Perth.

But they didn't get George's letter. When I got to Perth, I copied out George's letter in my own handwriting onto a blank with the company office address. Then I signed it, George Archer. The bank officer was more than pleased to receive a new account. He'd heard of our company and was anxious to please. To him, I was George

Archer, the owner. All I had to do was to make sure that he and George never met. I knew that this wouldn't be likely. George thought banks were parasites on businesses, charging excessively for looking after his money. He seemed to hate their stiff shirted manners. Even if he did go to the bank, I knew that he would more than likely deal with a teller and not the principal officer. They only checked to make sure sufficient funds were in the account. As it was, they sent out regular statements indicating our financial status and this kept George content with the new account arrangement. He did go into town one day; I remember him coming back and telling me he'd withdrawn one hundred pounds for supplies and wages. I sweated blood for the next thirty seconds expecting at any moment that George would grab a pickaxe handle and start swinging; but he just flipped off the top of a beer and offered me a swig. I think he mistook my sweat-stained anxiety for heat stroke—anyway, the moment passed."

The old man grinned as if pleased at the elaborate efforts he had gone to all those years ago. The strain of telling his story was beginning to show. His cheeks suddenly became very flushed and beads of perspiration appeared on his forehead. They didn't move, but sat on his wrinkled skin like glistening pimples waiting to be squeezed. I poured him some water, which the old man gulped at, spilling from the corners of his mouth as he did so. He reached for the trapeze above his bed and pulled himself up against the pillows.

"Give me a few seconds, then I'll go on. I need to tell you everything…

It was about two years later when the accident happened. A farmer called us in because a dam he had started to construct was slipping, moving down stream. George and I were walking along the top of the dam looking for major cracks. George decided he would drive in a row of planks to create a temporary wall. The idea was to excavate behind the plank wall and dig down to build a bigger and stronger foundation. It was raining hard that day and the stream was rushing down the narrow opening past the dam. I thought I felt some movement and I think I remember telling George we should get back. He wanted to make some measurements." The old man paused for a few moments and leant forward squeezing his eye lids as if holding back his pain. He regained some semblance of composure and continued.

"George climbed down the bank of the dam on the downstream side. He drove in a couple of stakes to the rock bed and began taking measurements to find the slope of the wall. I was at the top recording the measurements and sketching the position of the stakes. The whole end of the dam suddenly gave way. The roar was nearly deafening. I ran back to the edge and caught sight of George scrambling up the mud; but he didn't have a chance. A huge shower of mud and rocks engulfed him—it was an instant grave.

There was nothing I could do. There wasn't a sign of George. With the subsiding of half the dam, the rushing of the water eased. It went very quiet. Just the rain splashing into what was once a raging torrent. George was dead. The realization of all I had dreamt of went through my mind as quickly as the bursting of the dam. I got back to the farmer's house and told him what had happened—except that I reversed the roles. At that instant I became George Archer."

"Didn't you feel sorry, or even guilty?"

"Why should I," shouted Charlie. "It was my chance and I grabbed it. I didn't kill him, I just took the chance when it was offered. If you don't grab with both hands you rarely get a second chance; you'll do well to remember that. I was prepared—and quick-witted enough to seize the opportunity. It gave me a start, but that's all. I made that small company into a major business. I didn't rob anyone, I operated strictly within whatever law a country threw at me. In those early days, there were fewer restrictions. You could hire who you pleased, pay them what you liked and treat them like dirt. But I abided by every aspect of legality that came my way.

Once I got hold of the business, I operated for a year or so just as George and I had done. I hired people around the state and paid them off after each job. I didn't want anybody getting too close or asking too many questions. Some knew me as Charlie, some called me George; it was difficult in those first couple of years. I soon realized that it would be much safer if I kept a low profile and so I started contracting work out. I did the bidding, drew up plans and then contracted the work out to local builders. There were always contractors and builders in Perth and Geraldton willing to take on work for a couple of months. I then realized there was more money to be made because I could contract out several jobs at one time. I became the middleman, the contact between the farmers and local authorities who wanted construction work, and the building firms. It was a good living, busy, even hectic, but reasonably profitable."

Charlie paused for a couple of minutes, as if resting from the physical strain of talking for so long. But he was obviously enjoying this foray into his past. Even with his head resting against the pillow, and his eyes closed, he was smiling with a self-ingratiating satisfaction. He started talking again with his head against the pillow, his eyes fluttering.

"Of course, I made real money later, in Africa in the fifties. I contracted for preparations for the Kariba Gorge dam."

It was at this point that I interjected, "That was some step up from farm dams in Australia." The old man smiled, almost laughing in a gurgling sort of way.

"No, hell no, I had nothing to do with building the thing. That was a real dam, a monster. I got the contract to catch and clear wild animals from the area." I looked at him in amazement. I thought he was joking at first, but the intensity in the old man's eyes convinced me otherwise.

"I supplied the transport; helicopters, small planes and trucks. Game wardens and hunters directed most of the operations. We used the planes to buzz herds of eland, springbok, gazelle and giraffe. We also airlifted hundreds of tranquilized lions, monkeys, apes, gorillas, even the odd reluctant hippo. I spent five years flying and carrying whatever they caught to wherever they wanted. It was a marvelous contract, it set me up for the rest of my life. That little Aussie business grew to become a major international transport service. I took that company and made it grow into something neither George nor I had ever dreamt of. A lot of luck, but I did it." Charlie was breathless with excitement. His small dark eyes were sparkling with enthusiasm and his thin white hands were trembling with admiration at his own success. It was as if he wanted grateful hands to shake his in recognition of his achievements.

I became annoyed at this man who was not George Archer, but my Uncle Charlie who had caused my mother so much anguish. I hated the deception; and yet I couldn't help but feel a tinge of admiration for the old bastard. I spoke angrily.

"That letter—the one you wrote to my mother...your sister...it killed a part of her. Didn't you stop to think?"

"I couldn't...the risks were too great," Charlie protested. "I wanted to tell her, explain everything...but I had to wait until it was safe. I kept saying to myself, just one more year...but ..."

"But then she died," I interjected, vigorously. "You sacrificed your sister for your precious money and ego."

Charlie protested yet again. "It wasn't like that. She was never far from my thoughts, you've got to believe that. I've always been proud, stubborn and sometimes hot-headed. I needed to be able to show her how well I had done, I..."

"Hell no!," I shouted, "let's not kid ourselves. I don't believe you thought about anyone but yourself. It had to be your way or nothing. The contact with my mother, if there ever was to be one, was to be on your terms, to satisfy your needs. Didn't you ever think about her needs, her love and admiration for you?"

Charlie's face turned pink. His lower lip trembled like that of a scolded child. "When I went back to her funeral, I realised how foolish I had been...not at the service, but at the house. It was as if I felt her presence ...and her questioning stare. Just as if we were kids again.

She would stare, reproachfully, when I had stepped over the limit; gone too far."

Charlie's head flopped back against the pillows; his eyes were tightly closed seemingly clenched against the tears that welled within him. The protruding adams-apple bobbed violently and his extended arms banged against the sides of the bed. His thin frame weltered agonizingly on its white lined shrouds.

The nurse had crept stealthily into the room and was leaning over the side of the bed rail trying to calm her irate patient.

"You'll have to go now, Mr. Archer needs rest; you've succeeded in upsetting him; it's not good for him you know." I didn't know, I didn't really care; but I took her advice and left the room.

I decided to get out of the building for a few hours and think things through. I walked a few blocks heading in the direction of a huge McDonald's sign. A vacant, wide eyed, youthful blonde was serving behind the counter. Her jaw moved with wide rhythmic motions revealing the natatorial movement of a wad of pink gum in a saliva pool. Her teeth carried macabre looking retainers and a rubber band tensioner gave the appearance of an ever present thread of saliva. She was able to move her tongue dexterously in retrieving all but the smallest fragments of her gum. Closer inspection revealed thin splatters of gum that had fixed themselves to her upper lips, chin and cheeks; symptoms of a morning's work at the breakfast bar.

"What dya want?" Her saturnine elegance contrasted beautifully with the violent lighting and brash yellow countertops. The only thing missing, I thought, was an ash-laden cigarette dangling from her lips. Maybe her next job would allow her such privileges. I ordered a 'Big Mac' and a vanilla milk shake.

The cold glutinous drink didn't help my concentration. I sucked unceremoniously on the plastic straw and succeeded in moving a clot of ice cold liquid. It was rivetingly cold and caused a painful ache that extended from within my throat to the top of my head. As if not convinced of its effect, I tugged at the next clot, once the pain had subsided. It produced the same unwelcome effect. I gave up on the shake and ordered a coffee from the counter.

The old man had scared me with his revelation. I couldn't dismiss him and pretend I hadn't heard what had been said. But it occurred to me that the old bastard was probably very lonely. I was his one contact with the family he had forsaken, and especially with the sister he had been so close to. The old man had severed his family ties through pride, self interest, perhaps even lack of real concern, and now he needed to re-establish his links with his roots. Even a long term exile has a need to be in the cradle in which he was reared. But Uncle Charlie had been a man who never had much time, or need, to look back, I thought, and now that he had time, he wanted to be reunited. I hated the old bastard for ruining the uneventful predictability of my own life. Now that the vistas of Uncle Charlie's life had been revealed, my own would never be, and could never be, as it was. The anonyminity in which I had indulged for all those years had been destroyed. From now on, not only would I have to make a decision about Uncle Charlie, but also decisions about the direction of my own life. The garden gate had been opened and I was about to step through into another world; I had no choice. When I got back to the apartment, I asked to see Uncle Charlie (Mr. Archer I called him to the nurse). He was asleep and sedated.

"He'll be awake about two, you'll be able to talk to him then."

"Just how serious is the illness?" I enquired.

"Well, I shouldn't really be discussing my patient with you." The nurse made him sound like some prized ornament that she was cataloging. "But let me say this, he's suffering from cancer and is unlikely to last more than a month. But it's almost impossible to tell. I've known patients with similar complications hang on for over six months, others die within a week; it depends very much on their will to live, their willingness to fight the pain, and the futility of it all."

"You make it sound very depressing," I said.

"It is very depressing," replied the nurse, in a reprimanding tone. "A heart attack is much more humane, people who die from cancer suffer a long, lingering death that deprives them of all their independence. For a man like Mr. Archer, that's as hard to bear as the physical pain. We can control his physical pain with morphine, but we can't restore his loss of dignity, we can only help him see it through to the inevitable end. The morphine will probably cause his death first, and that's a blessing."

I was taken aback by the nurse's sudden proclamation. She was very protective of her patient and very understanding of his needs. This good and committed social worker gave no judgement on his past life, only compassion for his pain.

I found it difficult to talk to my Uncle for any period. The drugs had taken their toll, making it impossible for the sick man to concentrate for any length of time. The mornings were the best. After a late breakfast, we often talked for a couple of hours. The old man wanted to know every detail of my life; especially my early years, my school and my mother... mostly about my mother. I found it increasingly difficult to resent this courageous individual. This one-time adventurer exhibited tremendous inner strength and discipline in controlling his pain and fighting the slowly debilitating effects of both the cancer and the drugs he took. But, just as I was beginning to get to know my remarkable Uncle, death was moving inevitably closer. Life had ravaged the old man's body; only death could bring him the peace he sought.

Chapter 6
Tracy

I found myself increasingly concerned with the role of my Uncle's diminutive companion, Tracy. She seemed to have no affiliation with him and, on his particularly bad days, she made herself scarce by opting for shopping trips or visits to friends in Washington. She was rarely mentioned in my conversations with my Uncle. We inevitably talked about the years my Uncle hadn't seen; my boyhood and recollections of our family life. I did ask about Tracy on one occasion, just as I was turning to leave the old man to rest. "She's been good to me Joe, good for this old man." He smiled and closed his eyes as if signaling an end to this line of enquiry. I took the hint and quietly left the room, leaving the old man to his memories, his dreams and his pain.

It seemed to me that Tracy was going out of her way to avoid me, particularly since it was evident that my Uncle and I were getting on well. But that night she announced she wanted us to have dinner together. This was a first. Up to now I had been provided with all my meals in complete isolation, eating at a large rectangular polished dining table with an almost regular menu of burgers, fries and coleslaw salad. Dinner was to be served at seven thirty that evening. I glanced into the dining room earlier in the afternoon. The large mahogany table had been set for two, with cutlery and wine goblets positioned at either end of the table.

I showered and dressed; glad of the change of pace, and the slightly tantalizing hint of excitement that was, in my mind, associated with Tracy. I donned my gray slacks and a white long sleeved cotton shirt. I slipped a two tone belt into the loops and rolled the cuffs of my shirt to just below my elbows. Tracy stood on the other side of the mahogany table pouring wine into her glass as I approached. The single lamp hanging over the table illuminated her skin in its soft glow. Her cheekbones sparkled as the light reflected on the glitter make up she wore. She raised herself erect as I approached, holding the decanter wide of her body in her left hand with her right arm flung deftly in gentle balance towards me. Her nipples pushed at the edges of the wide plunge of her body hugging silk dress. I stood gaping at her, awe struck.

She smiled at me. "Why Joe, how splendid you look." I shuffled with a couple of awkward half steps. I quickly recovered my composure, pulled myself erect and strode in to take my place at the table. I caught the bouquet of the red wine as Tracy leaned forward with the decanter.

I raised my glass; "to a beautiful dinner."

"To a beautiful evening," she replied, with a smile. I was hungry and attacked my food. My mouth was full; I couldn't speak. I could only watch as she slowly pushed a morsel of food around her plate before piercing it with her fork and lifting it delicately to her parted lips. Her eyes rose to meet mine as she did so. I stared, transfixed for the moment by her pale blue eyes and smooth, taught skin. She, in turn, held her position, with her right elbow raised and her fork held to her mouth as she gripped the morsel of meat with her teeth. She leaned forward slightly to prevent the juice and sauce that dripped from her fork from spilling on her dress. As she did so, the clinging dress parted from her breasts. My gaze fixed, waiting for the dress to reveal its contents again. Saliva flowed across my bottom lip and over my chin.

Tracy smiled. "Joe," she commented, "you're dribbling." I felt admonished. I quickly grabbed my napkin and mopped the rivulets from my lips.

Tracy's facial expression was slightly condescending and mocking; but her sudden laughter relieved the moment.

"You are obviously starved of the finer niceties of life," she added with a rapturous gaze. I ate steadily using both knife and fork in the European manner, only punctuating my steady consumption of the delicious meal to sip my wine and to grunt in appreciation at the quality of the food. There was little conversation; we glanced at each other from time to time, smiled and watched each other eat. It seemed to slow down our eating. I was reluctant now to finish my meal in case it would break the intimacy that I felt we had. I was sure Tracy was doing exactly the same; in fact, she seemed to be leading the action, like a conversationalist leading a discussion. We devoured not only the food. As we sated our appetites, we seemed to be devouring each other with our eyes. We were increasingly smiling at each other, and Tracy made no attempt to redirect my obvious staring at her moist mouth, her long neck, and her breasts.

Tracy served black coffee with the chocolate mousse desert. I found the coffee bitter and the mousse too sweet for my tastes, but sipping the aroma filled liquid gave me time to appraise her from a more detached perspective. She seemed out of place. Excessively beautiful with a wanton manner that paid little or no heed to the affairs or condition of my Uncle.

"Joe, tell me," she said, with a sudden abruptness, "why have you come here?"

"You've no idea?" I asked.

"None at all. I assume you are a relative of George's. Which side of the Archer family do you belong to?" Tracy's question was almost in the form of a demand for further information. Her tone caused me to be suddenly alert, almost defensive. I chose my words carefully.

"I'm not related to the Archer family." As if sensing something inconceivable in this reply, Tracy probed further.

"Then why are you visiting George, what's the connection?"

"He's an old friend of the family. He knew my mother many years ago." I decided not to reveal exactly my connection with the old man at this stage. Uncle Charlie and I had shared many private family connections and I felt no compulsion to reveal George Archer's true identity to this girlfriend of the old man's. Let him tell his story when he's ready and if he wants to, I thought.

"Er, how long have you been with George?" My question seemed to hit her out of the blue. It was her turn to look slightly befuddled; but she quickly recovered her poise.

"Three years I think; let me think, yes, three years." I sensed that extracting information was, for some reason, likely to be difficult.

"Tell me Tracy," I tried hard not too sound too serious, "why do you live here, what do you do here?" Tracy looked at me quizzically before answering, perhaps looking for some hidden meaning.

"I don't do anything much now that he's so ill, I just hang around, waiting. "

"For him to die?" I interjected.

"Yes, but you don't have to put it so coldly. I've done my share. When I came to work for the firm, I was just a secretary for one of George's executives in his downtown office. I got noticed; I made sure I got noticed. I wanted to get on, just like anybody else."

Tracy became flushed with excitement at recalling, with some pride how she had out maneuvered others so as to be recognized by George Archer.

"It wasn't that difficult. He had a reputation for pretty girls." And she was exceptionally attractive I mused.

"I also made sure I was identified with those who did the best work. The other managers often commented how efficient I was. They liked my ideas...actually I borrowed the best of them from discussions I overheard from the other managers. Anyway, they soon recommended me to Mr. Archer."

* * *

With the passage of time, and success of Archer Enterprises, Charlie gave almost no thought to his alter ego; he was, in his mind, George Archer and save for the death of his sister, Charlie was a well-hidden memory.

He had quickly realized that they had, if anything, understated the skills of his diminutive personal executive; and she had other qualities. She made him feel good. She flattered his manly ego with effective praise; the occasional brushes of her hand on his excited him. He also loved the fragrance of her perfume. It filled his nostrils as she approached and lingered in the room after she had gone.

At times, she could be aloof and distant. It added to her mystique and heightened his urgency for her. But he was afraid. Afraid of rejection; afraid of her youth, afraid of her blatant cunning and afraid of himself. He hadn't felt well for some time, although he had periods when the pain was less intense, the nausea less sickening. And she made him feel young. Her presence anesthetized his illness; he felt a youthful passion for her, a longing in his loins. But he knew that if he took her, a little of the mystique would vanish, the power of the anesthetic would wear off. And so he contented himself with closeness, allowing her to linger affectionately on his shoulders, to caress the nape of his neck, to rub his shoulders with her small but strong hands.

He soon needed more of this drug. The evenings were long and silent. His cook, housemaid and valet were discrete to the extent of being boring. They melted in and out of the background like ghostly aberrations, providing only infrequent and terribly polite conversation. His suggestion to Tracy that she move in to his apartment didn't receive an immediate response, but within a few days, Tracy approached him about his offer.

"Mr. Archer..."

"Call me George, please."

"George, what is it you want from me? I mean, what do you want me to do? What do you want me to be?"

"Look Tracy, let me put it as plainly as possible. I don't think that I have a lot of time left, maybe a few months the Doc says. But I need something, someone to make me feel good each morning, someone who makes me smile, someone who is bouncy and beautiful and alive. I don't want sex, I want a sexy companion, someone who rekindles my interest in life without making it seem as though it's all gone by me."

"A play bunny, that's what you want, a sexy toy to have hanging around."

"I'm not trying to force you to live with me Tracy. I'm sorry I started this now, it's just that I enjoy your company, I like looking at you, I enjoy having you look after me..."

"If I did agree to some arrangement George, what is in it for me?"

"Well, as my personal secretary, you'll get double your current salary, and you'll be responsible for all my personal arrangements. I need someone to arrange my schedule, help me contact my department managers, help me keep them on their toes. I want you to help me give the impression that I'm still very active, still very concerned with all my business interests...what do you think?"

There wasn't a hint of hesitation. It was as if this was just what she wanted to hear.

"I think I'd be crazy to miss the opportunity."

Chapter 7

Concerns

George Archer died peacefully in his sleep two nights later. That morning, Tracy woke me early; it was about seven.

"Joe, Joe, wake up." Tracy was standing over me shaking my shoulder. I peeled back a lazy eye and winked at her lasciviously.

"Tracy, Tracy," I murmured, "climb in with me, it's wonderfully warm in here." She glared at me as if she was about to scold me severely. She then gave a half smile and slid an ice-cold hand across my chest. I shivered in response. Tracy leant forward and kissed my cheek, letting her hand slide down to reach my morning glory. She stuck out her tongue to lick the lobe of my ear and whispered.

"We'd better wait until after the funeral."

"After the what?"

"The funeral, he popped off in the night, sometime early this morning the nurse tells me." I sat bolt upright, grabbing her by the shoulders with both hands.

"Why the hell didn't you tell me? What game are you playing?"

"Game? Me playing games! It's you who wanted to play games. I just came in to give you the news of George's death, that's all." I pushed her roughly to one side and leapt out of bed. I grabbed a dressing gown from the door and rushed down the hallway in the direction of my Uncle's room. The nurse cut me off before I could enter the room.

"Mr. Archer passed away about four thirty. It was apparently a peaceful death. I was on the cot bed in case he should need me, but I didn't hear a sound. My alarm woke me at five so that I could administer his usual dose, but he'd already passed away. I immediately called the doctor who verified he was dead, and gave me an approximate time of death. I'm very sorry, Joe. I do believe that your coming gave him some comfort. He seemed to let go after you both became quite friendly. You can go in and see him if you like."

Two other nurses were finishing pampering and washing the corpse. His hair had been combed, his face washed and his hands folded across his chest. He looked extremely well; the best I had seen him since my arrival. He looked more like the mystery man who had visited my mother's funeral. I offered a silent prayer over my dead Uncle. As I kissed his forehead, I felt tears gathering in my eyes. I watched almost in amazement as they splashed onto the pale face of my Uncle and rolled down his pale cheek. A weeping corpse. I pulled away, startled.

* * *

George Archer was wheeled into the funeral service in a black and ornate mahogany coffin with brass handles and fittings. Its old fashioned appearance contrasted with the red and black silent rubber wheels that supported the trolley, one of which squeaked rhythmically as the coffin trolley rolled forward on the red flagstones. The service followed the script ordained by the deceased. George Archer had been thorough, even in death. The congregation was small, but there were one or two that I didn't recognize. Tracy was there, of course, as were most of the nurses and the house staff. George had made arrangements to be cremated. It seemed a fitting end for someone who had become so neat, ordered, and ordering. At the end of the service, the coffin was wheeled behind a red curtain as the last hymn played.

The small hitch in the arrangements soon became self-evident. The sleek black hearse at the back of the church, which was to discreetly usher George Archer's remains to the crematorium, was still in its parked position some ten minutes after the small contingent had filed from the church. I indulged in small talk with a church usher at the same time keeping an enquiring eye on the stately and stationary black coffin carrier. An ambulance arrived near the rear entrance to the church and drew alongside the hearse. At last the coffin carrying Mr. Archer's body was wheeled from the church toward the parked vehicles. But instead of being loaded into the hearse, the coffin was lifted onto a stretcher from the ambulance. My jaw dropped in amazement as four ambulance men in blue uniforms attempted to lift the stretchered coffin into the rear of the ambulance. They struggled to lift the frail body in its mahogany shroud and had to enlist two church officials to help with the exercise.

"The deceased is to be examined by the local Coroner," explained one of the church officials who had been commandeered to assist in lifting the coffin into the back of the ambulance. "I was asked to tell you that a meeting will be held in the Coroner's office at ten tomorrow morning."

"Who told you?" I demanded. "What the hell's going on?"

"There was a guy with an accent like yours, and an official from the Coroner's office. They have been here since first thing this morning. They didn't want the service to go ahead, but the Chaplain insisted." I turned to the Chaplain.

"Tell me what's going on? Who the hell are those people and why are they interfering with this service?"

"They didn't want the body to be cremated without first examining it," explained the Chaplain, somewhat reluctantly. "In fact they wanted to remove your Uncle's body this morning, before the service had started, but I insisted. After all, the arrangements had been made."

"Who's they?" I demanded.

"Well, the Coroner's Office had instructions from the State Department. The other fella is from the Australian Embassy. A matter of routine, they said. Something to do with his being an Australian citizen. There will be a meeting at the Coroner's Office at ten tomorrow morning."

"Hopefully with some explanation," I added.

"I expect that's the purpose of the meeting," offered the Chaplain with a tinge of sarcasm in his voice.

The Coroner's office was housed in a small complex comprising an estate agent, a lawyer's office, an insurance office and a doughnut shop. I arrived with twenty minutes to spare. The pleasant aroma wafting from the shop when the sliding access window was pushed open caught my attention. I ordered a small black coffee and a plain doughnut. The doughnut was virtually tasteless and quite hard. I dunked the end of the doughnut into the steaming black liquid and quickly bit into the coffee soaked cake. It was surprisingly good. I could hardly swallow the first bite fast enough in anticipation of the next coffee soaked morsel of softened doughnut. I managed to get five coffee soaked chunks before exhausting my supply of dunkable cake. What remained was a third of a cup of dark brown liquid with lumps of doughnut adhering to the sides of the cup just above the coffee line. I pitched these unappetizing dregs into a plastic lined bin fastened to a concrete post.

I nodded to the Chaplain, who was waiting outside the door. We exchanged brief greetings and then went inside to the Coroner's office. The Coroner introduced himself; "I'm the Coroner for this county. The Chaplain I know, which leaves you to be the deceased's visitor from England."

"Joe, Joe Jackson." I extended a hand toward the thin and emaciated fingers of the Coroner. The fingers were long, like tentacles. They wrapped around my hand in a soft and distant manner, which prevented our palms from touching. The tentacles released their wrap almost as soon as they touched my hand. It was a quick and impersonal handshake. The owner of this unfortunate hand kept his head bowed throughout our greeting as if embarrassed by the repulsion that his hand might convey. I glanced at my own hand as I lifted my arm away from the unctuous coroner. I half expected to see some slimy rash and was relieved to find no obvious contamination. I hoped the coroner didn't see my surreptitious glance.

A large and square jawed man introduced himself. His broad Australian accent conveyed his origins in his first half sentence.

"G'day Mr. Jackson... Joe, right? I'm Max, Max Jordan. I represent the West Australian Government. I'm with the Australian Embassy here in Washington." He wore a camel coloured blazer with an embossed black swan surrounded by a shield on his breast pocket. The gold lamé thread caught the morning sunlight as it streamed in through the slatted wooden window blinds.

"I should tell you that I was asked to intervene by our Fraud Squad."

"Fraud Squad!" I repeated, with obvious alarm in my voice.

"Let's not get ahead of ourselves Max. I think we owe Mr. Jackson some explanation before he becomes unduly alarmed." The sudden intervention of the third man in the office caused them all to turn in his direction. "Let me introduce myself. I'm John Taylor with the State Department. I'm here to help Mr. Jordan with his enquiries and to provide any assistance I can to the family members." He spoke with a soft, almost disquieting manner that left me feeling uncomfortable. "We have reason to believe that Mr. Archer may have been able to help us with enquiries into the death of his partner some time ago."

"In Australia you mean?" I blurted.

"Exactly," interrupted Max Jordan, "and not to put too fine a point on it, we would like to know how his partner died. You see, a body was found about six months back. Well, a skeleton really, but some of the body was amazingly well-preserved. It had been covered for years in a clay layer at the base of one of those dams your Uncle was involved with before the war. The old dam wasn't needed any more. When they bulldozed away the base they unearthed this body."

"How do you know it was connected with my Uncle's firm?" I asked.

"Well," continued Max in his twangy drawl, "we don't have proof of any connection in the formal sense, but a couple of the old Abos and a cockie or two - farmers to you," he added with a grin, "tell a tale of one of the partners being caught in a collapsing dam. It was even reported in the local newspaper. Apparently Mr. Archer was lucky to get away with his life. We would have liked to interview him about the accident, just to set our records straight."

"There were also other suspicions," added the rather strange John Taylor. "It seemed that Mr. Archer's business started to flourish shortly after that incident. There may be a suggestion of impropriety."

"What exactly are you suggesting," I enquired.

"You see," interrupted Max Jordan, "George Archer's partner was a bit of a hot head. He'd been in trouble when he first arrived in West Australia. Our view is that he may have become something of a liability, or maybe he was fiddling the books. George Archer may have simply taken the opportunity to get rid of this character and move on. His firm certainly grew very quickly from that point onwards."

"But why hold up the cremation ceremony?" I asked. "It doesn't make sense. Even if your suspicions are true and Mr. Archer did murder his partner, what does it mean after all this time? Surely you cannot have taken all this trouble just to clear up some old suspected murder?"

"There's more to this Joe," replied Max Jordan. "We found a letter in a leather wallet in the inside pocket of the body. It was amazingly well-preserved. Partly due to the leather wallet and partly to the sealing of clay, so the forensics boys tell me."

I turned quickly to look at Max Jordan, hoping I wouldn't betray my rising concern. I felt I was hiding some secret that had at first seemed inconsequential, but now assumed mammoth proportions.

"A letter!" I exclaimed. "Does it tell you anything, how does it help?" I hoped I didn't sound unduly anxious or nervous. My heart was now pounding in my chest and my face felt flushed.

"Well," drawled Max, "the most unusual thing was that the letter was addressed to George Archer." I was almost relieved.

"So what?", I probed, "how does that lead to so much suspicion. They were partners weren't they? He could simply have been given the letter by George Archer." I felt I was suddenly getting deeper into this than I wanted. I felt I was deliberately withholding evidence in case my own fortunes should be affected in some way.

"But the letter was of a very personal nature; and the wallet had been embossed with the letters G.A. – A strange combination of circumstances I think you'll agree". I nodded slowly as I let this all sink in.

"And the letter, what did it say, can it be read?"

Chapter 8

DORIS CHAPMAN

Derbyshire, 1924.

Doris Chapman first met George Archer at the home of his parents in Reading. Not that she met him in any traditional sense of the word; hers was a different status from his. She was employed by the Archer family to serve as a hostess at the weekend parties they occasionally held. She welcomed the chance to supplement the somewhat meagre income she received working as a secretary for a local firm of solicitors. But it wasn't just the extra income she enjoyed. It was the chance to dress up and select from one of her three silk dresses; the chance to mingle with some of the upper-middle class and engage in conversation, even if her role was merely one of a facilitator. The Archers had discovered her quite by chance. Mr. Archer had wiled away some time in the front office while waiting for his appointment and found the young Doris to be very well-informed, well read and very amusing. She had the engaging habit of saying the most outlandish things and then retreating into a shell of embarrassment. She could be very blunt and pointed and suddenly equally coy. She had sparkling, lively eyes and a pert mouth. Her ability to engage Mr. Archer in what he considered to be amusing, almost daring, conversation intrigued him. He relayed his chance encounter to Mrs. Archer who suggested it might be amusing to have her help at their next party.

Doris was delighted by the invitation. Mr. Archer dropped by the office to explain, in the rather stuffy and formal way so typical of the upper middle class in the 1920s.

"Miss Chapman, nice to see you again. Now, Miss Chapman, I have a proposition for you."

"Mr. Archer!" squealed Doris in mock indignation. "What a way to start the morning."

"Miss Chapman..."

"You'd better call me Doris if you are going to proposition me."

Mr. Archer gave a brief snigger. He wasn't above sniggering.

"Perhaps I should start again. My wife and I..."

"Lost its appeal already," quipped Doris.

"Really Miss...er, I mean Doris. You really are a most amusing young woman. Well look. This weekend we are having a party for our friends. We really need someone who can help organize the staff and also make everyone feel comfortable. We would of course offer you a reasonable reimbursement... how does ten pounds sound?"

"That's more than I make in a month Mr. Archer. I'm staggered."

"Is that a yes or a no Doris?"

"Why yes, of course."

"Good. I am sure you'll do wonderfully. Mrs. Archer needs you to pop up to the house on Wednesday evening at seven. She'll go through the guest list, and give you all the details regarding your duties."

"Seven on Wednesday...yes I can make that."

"Good, I'm glad you will be able to help. I'm sure you'll have a splendid time. Good day Doris."

"Bye Mr. Archer."

Doris was a huge success. Not only did she organize the servants and instruct the cook, just as Mrs. Archer would have wished; she also delighted and amused the guests with her homespun charm. Her seemingly casual remarks teased the egos of the male guests and yet flattered their wives. She skillfully interjected only when the conversation lulled, or when Major Thornton went on with one of his endless stories about shooting grouse in Scotland. He was rather proud of the fact that he was a regular guest at Lord MacKay's estate near Dumfries; however, he had the unfortunate tendency to belabour his reminiscences.

As the evening progressed, the women chatted on exchanging gossip for pleasantries. Their heads leaned forward to capture and savour the racier items of intrigue with interjections of "well I never!" interspersed with cackles and giggles which resulted in their flinging back coiffed hair and pillbox hats almost in unison. The men took refuge at the far end of the long drawing room where they could light their cigars and blow billows of aromatic smoke in the direction of their spouses. They talked of politics and hunting, of the Empire and of Europe. They persuaded each other of their own security and reassured one another as to their attitudes and values. Young George

Archer seemed at odds with this sober group. Doris heard his voice raised in protest on more than one occasion.

"I don't see any adventure or future for me if I remain in England," he explained. "I don't agree with your ideas that suggest the status quo should be maintained, seemingly at all costs."

"Now George," interjected Mr. Archer, "we are all very aware of your call for the rights of all men."

"It's not just a question of rights; it's more a need for equality. Men must feel they can progress because of their abilities, not because of their birth."

"But surely George, you cannot deny that many more of us have opportunities that a hundred years ago would have been only for the privileged few," added Mr. Blackmore, a local banker.

"Oh, I admit some progress has been made; but it's a slow inevitable progress that does virtually nothing to create new opportunities or to encourage new ideas."

"So, it's revolution you seek," teased Mr. Turner, the owner of a local cattle auction business.

"No, I don't want to see turmoil, merely the acceleration of the rate at which new ideas are accepted and nurtured; and that means encouraging all who are entitled to vote to seek the highest office. Women too have more to offer than we seem prepared to allow."

Doris had been lingering on the edge of the group and couldn't resist the chance to encourage these bold statements of George Archer's.

"Oh, I must agree. We women are strong and intelligent. We can rear your children, labour in the garden, keep the house budgets, purchase fittings and furniture, supervise staff and outlive all our men, but we are considered barely capable of running a local sweet shop. Give us a chance to make a difference and we will, you'll see."

"Well said, er Doris, I couldn't agree more emphatically," added George Archer. "It's time we had more bold talk, not just from women, but from all groups; skilled workers, semi-skilled workers, craftsmen, clerks and shopkeepers. Every sector of our society must feel able to make a difference. If we don't encourage this investment in talent we'll be left in the dust by the Germans, the Canadians, the Australians and especially by our American cousins."

Mr. Archer saw his chance to change the direction of this mildly seditious conversation.

"Of course you all know that George is planning to flee this country he so berates and move to Australia."

"It's only for a few years you understand. I have the opportunity to be the engineer for a mining company in Kalgoorlie. I regard it is an ideal chance to gain some invaluable experience. I could never hope to get such a position in this country, not until I had at least fifteen years of prior experience."

"Australia!" gasped Doris. "Sounds so very exciting!" George smiled at the admiring Doris. "You may just make something of yourself!" she added, in a teasing voice. George found himself enthralled by this bold young woman. Her bright and lively eyes twinkled with charm, especially as she added her teasing remarks. It was as if she found some inner delight in getting the better of her male companions. George contented himself with observing Doris as she flitted from group to group, leaving them smiling in her wake at her wit and charm. The women sent subtle semaphores with wispish waves of their silkish hankies accentuated by nods, hand gestures, and errant eyebrows. Their signals were generally favorable, something of a coup for Mrs. Archer. The men exhaled their smoke and invoked, rhetorically; "Charming girl, what?" "Yes, simply charming." Their eyes turned in unison to observe their young hostess. "Good looking, too." "Hell of a figure." "Delightful. Makes me think of earlier days." The women caught sight of this vulgar voyeurism. Hands twitched, eyebrows reached new peaks, and legs crossed in an angry screech of silk, wool, cotton and tweed.

The next day, George called in at the office where Doris worked on the pretext of thanking her "for the splendid job she had done last evening."

"Do you think it went alright? I thought it started well enough, but it seemed to get a bit strained toward the end of the night. I wondered if I had said or done anything inappropriate?"

"Not in the least," insisted George. "You were caught in the difficult position of having to appeal to the vanities of both sexes without offending either of them."

"Yes, that did occur to me, especially when one or two of the husbands had their eyes transfixed on my behind." George laughed.

"Look, let me repay you for the trouble you encountered..."

"Or caused," interjected Doris.

"If you are free this evening, I'd like to take you to dinner; there's a new restaurant about 20 miles away. I could pick you up at seven." Doris looked at him with her large soft brown eyes, and smiled.

"You can tell me all about your plans for Australia."

"Great. I'll see you at seven."

George Archer found he was enjoying Doris' company more than he had anticipated. It was not what he had planned. With his imminent departure to Australia, the last thing he wanted was a romantic entanglement which might interfere with his plans to work in the rough and male dominated world of mining. He hoped to be totally free to work in Australia, returning to England for the odd visit, and eventually settling down in Australia if he really liked it there, or returning to England armed with experience, if he did not. George had omitted to tell his parents that he might decide to stay in Australia. He would deal with that eventuality if the time arose. He did, however, explain all this to Doris; or at least try to. She joked, "Why don't you take me with you?"

George became very defensive. He insisted that he must travel alone.

"I was only joking George, why we've only just met, and I certainly don't want to interfere with your plans." George hadn't reckoned on meeting someone like Doris. He resolved it wouldn't change his plans though and he carefully and painstakingly explained his situation to Doris. She called him "a boring old fart"; despite being quite swept away by this romantic would-be explorer.

Doris; this liberated charmer, this wonderfully candid and contrary conversationalist; beautiful and yet branded by her accent, her attitudes and her criticisms, made George feel so comfortable and brave. She reassured him about his plans to work in Australia. She could see all the benefits and excitement of what he was planning. His family, on the other hand, sensed only some awful and protracted separation. Mrs. Archer complained with increasing frequency to Mr. Archer, imploring him to save her son from this "miss-adventure". Mr. Archer felt increasingly powerless to influence his son. He secretly admired his son's bold initiatives and was determined not to let Mrs. Archer's motherly concerns affect his judgment, or result in some friction between them and their son. George was glad of the opportunity to find reassurance for his plans. His mother's obvious concerns were making this last few weeks before his departure very difficult. His father, he sensed, was trying his best to control the situation, but his attempts at directed conversation were becoming more and more contrived.

"Doris, I've got to go up to London next week to buy essentials for my passage. Care to come?"

"A dirty weekend eh. Really George, all you need to do is ask. All this beating around the bush!" George blushed.

"That's not what I meant..."

"Well, that's nice I must say. Next you'll be telling me that you respect me for my mind."

""But I do..."

"And you don't notice my body?" teased Doris.

"You know I do," replied George, "I can't keep my eyes off you."

"It's not your eyes that concern me," she replied with a broad smile. George laughed. Doris laughed... they laughed so loud and hard they had to support each other.

"Of course I'll come. But with one proviso. None of this separate room nonsense, and none of this pretending to be husband and wife. We'll simply sign in as who we are. You need to know what you are missing before you trek off to Australia."

"Ah, now you sound just like my mother."

They laughed again, hugged one another, and laughed, and laughed.

London was exciting. They took a taxi to Bond Street from a nice hotel near Charing Cross Station. Doris had added several items to the list George had prepared. She took great delight in selecting his shirts and socks, carefully picking a mixture of sensible cotton shirts for work and a smaller number of dress shirts and dress collars. They worked feverishly; Doris picked out, discarded, selected and discarded again before settling on the most appropriate and practical series of selections. A small shop on the second floor just near Fleet Street offered "everything" for the tropical traveler. The tropics weren't on George's itinerary, however, their selection of calico shirts, sun hats, leather boots and camping equipment provided many of the essential items for George's list. Doris found a small, leather bound writing set to go with a leather hold-all which George had selected with considerable care. Instructions were left with every store to box and send their purchases to George's home address. Most willingly agreed to offer this service, given the number of items being purchased. The Fleet Street specialists even offered to ship George's order direct to Australia. George declined their generous offer, preferring to check his purchases prior to packing them off to Western Australia.

The Garrick Theatre entrance appeared bright and appealing. It was in stark contrast to the yellow and diffuse light emitted by the hissing street lamps still lit by gas. The play was Major Barbara by George Bernard

Shaw. Doris had seen many plays at their local theatre, but this was her first experience of the famous London stage and its celebrated thespians. She marveled at the intimacy of the small and compact theatre. Their seats were in the third row; so close that Doris felt she could reach out and touch the actors. The beating of Major Barbara's drum and the clash of symbols emitted a deafening ring, which startled Doris so much that she gasped and grabbed George's arm. George wrapped his long fingers around her hand and held her hand in place against his arm. Doris smiled and gently squeezed his forearm. Major Barbara appeared to witness this display of affection and smile at them both.

George and Doris spent three days in London. It took about a day and a half to get the items needed for George's trip. The rest of the time was spent visiting London museums, art galleries, Buckingham Palace and Holland Park. Doris particularly enjoyed Holland Park. A brass band played at the edge of a small lake. The ground sloped toward the lake forming a natural amphitheatre, which elevated the tone and quality of the deep base notes. The resounding marches echoed around them making them bristle with excitement.

"Makes you proud to be in England," whispered Doris. George's reply surprised her.

"I'll miss all of this." His eyes were wet and misty looking. "Doris..."

"Yes George?"

"I want you to write to me in Australia. We must keep in touch."

"Only if you write to me," urged Doris.

"Why don't I believe you'll write?" queried George.

"George, of course I'll write. This has been the most wonderful period of my life. Meeting your wonderful family and their odd friends, and then you..."

"Which category am I in, wonderful, or odd?" asked George.

"Oh, wonderfully odd of course," teased Doris.

On the day of departure, they all traveled down to Southampton on the train to see George off. They had a first class compartment to themselves, but conversation was stunted by the thought of George's approaching embarkation. It hung over all of them like some dark cloud. Even Doris was unusually silent. She felt as if either she or George's parents didn't belong on this unpleasant journey. They both wanted George to themselves; both had personal claims on the imminent traveler. George quickly realised that this collective and protracted farewell was a mistake. He wished he had insisted on traveling alone to Southampton. They had each exhausted their 'goodbyes' over the last days.

"Write soon," pleaded George as he embraced Doris. The purser was making his last request for guests to leave the ship.

"As soon as I hear from you," answered Doris.

It was almost six weeks later when Doris received her first letter from George. She eagerly opened the letter and quickly skimmed the sentences, searching for the ending.

With all my love,
Yours,

His scrawled signature followed. Doris then read the letter slowly and methodically, absorbing every word and phrase, trying her best to imagine the dry dusty streets of Kalgoorlie, which George had described. Doris replied to George the very next day. She hadn't been feeling very well the last couple of weeks, but simply ignored her condition in her reply to George.

Doris suspected and then confirmed that her "condition" was in fact a pregnancy. She felt so foolish and ridiculous. How could she, a pragmatic feminist, allow herself to become pregnant? She had been somewhat careless with George, that was becoming painfully obvious; but she had hoped that she had taken reasonable and sufficient precautions.

But what to do? She felt trapped by the circumstances. She desperately wanted to write to George and give him the news; but it all seemed like a trap, as if she had planned this event to get George to marry her. Doris simply gave up writing to George.

Mr. Archer heard the startling news from his solicitor.

"Pregnant…pregnant, I can't believe it. She seems such a decent girl. High spirited, full of fun, but decent. Have you any idea who the father is?" His slow brain refused to accept the obvious.

"You mean you've no idea?" probed the solicitor, not wanting to offend his old friend and client. "I'd rather not say. You know what village gossip is like."

"You don't mean…"

"I'm afraid so. It is only rumour. She's been stubbornly unwilling to name the father. I asked her myself, since I am her employer, but she refused point blank and urged me not to ask her again."

"George, the fool, I can't believe he could have allowed himself..." His voice trailed off as he realised the obvious.

"Thank God he's in Australia away from all this. I'll need to speak to Mrs. Archer. She needs to hear it from me before the village gossips get to her. What's going to happen to Doris? Can you continue to employ her?"

"For a couple more months I think. But after that it's going to be impossible. The gossip, the stares, the nudges; she'll need to leave the village, it's the only chance she, they, are going to have."

The letter Doris received from the Archers was very brief, curt and to the point.

'Dear Doris,
We would like you to come to afternoon tea on Saturday next. We believe that there are things that need urgently to be discussed and plans made for the future.
Yours sincerely
Mr. and Mrs. Archer.'

Doris pondered for some time before deciding to visit the Archers. She felt, on refection, that she really had no option but to visit them, even though their motive in extending this invitation was less than clear.

The Archers were alone in the house when she arrived. There was no sign of the cook or the gardener. Even the maid had apparently been given the afternoon off. Her bicycle was not in its usual place with its front wheel lodged between the fence and the gatepost. A rather frosty Mrs. Archer opened the door in answer to Doris's hesitant knock. Doris was taken somewhat by surprise. She hadn't expected Mrs. Archer to answer the door, and the almost instantaneous response to her quick double knock suggested that she had been waiting for her visitor.

"Come in Doris, Mr. Archer is in the living room." Doris presumed this was an invitation to proceed to the inner sanctum. Mr. Archer was sitting stiffly on a high backed dining chair. He motioned Doris to join him at the highly polished table. Mrs. Archer moved toward their table, paused, and then veered off to take a winged chair next to the fireplace. She sat poised on the edge of her seat with a very erect posture.

Mrs. Archer spoke first.

"Doris, we have been informed that you are pregnant." She seemed to place great emphasis on the word "pregnant", dividing it into two distinct syllables.

"Really, do we have to start like this?" asked Mr. Archer in more conciliatory tones.

"It's quite alright. I am pregnant and there is no point in trying to avoid the issue." Doris surprised herself with her ability to speak for herself. She had been dreading this encounter and had contemplated not coming many times.

Mrs. Archer forged on.

"Whose baby do you think it is?" There was the distinct implication that someone other than her son must be the father.

"Really dear, I think we know the answer to that." Mr. Archer tried to sound apologetic.

"Do we, do we, I'm not convinced?" Mrs. Archer's retort rose in crescendo.

"Look, I've come here at your request to try and explain my side." Doris spoke with cool resolve, but inside she was literally boiling. Perspiration gathered under her arm pits and dropped on her upper bodice. She felt very uncomfortable. Mr. Archer interjected.

"Look dear, we must be calm about this. I'm sure it's just as difficult for Doris, after all she is the one who's with child."

The silly old bugger couldn't bring himself to say 'pregnant', thought Doris, but at least he's being more helpful than that bitch who claims to be George's mother. Doris caught herself glaring in Mrs. Archer's direction. Mrs. Archer sat very still as if struck dumb by her husband's mild rebuke and Doris's hostile glare. The lull in the conversation seemed to clear the air, giving Doris time to compose herself. She decided to explain things from her side, as least as much as she could.

"I love George and had I not become pregnant I would be writing to him daily to tell him just that. Since I found out I was pregnant, I stopped writing to him. The very last thing I want is for George to feel that he must sacrifice his career and return here to marry me. Nor do I want George to feel he must ask me to live in Australia, at least, not under these circumstances. The baby I am expecting is George's; he is the father. We spent a great deal of time together before he sailed, as you know, and although I thought we were being careful, I'm afraid we weren't careful enough."

"I can hardly believe my ears," whispered a shocked Mrs. Archer. "I could weep for my poor George."

"What about me? I'm carrying his child, your grandchild..." Doris suddenly burst into tears and sobbed uncontrollably for several minutes. Her head remained bent and pressed into her hands long after the sobs subsided. She suddenly felt she was quite alone. Mr. and Mrs. Archer were not making a sound, not one pathetic little comforting word, not even a rebuke. But they were there, looking uncomfortable and restrained. She could see their blurred outlines through eyes misted with tears. Doris took a deep breath and continued.

"I have no intention of entrapping your dear George." Doris gave Mrs. Archer an icy stare. "It's precisely because I love dear George that I don't want to entrap him in any way. I couldn't agree to any form of forced marriage, no matter how correct or honourable it may be. I want to be free to contact George once the baby has been born, and then let him make the right decision. I don't want to start any long-term relationship under any direct or implied threat."

Mr. Archer coughed as if signaling that he wanted to speak. Both Doris and Mrs. Archer turned in his direction, but he just sat staring in the direction of the fireplace. He shuffled as if embarrassed by their stares. He gave a second nervous cough, and then spoke.

"I honestly believe you are approaching this in a very courageous way, Doris. It will not be easy for you to face the villagers and continue working. How will you manage financially?"

"I've no intention of staying on here," replied Doris. "I've an Aunt who lives by herself near Birmingham. She has been a nurse for a number of years and I know she will help me get through this. I've also got some savings, a couple of hundred pounds I think."

"That's not going to support you for very long," said Mr. Archer. "You'll have an extra mouth to feed." Mrs.

Archer surprised them both by nodding in agreement with her husband.

"You will have to let us help you financially. It's the very least we can do for your baby, for our grandchild." She seemed relieved that Doris wasn't going to force herself on George. In fact, Mrs. Archer was delighted and relieved that Doris had decided to leave the area. She felt sure that would be the best thing for her and Mr. Archer.

"Yes," added Mr. Archer, "we want to do what ever we can to help you and our grandchild. We will also want to help with the child's education, boarding school, that sort of thing." Doris smiled at them both. She had no intention of letting them help by sending her child off to some private boarding school. She would write to George after the baby was born and he would send for them both, she was sure of that. The conversation got a lot lighter and brighter after this. The Archer's were delighted that Doris was leaving, and seemed equally pleased that she was prepared to accept their offer of financial assistance.

"I think I'll move to my Aunt's at the end of this month. I'm going to hand in my notice at the end of the week."

"Good for you," added Mrs. Archer, sounding a little too pleased at the plans Doris was outlining. Mr. Archer interjected quickly.

"We want to help you in any way we can. I'm going to instruct my bank to send you a cheque each month."

"You don't have to do that. I'm sure I'll be able to manage." Doris was, however, secretly glad of the offer and hoped Mr. Archer would follow up on his proposal. It could be very difficult for a single mother with no income, she knew that.

"Nonsense," replied Mr. Archer in very emphatic tones. "I mean to do the right thing for you and for our grandchild. If you don't need all the money I send, you can save some for the child's education."

"We really must put the child's name down for school. If it's a boy, it will be important for him to attend a school similar to the one George attended," added Mrs. Archer. Doris knew what that meant. A small, private, preparatory school run along military lines, followed by a mid-sized private school with a reputation for discipline. She shuddered at the thought.

The next couple of months passed very quickly. Doris packed her portfolio of things in a trunk given to her by the Archers. They had been good to their word, and had started by putting the sum of thirty pounds in Doris's account. This was an amazing sum to her, and she presumed that this must be an exceptional payment. She was staggered when a similar deposit was made in the subsequent month.

Mr. and Mrs. Archer ran Doris to the station and helped her onto the train. Mr. Archer had bought her ticket and arranged for her belongings to be handled by the porter. Doris knew that they were buying her silence, but in a strange way, she didn't mind. She had every intention of contacting George after the baby was born, something the Archers seemed intent on ignoring. She was also glad to leave the village. The gossips and the wags were beginning to annoy her. She'd had to restrain herself, more than once, from confronting those who were the most malicious.

Chapter 9
Aunt May

Aunt May met Doris at the railway station. She was a tall, thin woman with sharp angular features. She was only ten years or so older than Doris.

"Aunt May, May, May..." called Doris from the carriage window. May waved enthusiastically. She had always liked her niece and was very pleased that Doris had approached her for help. She felt a close kinship with Doris, in part because they weren't that different in age. She had assumed some responsibility for Doris since she was a young girl. Doris' parents had a difficult marriage, which was compounded by financial problems. May Carter had offered to help by having Doris to stay at every school holiday since her twelfth birthday. She had been a very shy and withdrawn child when she first started visiting. Doris enjoyed her Aunt's predictable ways and listened intently as Aunt May talked endlessly and incessantly about her work as a nurse, her interests in local politics, and attitude toward men. Aunt May was still young and a very good-looking woman. She had many opportunities to be married, but her strong will coupled with her inflexibility resulted in her never finding one that she thought could offer anything exceptional. Her suitors rarely lasted more than a few months before May became more and more disinterested in their attentions. "I got what I wanted from them," she would recall with a hearty laugh.

When Doris was a teenager, Aunt May had insisted that she drop the term 'Aunt', which seemed, she said, to age her prematurely.

"Call me May, Doris, that's my name and I want you to get used to using it." May often talked freely about some of the men she had known. She even remarked on their ignorant attitudes toward women, and toward sex in particular. Doris had been shocked, at first, by her Aunt's revelations but soon found that she was learning about life from her practical, pragmatic and independent Aunt. Her own Mother was a complete contrast to her strong younger sister. Doris's mother was a very nervous, almost neurotic woman, who worried as if her life depended on knowing the outcome to everything she encountered. Her nervousness was in part due to the loneliness she felt. Doris's father was a distant and uncaring man who preferred to keep company with the bottle. He had left home about seven years ago and none of them had heard from him since.

Aunt May had supported her sister; but she had also encouraged, almost insisted, that she become more independent. She would find strength, May urged, by being independent. It hadn't worked, and Doris's mother was now a nervous, shell of a woman.

Aunt May and Doris hugged.

"It's lovely to see you again," said Aunt May, looking her niece up and down. "You do look well, I'm impressed."

"Thanks May, it's great to see you."

Aunt May told Doris to unpack in the spare room and to take a long relaxing bath. They would talk after dinner if she wished.

"Thanks May. I feel comfortable already. I feel as though I've been living with my feet stuck in the village stocks. Everyone I know seems to be whispering and talking about me."

"You won't be bothered here. The one advantage of these large towns is that most people don't want to be involved with their neighbours. It's why I like living here."

Doris soaked herself for almost an hour in the large cast iron bathtub. Her breasts were becoming large and firm. She raised herself above the water line and admired her plump, smooth skin. Her stomach was slightly distended, yet it appeared quite in proportion to her enlarged breasts.

She flopped noisily back into the bath water, sending a wave of water splashing over the rim. Doris wrapped her partially dried body in a man's dressing gown she found on a shelf in the towel cupboard. She felt wonderfully warm and content. She slipped her feet into a pair of her Aunt's slippers, which were two or three sizes too big, and flopped down the small carpeted staircase. Aunt May was laying out plates on a small table in front of the coal fire. May laughed at her niece with her glowing pink cheeks.

"I thought you might have drowned. You were ages." The mild rebuke was followed by a wide smile. "I see you found one of my ex's dressing gowns. Maybe he was of some use after all." May laughed to herself as if sharing a private joke. "Sit over here where it's warm. We can eat by the fire. I've made Welsh Rarebit, is that alright?"

"Great," declared Doris.

It didn't take long to clear away the dishes and wash up. May shoveled more coal onto the glowing fire and poured two large glasses of cream sherry. Doris stretched out in front of the fire taking frequent sips from her slim glass. May sat more upright and leaned back against the soft folds of her favourite lounge chair.

"You'd better not drink too much in your condition." May finally broke the comfortable silence.

"What do you mean?" queried Doris in a lazy voice, not at all surprised by her Aunt's pointed remark.

"You're pregnant aren't you?" Doris pushed herself up to face her Aunt.

"It's that obvious is it?" she asked, feeling herself suddenly become flushed with embarrassment.

"No, not really, but there had to be a very good reason for your suggestion of an extended visit…"

"Apart from the fact that you are my favourite Aunt?"

"I'm your only Aunt."

"That too," retorted Doris. They laughed. Doris spent the next hour explaining the events of the last few months in her 'matter of fact' way.

"And you are sure that George feels the same way about you?" asked May.

"I know he does. I've absolutely no doubts on that score."

"You're lucky. It's not everyone who has the good fortune to feel that sure about a relationship; I envy you."

"But I feel so stupid for getting into this condition."

"There but for the grace of God," suggested May.

"I wasn't given any divine protection," replied Doris.

"Yes, I'm sorry, I shouldn't be so flippant."

The first few weeks at Aunt May's house were almost idyllic. The two women thoroughly enjoyed each other's company. They spent long evenings reminiscing about the summers Doris had previously spent with her Aunt. Doris gave May a full account of George and his parents, trying to conceal her discomfort at discussing George's mother, and making her love for George perfectly obvious. Doris and May began doing the practical and sensible things. They planned for the arrival of the baby, making long lists of names and speculated on everything from the sex of the baby, to its hair colour, its dimples, who it might take after, and what it might become.

May made simple meals with plenty of nutritious food, glasses of milk and the occasional bottle of wine. Doris felt the occasional twinge of pain in her side after some of Aunt May's more filling meals. She decided to eat more selectively, and to avoid the fatty foods, which seemed to give her so much discomfort. Aunt May laughed when Doris explained her problem.

"I seem to be getting stomach cramps when I eat fried foods. I'm also passing wind like never before."

"Farting or belching?" enquired the phlegmatic Aunt May.

"Well both, if you must know."

"You're developing a good dose of morning sickness. It'll pass eventually."

"But its not just in the morning, it seems to be just after I eat, and it's becoming quite painful."

"I'll keep a good eye on you, and in the meantime, I'll make sure we have mostly poached or boiled foods; especially if fried foods are doing you the most harm."

It wasn't just the sight of food, or the smell of food; it was simply the thought of food. Air and gas refluxed into her mouth with almost every morsel of food she attempted to eat.

"I'm sorry, May, I just can't understand it. I've gone from having the biggest appetite and strongest stomach to feeling perpetually nauseous. And my ankles, they're quite swollen, look." Aunt May laughed.

"Sheer vanity, that's what it is. But not eating won't help your swollen ankles."

"I think I'll try some fruit, perhaps some pears." Doris spoke without conviction as if she had already decided that even the most delectable pears would still have the same effect. May picked her up on it immediately.

"You're not very convincing Doris. But if you go on like this you'll become ill. I feel I should take you to Dr. Gillan. You need to get a thorough examination anyway." Doris was becoming too tired to argue. She just wanted to steer the conversation away from food and rest. She felt very tired almost all the time. The first couple of hours in the morning were all right, but as soon as cooking smells wafted into the house their pungent odours brought on her nausea and tiredness.

May liked to have a cooked breakfast before she left to catch the 8:15 bus which took her almost to the main door of the hospital. May was methodical and punctual. She lived by a certain regimen of order that ensured her independence. She was delighted at her niece's arrival, yet equally reluctant to veer in any way from her daily routine.

Doris could hardly wait for her Aunt to leave. It signaled a chance for the air to clear of breakfast aromas and a respite from the now incessant and almost insistent advice on eating for two from her well-intentioned Aunt. Last evening had been quite tense.

"Really Doris, you can't go on like this. You'll make yourself ill. You haven't eaten for days." The discussion on food caused Doris's stomach to rumble. A vile bile gushed into her mouth and halfway into her left nostril. She snatched at her handkerchief, spitting and blowing the green phlegm and frothy brown bile into the folds of the white linen.

"Sorry Doris, I should leave you alone, I know. It's just that I'm so concerned."

"For God's sake, May..." Doris wretched again.

"Sorry dear, I'm so sorry." Doris smiled at her Aunt.

"I know, May; I'm sorry too. It shouldn't be like this, should it?"

Dr. Gillan was a stout Scot with wild wiry hair. He wore rimless glasses with thin wire frames that disappeared into his thatch of graying hair. Tufts of black hair sprouted from both his ears and from his nostrils. He probed at Doris's stomach with firm, practiced hands. Doris felt reassured by his confident manner.

"How are we progressing Doctor Gillan?" enquired a pale Doris. Her voice had lost its usual verve. She sounded tired and lethargic, but she tried to appear confident and able for the benefit of her attending physician.

"I don't think you should be trying to pass this off too lightly young woman. You need to eat more and drink plenty of fluids. You keep this up and I'll whisk you to hospital."

"I'm trying Doctor, it's so awful. I can hardly explain it."

"I expect it will pass; it usually does. I'll pop in next week and see how you are doing."

"And my baby Doctor Gillan, how is my baby doing?"

"The bairn has a strong heartbeat and is well-positioned. It will be an easy birth, you'll see."

"There's no such thing!" retorted Doris.

"Ah, I see you haven't lost your spirit. That's excellent, excellent. I'll be back in a week, but get in touch with me before that if you are experiencing any difficulties. In the mean time, I'll expect you to eat sensibly. Bye Doris." The mention of food was making Doris queasy. She waved a hand in the Doctor's direction and rolled onto her side.

"Well Dr. Gillan, how is my niece?" asked May as the Doctor closed the bedroom door behind him.

"For the moment she's holding her own. She was obviously in fine health before she became pregnant. Her blood pressure is high; we'll need to keep an eye on it. I'll not deny that I'm worried about her eating. I'll visit next week. Make sure she drinks plenty of fluids and try to get her interested in eating; dry toast, fruit, anything."

"I've tried the usual remedies. She's got the worst case of morning sickness I've ever seen."

The next day Doris felt a little better. She drank two full glasses of water, which May insisted she attempt to drink each morning. She even managed to eat two thin slabs of crisp toast, each with the faintest scraping of butter. May was very encouraged.

Doris was quite pleased with herself. She actually enjoyed her toast after she had digested the first few bites without experiencing any bilious reactions. Doris poured cold water into the washbasin and splashed her face by dipping in with her cupped hands. She felt cool and refreshed. Doris slipped on her Aunt's dressing gown and eased her way down stairs to the sitting room. Although Doris wasn't yet displaying a large distended stomach, she felt large and had a compulsion to walk with her feet splayed and waddled gingerly to the couch, grabbing the writing pad from the desk as she did so. Now that she felt a little better, Doris felt it was time do something she had been putting off for weeks; write to George.

Writing the letter took longer than she had expected. She wanted to get to the point so quickly, but seemed unable to do so. She tried several paragraphs on largely irrelevant information. She eventually decided to just address the real reason for writing to George.

'Dearest George,

Please forgive me for not writing to you earlier. It seems an eternity since we were last together and I've wanted so many times to write and tell you how much I miss you. I've delayed writing because I love you and because circumstances have changed so dramatically. There has been a very good reason for my not writing.

Let me get straight to the issue (Oh dear, that sounds terribly blunt – but blunt I must be).

What I've been putting off telling you, and what I'm desperately trying to put into words is that something wonderful and exciting is going to take place; and yet it fills me with dread!

The fact is that I am pregnant. And you, George, will soon be a father!

I'm so proud to be having your baby, but so disappointed at the circumstances. I feel guilty as if I've done something deliberate and cunning; something that would make you marry me. It's precisely because of this feeling that I haven't written, but I now know I must. You'll be a father by the time this reaches you.

I do hope you're not angry.

You'd better not bloody well mind, George. This baby is kicking me to death. He or she obviously has some of your adventurous streak. George, it's time we got together and planned for our future and for the future of our child.

I love you George. Please write soon.
Doris.

Doris popped the letter in a large white envelope, sealed it, and addressed it to George Archer at the same address in Kalgoorlie where she had arranged for his packages to be shipped. She left the sealed envelope on the corner of the desk together with other correspondence her Aunt had assembled for posting.

The pain, which suddenly gripped Doris, was excruciating. A sharp, stabbing pain in her right side. Doris gasped. She tried to move but was completely immobilized by the severity of the acute cramps that burst in her side. She gripped her side with both hands and tried to cry out. Her breathy gasps only heightened her pain. She got some modicum of comfort by clenching her teeth and rocking back and forth in her seat. The pain subsided for only a few seconds and suddenly attacked her with even greater venom. The severity of the pain caused Doris's body to shudder. She grabbed at her side, as if trying to tear away her afflicted flesh. Doris felt helpless and powerless, completely in the grip of a pain so intense and extreme. It was beyond anything she had experienced before. Just when she thought she couldn't stand anymore of these excruciating waves of pain, a welcome blackness engulfed her, numbing the pain as it did so. At last there was only a relieving, smothering, silky blackness.

When Aunt May first discovered her niece, pale and quiet and lying on the couch, she thought she was asleep. She quickly realized that something was amiss. Doris's black hair was matted against her forehead, her cheeks were white and clammy and her hands were twisted in the folds of her dress. What frightened her the most were Doris's eyes. They were half open but her eyes were rolled back in a death like stare. May gasped. She felt for a pulse. It was weak and erratic. She covered her niece with a tartan blanket and rushed out for help.

May paced restlessly. It had been over an hour since they had arrived in the white, clanging ambulance to the casualty door of the hospital. May had called Dr. Gillan at home. He was in the hospital within fifteen minutes. She stared at the hideous green tiles that lined the wide corridors. Their straight lines drew her gaze toward the door of the operating theatre. Its bright fluorescent lights cast a diffused beam through the glazed glass windows in the upper half of the heavy wooden doors. The glistening beam offered hope and expectation. Dr. Gillan would not allow her into the operating theatre. He was quite right of course, thought May. She had been so decisive and confident in dealing with the immediacy of the situation, but now she felt weak and nervous, almost jittery.

Dr. Gillan peered around the theatre door, beckoning to May. A white mask was dangling below his chin. It fluttered slightly as he talked.

"She's eclamptic May. I should have spotted this earlier. The symptoms were all there. She's had a couple of major convulsions. We managed to get those under control. The last convulsion resulted in the premature birth of her baby..."

May gasped. "How is the baby, is it dead, is it...?"

"The baby seems to be alright. We won't really know for a few weeks. You can never really tell with a premature delivery at seven and a half months, especially like this. It's Doris. We couldn't get her blood pressure under control."

May let out a low groan. "You don't mean ... she's dead?"

"I'm sorry May. There was nothing we could do. She had signs of edema when we brought her in. She died of heart failure shortly after her baby was born." May's knees felt very weak. Her head began to spin. Dr. Gillan caught her just as she collapsed.

Chapter 10

Georgina

May peered into the lace edged cot. The tiny baby wiggled a doll-like finger over the edge of its pink trimmed blanket. May wondered what was to become of this fettered neonate. It was still, to her, an ugly troll like creature; its soft pericranium pulsing rhythmically, like a deep blue pulsing vein. This gurgling, supine creature was the cause of a great deal of suffering. May blamed herself for not recognizing just how ill Doris had become. She blamed Dr. Gillan for failing to diagnose Doris's condition, and she blamed this impudent baby for daring to survive her beloved niece. Dr. Gillan also blamed himself. He said as much to May. In truth, he had assumed that having a superb nurse like May in the house made his visits rather superfluous. He admitted to himself that he had paid only scant attention to his patient. When he saw Doris lying in a comatose state, his immediate reaction was to look for some unrelated reason. A brain hemorrhage, perhaps. His detailed examination failed to confirm anything but the ugly truth. He had made the unforgivable error of complacency; of assumption. Beads of sweat gathered on his brow and ran along his temples causing him to rub his eyes with the back of his hand. He tried to console May, he even attempted to explain; but then realized he could not, and must not, admit that he had made a misdiagnosis.

May found herself visiting the baby several times a day. It was as if some magnet, some genetic bond, drew her towards this unfortunate child. Its future was unknown. One parent dead, the other an unsuspecting father half a world away. She had posted the letter Doris had written; she'd write and explain as soon as he replied. She didn't feel like trying to write and explain all this to George Archer just at the present. And the Archers. She must write to the Archers and tell them what had happened.

Within a few days, May realized how deeply attached she was becoming to this giggling, gurgling baby. She could hardly wait to see her again. May could see family resemblances in the facial folds of flesh. Her delicately tipped nose and the tiny proud chin reminded May of the vignette of herself as a baby which had been given to her on her tenth birthday by an uncle. The baby was christened Georgina. May thought this was an appropriate recognition of the girl's distant father.

May's letters to George Archer went unanswered. Little did she know that George Archer had been killed in the same year his daughter had been born. Charlie, as George Archer, received her correspondence, but simply threw away any letters addressed to George Archer that appeared to be personal. He didn't even bother to open them. He burnt them as soon as they arrived. It was as if handling them for any time would somehow further implicate Charlie in George Archer's death and deepen the complexity of his subterfuge. After her third letter went unanswered, May decided that George Archer was an uncaring and contemptible young man; not fit to have any association with his daughter, the delightful Georgina.

The Archers were devastated by the news of their son's death. Charlie had cunningly written to the Archers telling them that their son, George Archer, had been killed in a landslide on a dam he had been constructing. He even sent a carefully selected newspaper clipping which simply reported

'A tragic death: engineer killed by collapsing dam.

A young engineer from England was killed on April 5th, 1926 when a dam collapsed on the property of Malcolm Thomas, near Merriden. The body was completely buried and could not be recovered.'

Mr. Archer had been ill for some time with lung cancer. The news of his son's death sent him into an accelerated decline. He was berated by Mrs. Archer for encouraging her son to undertake the crazy mission to Australia. Mrs. Archer began to see her husband's illness as some retribution for his part in supporting their son's adventurous ways. She had little sympathy for her desperately ill husband. Poor Mrs. Archer. When her husband eventually succumbed to his debilitating disease, she sat in a chair in their bedroom, talking and further berating the dead corpse. A visiting nurse found her still jabbering away almost three days after Mr. Archer had finally wheezed his excruciatingly painful last breath. The nurse had rapped at the front door and stepped into the hallway as she always did on her weekly visits. She could hear Mrs. Archer talking at her husband, something she had come to expect. But it was the foul smell that attracted her attention the moment she set her foot on the bottom step of the staircase.

"Mrs. Archer, Mrs. Archer?" Her second call was louder as she quickly ran up the staircase. The bedroom door was half open. She could see Mrs. Archer sitting on the edge of a chair at the far side of the bed. She appeared to be muttering to herself. The nurse gasped as she stepped into the bedroom. The source of the putrid smell was readily apparent. The stiff white corpse of Mr. Archer stared in her direction, propped up as it was against several pillows. She could see now that Mrs. Archer was muttering to her dead husband. She appeared not to have noticed the nurse.

"Mrs. Archer, it's Nurse Moran, Janet Moran. I want you to come downstairs with me Mrs. Archer. I'll make you a cup of tea." Mrs. Archer appeared to respond to the calm strong tones of Janet Moran's voice. She turned her gaze away from her dead husband.

"That would be nice Janet. I've been waiting for you to come. That awkward husband of mine has been giving me some trouble..." Her voice trailed off and she allowed Janet to lead her out of the bedroom and down the staircase.

May tried to write to the Archers. This time her second letter was answered, not by the Archers, but by their family solicitor. He pointed out that Mr. Archer had recently died and that Mrs. Archer was unlikely to be able to manage her own affairs ever again. He suggested that either Georgina be put up for adoption, or that May consider bringing the girl up herself. May was quite taken aback by this turn of events.

"Poor little Georgina," she cooed over the edge of the cot; "whatever will become of you?" Despite some reservations, May soon convinced herself that the only option was for her to adopt Georgina. Georgina Archer became her adopted daughter, Georgina Carter. May relished her new role. She enjoyed having this "daughter"; it took her mind away from any thoughts of loneliness and filled her days and nights with excitement and anticipation. Georgina was a delightful child; inquisitive, bright and alert. She was strong willed and determined: just like her mother, thought May. She did well at school but had difficulty in keeping friends. May spoiled her excessively, lavishing treats and gifts, catering for every little whim that took Georgina's fancy, as if they would compensate in some way for her inability to make friends.

Georgina's teenage years were difficult for May. An estrangement between them seemed to grow with every month that passed. To add to May's problems, Georgina's schoolwork was going very poorly. The Head Mistress had written a stern letter to May advising her to 'get to the bottom' of Georgina's poor display over the last two terms; "after all, she is a very capable girl."

"Georgina, Georgina," May called from the bottom of the stairs.

"What now!" came the exasperated reply from her truculent charge. It was about a year ago when May had explained to Georgina that she was adopted. It seemed to May that most of her troubles stemmed from that revelation.

"Come here, Georgina, we need to talk."

"What about?" replied Georgina as she ambled down the stairs, "I suppose that cow of a head mistress has been on to you again."

"As a matter of fact she has, and I'll thank you to refer to her with more respect."

"That's all she'll get from me."

"Enough, Georgina! That's not what I called you about, although heaven knows I should be making a bigger issue over your attitude to school. You need to know...you're old enough now... who your parents were." Georgina shuffled her feet and leaned against the kitchen wall.

"I told you, you were adopted..." She broke off, realising Georgina had suddenly changed from being disinterested to being very attentive. They both reached for chairs at the kitchen table. Georgina leaned forward looking bright eyed for the first time in months. She rested her elbows on the table and planted her chin in her cupped hands.

"I told you, you were adopted, that I am not your real mother. I also told you I would tell you the full story when you were old enough. You're nearly sixteen now. It's time you knew more about your family." May paused, trying to find the right words.

"Go on Mum," insisted Georgina, breathlessly waiting for more.

"As you know, your mother, Doris, was my niece. That makes me your great Aunt. She came to stay with me when she was expecting you. She was a beautiful girl. Bright, intelligent and headstrong; just like you..." May paused, causing Georgina to raise her head, May continued. "She died shortly after giving birth to you."

"Did I cause it...her death?" asked Georgina in a subdued tone.

"No," replied May. "She was ill and died from heart failure. It was a very sad time. I was very, very fond of your mother."

"Is that why you adopted me?"

"I suppose so, yes. I couldn't bear the thought of some stranger looking after you for the rest of your life."

"What about my father?"

"I was coming to that. His name was George Archer. I never met him; he had gone to work in Australia before he knew that Doris was expecting you. Doris was sure she would be joining him, once you were old enough to travel."

"Why didn't he come if my Mother was so ill?"

"It seems all so simple now, but at the time...." May paused again, staring off to the side.

"Mum, Mum!" Georgina's urging startled May.

"Sorry dear, I was back with your Mother there for a moment. She was taken ill so suddenly. We had no idea how ill she was. After she died I posted a letter Doris had written to George Archer. I found it on the mantelpiece a day or two later...it must have been the last letter she wrote. I wrote to him twice myself, telling him what had happened to Doris...telling him that he had a daughter."

"What happened, did he come?"

"No dear, I'm afraid not. I found out some time later that he'd been killed in an accident of some kind. It's an awfully sad tale."

"So you adopted me when my Mum died?"

"Not straight away. I knew George Archer had come from Buxton in Derbyshire. That's where Doris, your Mum, had met George. George's father died shortly before you were born, and Mrs. Archer, well... she went a little strange when she heard of George's death. She spent her last few years in a home."

"That's awful," added Georgina. Her expression of concern surprised May. She'd become so used to having only distant and non-committal responses. It occurred that Georgina might be mimicking May's earlier remark; but the open and sincere look on Georgina's face convinced her otherwise. "But I need to know all you can tell me about this Archer family, especially my father."

"I know very little about the Archer family, apart from what I've already told you." May was delighted to have a heart to heart conversation with Georgina. It was the first time in many years that they'd talked like this.

"The family was comfortably well off; in fact Doris worked for them for a short while; that's how she met George. George was a Civil Engineer. He'd obtained a position in Western Australia before he met Doris. She helped him buy things he would need. I remember Doris telling me of a marvellous time they had together in London."

"Why didn't she just marry him and go with him to Australia?" It was all so simple and inexcusable in Georgina's mind.

"Why indeed!" May smiled when she thought of Doris's resolve, her determination not to interfere in George's plans.

"Doris didn't want to make George feel he was trapped into marrying her. She wanted him to go to Australia, just as he had planned. Doris had decided to tell him after you were born. She was sure he would send for her. It was her ultimate test. If he really loved her, then he would want her out in Australia. If he didn't, then she was at least spared the indignity of a poor marriage. She was a very strong woman, your mother."

"Well... did he really love her?" Georgina's romantic nature was coming to the fore.

"I think so. Doris was certainly very sure that he did. She spoke about him with such confidence. She positively glowed when we talked about him."

* * *

World War II was affecting all of their lives. The cities of Birmingham and Coventry had both been targeted by the Germans for heavy bombing. Although they lived about fifteen miles from Birmingham city centre, they seemed to be on the flight path taken by the Luftwaffe. Civil defence sirens were now an almost nightly occurrence. They were not the only targets, however. The heavy anti-aircraft fire, which had been established around Birmingham, resulted in some of the German bombers being eager to drop their ammunitions and return early to base.

May was very busy. She worked long ten-hour shifts at the hospital, occasionally having to catch only a couple of hours sleep in a ward bed before returning to duty. The hospital had been turned into a military centre for wounded airmen. May worked in the unit that attended to those who were not suffering from serious physical injuries; she looked after the shell-shocked and those mentally affected by their experiences. In many senses, they were worse off. No visible scabs and scars to heal, no crutches, bandages or splints to be discarded after they have served their joint purpose of healing the wound and eliciting sympathy. They wrestled with the complexities of their own fears and demons, ever conscious of their lack of obvious mutilation.

Johnny Jeffries had flown over seventy missions. He was a pilot, flying mainly Mosquito fighter-bombers with a crew consisting of a navigator and a rear gunner in addition to the pilot. He'd taken his share of hits and lost the entire crew on two occasions. But he had immense confidence in his own flying skills. He had always managed to limp back to land; not always making it back to base, but at least reaching dry ground. Johnny was always nervous before a mission. He sweated profusely and tended to talk extremely quickly. Other crews joked behind his back, calling him the nervous ace. But his reputation as a top pilot quickly grew. He was a different person in the pilot's seat; decisive and alert; always alert. He barked crisp clear signals in a no-nonsense manner and demonstrated extraordinary flying skills. He guided his aircraft with ability and confidence, nudging at controls and tapping at reluctant gauges, as if coaching the Mosquito to give of its best. They were responsive to each and all of his moves, as if the cockpit had been tailor-made to his requirements. The crew was simply extensions of his controls and his attitude demanded they respond as a team. Once on the ground, he seemed to lose confidence. His clearly barked signals became shorter and sharper; almost a whine. He was always at his worst during debriefing, so much so that the Squadron Leader had made a note, on two separate occasions, that this airman might crack, at any time. The crews, however, were always full of praise for their "nervous ace".

"Come in Jeffries, take a seat." The Wing Commander motioned to one of the cane backed chairs in his office. A red-faced, sweaty looking Johnny Jeffries hesitated for a moment, and then perched himself nervously on the edge of the seat. He knew what was coming and while his crew and other pilots were congratulating him, Johnny Jeffries was full of apprehension.

"Jeffries, you're a first rate pilot. You've flown over 70 difficult missions, your crews speak very highly of you; the group leaders rate you as one of the best we've got."

"Thank you sir," replied Jeffries, his face now even redder. The distinctive and disagreeable odour of stale sweat began to pervade the still air in the small room. The Wing Commander leaned forward and opened one of the steel framed windows, locking it on the third notch.

"Stuffy in here," muttered the Wing Commander. "Look Jeffries, Squadron Leader and I have recommended you for the D.F.C. You've earned it."

"Thank you sir," stammered Jeffries, "I'm...er...very grateful." He couldn't quite find the right words to say. It was the best he could do.

"There's more Jeffries. As you know, you've flown more missions than any other pilot in this squadron. We think it's time to give you a rest."

"Rest sir...you mean I'm finished with flying?"

"Not exactly Jeffries, there's still a war on you know"

"Sorry sir...I..."

"You have nothing to be sorry about Jeffries, we need good pilots like you. But we are humane, or at least try to be. We can't go on asking you to risk your life night after night. You've made a major contribution to the war. We need you to help train the new pilots." Johnny Jeffries took a quick gulp as if swallowing an imaginary pill. He was relieved to hear that he had flown his last combat mission, but the thought of being an instructor to raw recruits scared him. He knew the latest recruits were younger and less well prepared than those that had been so carefully screened and selected in the early days of the war. They couldn't afford to be so selective anymore. He had also heard that the training planes were less well maintained than those in the combat squadron. Able planes, like able airman, were enlisted for active missions over Germany. Only the used, the spent and the broken were used for training. New beads of sweat gathered like watery pustules on his forehead and reddened cheeks. One ran down past his temple and along the line of his lower jaw. He dabbed at the offending bead with the back of his hand.

"Are you alright Jeffries?" enquired the Wing Commander, "you look a little... er flushed?" By that I mean more than your usual rosy blush, thought the Wing Commander.

"Fine, thank you sir. And thank you for the appointment. I'll do my best."

"I'm sure you will, Jeffries. Close the door on your way out."

"Yes sir."

*　*　*

The air was cool and crisp at 0600 hours. The sky was clear, save for a few high wispy cirrus clouds. A perfect day for a short flight, thought Johnny Jeffries. He felt calm and relaxed as he strode around to conduct an early inspection of the Mosquito parked at the south end of the runway. The poorly patched wings and balding tyres caught his attention and he made a mental note to have a word with the maintenance technicians.

The training crew consisted only of a pilot and a navigator. They were both barely 20 years old but, outwardly at least, were full of confidence and bravado. Danny Ferris, the trainee pilot, had logged just ten hours of flying at the controls. As for his navigator, Pete Manning, this was his first flight. Johnny Jeffries introduced himself and then gave his instructions.

"I'll take her up and hand the controls over when we are at cruising altitude. Mr. Navigator, you inform me when we've reached altitude. We've been given clearance for a run due north from Norfolk. We'll move west and then follow the coastline south at Scarborough. Understood?"

"Yes sir," replied Manning. "I've already plotted our course."

"Good..." mumbled Jeffries. "Let's get on with it then." Settled into the cockpit, Johnny Jeffries went through the flight checks, making sure his trainee pilot repeated each of them with the same care and precision his own flight instructor had demanded. The cockpit had been fitted with makeshift dual controls. It made the controls feel unusually stiff, much to Johnny's dismay.

"Cleared for take off sir." Manning's voice shrieked through the crackle on their headsets. Johnny nudged her forward, gradually building up engine revs as he did so. He handled the plane with the expertise of a veteran, despite the dull response of the controls. They quickly climbed to cruising altitude, with Johnny barking instructions and observations to his trainees. Danny and Pete glanced at one another and exchanged quick grins. It was the smoothest take-off Danny had experienced and both were impressed by the confidence and obvious skill of their instructor.

"Cruising altitude sir." Johnny leveled her off and set the plane on course. Danny glanced at Johnny Jeffries, wondering if he should assume control. Johnny seemed to sense his questioning glance.

"Not yet Mr. Ferris, I want us to clear land first." Johnny felt himself gripping the controls with more intensity as the coastline approached.

"All yours Ferris," Johnny Jeffries suddenly announced. Danny was both surprised and excited. He grabbed at the controls too vigorously, causing the Mosquito to dive to the left and lose altitude.

"Hell Ferris," barked Jeffries, "you'll put this thing in the drink."

"Sorry sir," replied the anxious Ferris, over correcting as he did so, causing the plane to lunge even more violently to the left. Johnny Jeffries eyes bulged with a mixture of rage and indignation at the shear incompetence of his trainee. He glared at the pilot.

"Watch your controls," shrieked Jeffries, "keep her steady and learn how she handles for God sake. This is not a bloody battle ship!"

"Sorry sir ... I think I'm OK now." Johnny Jeffries relaxed slightly as he felt the aircraft straighten, regain altitude and hold her course. He couldn't prevent a sickening, nauseous feeling from gripping his stomach. It was, in part, a fear of being held captive by this poorly trained crew, and of the slipshod maintenance on the training aircraft; but most of all, it was a fear of not being in total command. He had prepared himself to function in battle by assuring himself of his own abilities and skills. He hadn't been prepared to share the command of his cockpit, least of all with a raw recruit; a trainee of very limited skills. He felt himself sweating profusely under the sheepskin lined flying helmet. He felt just as flushed and uncomfortable as he had in the Wing Commander's office. It was a new experience for Jeffries. This was his sanctuary, his operating realm in which he could demonstrate mastery with cool aplomb. But now he felt almost claustrophobic. His heart raced and his temperature seemed to soar. He wanted to get out of this damned cockpit.

"Head for base," Jeffries suddenly proclaimed.

"But sir..."

"Turn around NOW," screamed Jeffries. The navigator tried one more pathetic appeal.

"Sir, we've another half hour before..."

"NOW, damn it. I said turn now and I mean just that. TURN NOW!" His shrieking command alarmed the young crew. Without acknowledging the instruction, the pilot slowly banked the plane to the left, bringing the Mosquito back along their outward course. They continued in silence, with Jeffries continually fidgeting in his seat, his eyes constantly scanning the instruments.

"Anything wrong sir?" enquired the navigator, desperately trying to find someway to relieve the tension that pervaded the atmosphere in the small quarters of the cockpit. Jeffries didn't answer. His eyes were constantly flicking over the instruments with the occasional glance out of the window on the starboard side.

"Radio base, radio base," shrieked Jeffries, his voice suddenly splintering the quiet tension in the cockpit.

"Me sir?" enquired the dumbfounded navigator. Jeffries appeared to ignore him. "Radio base, we've been hit...coming in for a crash landing, alert all crews...landing gear jammed..." Jeffries broke off, breathless from his outburst.

"But sir, we're not hit, it's just a training flight." Jeffries ignored the protests of his pilot.

"I've got her now," Jefferies informed his pilot. "Leave her to me." His voice suddenly became calm and commanding. "Mr. Navigator, radio base, tell them I'm bringing her in." The navigator laughed, nervously. "Some sort of test isn't it sir?"

"This is the real thing Mr. Navigator. Radio base, all emergency crews needed."

The navigator followed the clear instructions of the instructor. To his relief, the airstrip base was coming into view.

"The tower wants to know our problem sir."

"I'm bringing her in... I need full assistance...we're badly hit, landing gear gone." The navigator paused for a couple of moments, and then relayed the message to the tower. This must be part of the exercise he thought, he hoped...he glanced at Jeffries, he wasn't sure. He glanced at Danny, who returned his anxious look. Danny's face was full of fright. His eyes and lips seemed to ask Pete for help...what do I do? They were coming in now, low and fast.

"Landing gear sir," urged the anxious pilot. Jeffries didn't respond. "Landing gear sir!" shouted Danny.

"Landing gear is locked," mumbled Jeffries in an irritated tone. Danny reached for the switch, but his hand was knocked away by an annoyed Jeffries. "Prepare for a belly landing...throttle back before we hit." Jeffries seemed to be running through some drill as if reciting from the manual. They were now very low and only two hundred yards from the start of the runway. Danny Ferris couldn't stand it any more. He grabbed the controls and flicked on the landing gear as he did so. The rumble of the slowly opening landing gear was barely audible over the din of the racing engines. Jeffries turned to Ferris in amazement.

"Bloody fool Ferris!" The wheel on the left wing of the half open landing gear caught the runway first. The plane dipped left; the wing and fuselage screeched along the tarmac. Suddenly the wing snapped causing the plane to flip. Jeffries was flung out through a gaping hole in the starboard side. The fuselage burst into flames in the next instant, engulfing the cries of the hapless crew. Jeffries vaguely recalled seeing a bright orange flash as the fuel tanks erupted with a loud, fierce explosion.

Jeffries was the only one of the crew to survive the landing. He had fractured his hip and was suffering from a combination of shock and concussion. Danny Ferris and Pete Manning weren't so lucky. They were trapped in the cockpit and died in the inferno. The Wing Commander came to see him on just one occasion; he was annoyed at himself, and at Jeffries. But the Wing Commander wasn't about to let this incident besmirch his record. Jeffries would be medically discharged and the cause of the accident would be a faulty aircraft. It happened all the time. There was a war to fight. The Wing Commander closed the door on the hospital ward, dismissing Jeffries from service and from his mind.

Johnny Jeffries was in a terrible state. He couldn't find anyway to close his eyes without seeing the terrified faces of his navigator and pilot as the fuselage spun on the runway. Their faces seemed to be pressed against his cockpit window for what seemed an eternity. The rapid spin dissolved into a slow timeless roll, with two young and panic-stricken faces gaping in bewilderment at their instructor as he slowly crashed through the hole, escaping from the death trap he had created. The dream seemed to get more bizarre and the events more distorted. I'm going mad, thought Jeffries.

Chapter 11
JOHNNY JEFFERIES

"Good morning, Mr. Jeffries," called May in her no-nonsense bedside manner. "How are we today?" Jeffries gazed at her with a vacant stare. He had been heavily sedated and was slowly awakening from his drug-induced sleep. He recalled being wheeled into an ambulance; at least he thought he did.

"Where am I?" he enquired, his voice still slow and his movements lethargic.

"You were moved yesterday to a different hospital...we can keep a better eye on you hear. It's a special hospital." Jeffries slowly looked around the ward, bringing his fellow patients into view. It was a small ward with eight beds, four along each wall. This alone was different from the usually jam-packed wartime hospitals he had encountered. But there were other differences he began to notice. The noise and commotion weren't there. He'd always encountered nurses scurrying with newly arriving patients, setting up makeshift beds to cater for the increasing numbers of injured. Doctors were constantly scanning patients to see which needed urgent attention; sisters were barking instructions and orders to overworked nurses and orderlies. There was always a sense of controlled panic in wartime hospital wards, with bandages, blood, catheters and cadaverous bodies being sorted by a small army of nurses, medical orderlies and doctors. But none of that existed here. It was as if the ministry had somehow overlooked this small secluded hospital ward.

"Is this a private ward, nurse?" May laughed. "There's no such thing these days. It's a psychiatric ward. You've been pretty badly shaken. You now need some time to get over everything you've experienced."

"A ward for nut cases. Am I a bloody nut case nurse?"

"Look here Mr. Jeffries, we don't tolerate that kind of language in this ward. You've been badly injured by the war and we are going to help you get better... but it doesn't help if you start off on the wrong foot. Now try and get some rest. The Doctor will be in to visit you in about an hour."

It was several days before Johnny Jeffries saw May again.

"No, I haven't been deliberately avoiding you," she said with a mocking laugh. "There are other patients besides you." Johnny Jeffries smiled at her mild admonishment. "You look well, more relaxed."

"Yes, I feel less tense. I don't know if it's just all the medication or the result of my sleeping for so long."

"Probably a combination of both the medication and the sleep."

"But I'm still having such awful nightmares."

"It'll pass, but it's going to take some time. What about this outbreak of hives?" Johnny Jeffries was covered in a red rash that extended from his waist to his shoulders, neck and forehead.

"The itching is driving me crazy. It started near my waist, but now its seems to have spread all over."

"It's not unusual for our patients to develop skin rashes. I'll speak to the Doctor about it. He'll probably recommend some soothing cream. If it gets very bad we'll need to cover your hands to stop you scratching."

"Thanks nurse. At least it takes my mind off everything else." May smiled at her patient. He was quite good-looking, if you ignored his ugly red blotches. His tall frame filled the standard ward bed and his shock of blonde hair and pale blue eyes gave him an angelic look.

The hives on Jeffries' body became very severe over the next few days. His upper torso was now covered in masses of bright red patches. He couldn't help but scratch at them almost constantly, and with such severity that several parts of his body, particularly his waist, back and thighs, were covered in inflamed and bleeding scratches. This served to merely exacerbate their effects, leaving him exhausted, frustrated and writhing in discomfort. Sleep was impossible. During the daytime, the brisk activities of the hospital staff provided some temporary distractions from his itching mass of sores. At night, there were no such diversions. The only noise Johnny Jeffries heard was the rasping of his fingernails on his inflamed iridescent skin. At night, he didn't have enough fingers to reach all the sources of his constant irritations. He simply had to scratch more vigorously and rapidly.

May was alarmed on seeing him a couple of days later. He looked drained and tired. He was sweating profusely, red and purple blotches covered his body and blood was trickling from several deep scratches on his chest and waist. May helped bind his hands with soft, white linen bandages after first cleaning his wounds and applying liberal doses of soothing lotion to his nettled skin. Johnny Jeffries felt better almost as soon as the first dollop of pink cream was smeared across his waist. May's strong, supple hands gently massaged the cream over his entire upper body and then along the backs of his legs. He felt a soothing relief, not only from her touch, but also through the alleviation of itching and burning her cream filled caresses seemed to provide. May reached for her scissors and snipped the ends of the neat and tiny knots, which punctuated her bandaging.

"Thanks nurse, that was wonderful."

"You, Johnny Jeffries, can call me May...at least when Sister isn't around."

"Thanks May. You've no idea how much better I feel."

"It's not going to last, I'm afraid. But at least you'll get some temporary relief, and you won't be able to scratch at yourself anymore."

"Not with these things!" Johnny held up the white appendages on the end of his arms.

"Take these pills, and try and get some sleep." May fed the sedatives into his mouth, one at a time, giving him a sip of water to wash them down. "I'll be cleaning you up and applying new cream tomorrow afternoon."

"I look forward to that nurse...I mean May," Johnny answered with a grin. May smiled at him.

"I think we might have to go back to nurse, especially if you start viewing these treatments in a non-professional manner."

Johnny laughed. "Nurse May, I've no idea what you mean." May walked away, pleased with herself. It was the first time Johnny Jeffries had really smiled since coming to the hospital.

May looked forward to her daily ritual with Johnny Jeffries. He was responding well to the medication and was gradually losing the blotchy and pink appearance he first had on entering the hospital. He was also becoming more confident. The night sweats were now occasional, rather than regular, and he seemed to be generally more relaxed. He had also started to assume an air of confidence, which May found particularly intriguing. He was going through a transformation from being miserable, frightened and depressed, to being confident, almost outgoing.

"The doctor says you'll not need treatment every day. Every other day this week and then once a week if you keep making progress."

"Doesn't that fool of a doctor know it's good for my soul as well as my body? You make me feel just great."

"So I've noticed," quipped May. "I'm not sure whether I'm doing this for your bodily excitement or your skin care."

"I'd like scented oils and deep body massage from now on," offered Johnny.

"You'll get cold pink cream just where you need it, and nowhere else," laughed May. "Let me have a go at your bandages."

Johnny was discharged from the hospital two weeks later. He had no family in the area, so May had learned, and he would need outpatient care for a month or so. May suggested he come and stay at her house.

"There's just the two of us, my daughter, Georgina, and me. We have a large house...and we... I ...could use some male company. I'd certainly feel more secure." She didn't really mean that, but she knew it would play to his ego.

"You're sure that I would be no bother?"

"Of course you would, but we'll just have to get used to your strange ways," teased May.

"As long as you let me pay rent; oh and I'll want my cream rub at least once a week."

"We'll see...about the rub I mean. As for rent, I won't deny that I could use some extra money." She gave a nervous laugh.

"How about £5 a week?" Johnny Jefferies replied." I can afford it, and if it helps..." May nodded enthusiastically.

"If you're sure that's alright ...? It was more than I had expected." Johnny grinned. "You shouldn't reveal your hand so willingly Nurse. But yes, I'm absolutely sure." It was May's turn to smile.

"Good, that's settled then. I'll meet you up at the front of the hospital at six tonight. That's when I get off my shift."

May suddenly felt very uneasy. What had she got herself into? She didn't really know this man; she hadn't told Georgina anything about him. What would Georgina say? Probably erupt in to some childish moralising thought May.

Johnny Jeffries was obviously nervous. He had seemed so confident at the hospital. He joked to May about his "release" from the hospital ward and appeared anxious to leave. But as they approached May's house, his manner changed; he stuttered and stammered and looked hot and uncomfortable.

"Relax Johnny, it's only my daughter Georgina; there's no one else. She's young and lively; you'll enjoy meeting her." Johnny smiled nervously at May.

"I expect you're right. I just get so uncomfortable in a new situation, with people I don't know."

'How on earth did I get myself into this?' thought May. 'It's going to be an absolute disaster'.

A rather recalcitrant Georgina shook hands with the stammering and shuffling houseguest. It was an uncomfortable beginning.

May persuaded Georgina not to go out that evening.

"There have been warnings of new air-raids Georgina. I get so worried when you are out at night. I've seen so many casualties; I'd hate for you to be one of them."

"I thought you'd want to be alone with the freak."

"Georgina, don't let me hear you talk like that again. He's recovering from shock that's all. There are hundreds of airmen in far worse condition."

"Not the ones I meet. The Yanks are great. Loud talkers and big spenders. I love 'em all."

"You'll end up getting yourself into trouble. I want no more talk like that, and I want you to stay away from those soldiers, you're only eighteen, much too young. Besides, they only want one thing."

"What about Jeffries, what's he want?"

"Look, Georgina, I've had enough of this. He's been very ill and needs some rest and relaxation. I want you to stay in tonight. And try and be more sympathetic."

"Sympathetic...to him. This is pathetic. You're the one behaving like a love-sick cow!" Georgina slammed the door and ran up to her room.

The air-raid sirens started early that night, at around eight o'clock. May turned out most of the lights and adjusted the blackout curtains in the downstairs rooms. The room was now dark and uneasily quiet. Johnny sat in the corner lit by the only remaining light. He was reading the evening newspaper but with such intensity that he appeared motionless.

May froze when she heard the low whistling sound. It was followed by an enormous bang and a flash of light. Windows cracked and several of the upper windows at the rear of the house were smashed by the blast. Georgina screamed from the landing at the top of the stairs. Johnny was on his feet in an instant. He sprinted up the stairs, picked up the hysterical Georgina in a fireman's lift and took her downstairs. May could only mumble a muted "thanks" as Johnny signaled to Georgina to lie back on the couch.

"There's been a direct hit, about a couple of streets away." Johnny was calm and in control. May marveled at his ability to respond to an emergency. So did Georgina. He was brave and decisive. So different from the miserable and uncomfortable man she had encountered earlier in the day. "Are you both alright?" asked Johnny. Neither offered a reply. They simply sat and watched their General taking command.

"I'm going outside; there are bound to be some injured."

"I'll come with you...I can help."

"No May, you stay hear with Georgina. I'll come back for you if I need you. Gas leaks and secondary explosions are very possible. I don't want you getting caught in something like that." Johnny ran round to the vicinity of the hit and quickly assessed the extent of the damage. The bomb had landed in the middle of the adjacent street, partly lifting the roof off two opposite houses. Roof tiles were scattered like playing cards, littering the street and the front gardens of semi-detached houses that had been so neat and tidy just moments earlier. Other houses were largely intact, except for shattered windows with billowing and torn curtains and splintered front doors, some with pieces of shrapnel embedded in their blackened paint work. Johnny was soon in control. He instructed two women, who had run from their homes in a nearby street, to go door to door, checking for anyone injured or missing. He ordered several members of the Civil Defence patrol to rope off the badly damaged houses. The fire brigade, accompanied by two ambulances, arrived some five minutes later. Johnny called them all over and briefed them as to what he had arranged. It was reminiscent of a field general briefing his lieutenants. They were summarily dispatched to attend to the injured inhabitants and the structurally impaired houses.

It was almost three hours later when May and Georgina heard Johnny at their front door. They both rushed forward, excitedly. Johnny looked tall and impressive. He strode down the hallway to greet them, whistling and smiling as he did so.

"Well girls, I think it's all clear now. We were lucky. That bomb landed just one street away. There wasn't a direct hit, but plenty of damage. A couple of houses lost their roofs."

"Any injuries?" asked May.

"A few, but mainly superficial; cuts from flying glass mostly. One poor old devil got a piece of shrapnel in his leg; nearly severed it, right below the knee." Georgina gasped. "Sorry Georgina...I should have...but you need to know, people can get pretty badly maimed."

"Is everything alright now?" enquired Georgina.

"I think so. The injured have been carted off, no one's reported missing, the two displaced families have been relocated. The fire brigade are busy blocking off gas lines and the Civil Defence are helping board up broken windows."

"It sounds as if you got them all organised...I don't now how they managed before you came along," teased May.

"Pretty poorly I think," replied Johnny, somewhat seriously.

The two women were proud of their hero. May was pleased to see that Georgina had taken an obvious liking to Johnny. The local Civil Defence commander, a bright and brisk bank manager who obviously relished his wartime role, called round to thank Johnny personally. For Georgina, it was as if some fictional adventurer was living in their midst. His exploits were discussed by almost everyone she encountered. Inevitably, the stories of his accomplishments tended to be exaggerated and embossed with every telling. His exploits as a pilot were equally well explored. It seemed as if everyone in the community had heard of Johnny and that every woman over fifteen and under forty wanted to meet him or find out from

Georgina some intimate detail that would further elevate his status. Georgina found herself swept along by this local hero worship. She enjoyed relaying every detail about Johnny that she knew of, or, alternatively, that she could make up with sufficient realism.

May was glad Georgina and Johnny were getting along so well. Georgina hadn't been so difficult of late, and she found it easier to go to her job at the hospital knowing that Johnny would be there to look after Georgina. It wouldn't last much longer, May thought to herself; Johnny was really very well now. He would be called back to service very shortly, at least to a desk job. In the mean time, their houseguest was proving to be a significant bonus; one she hadn't expected.

Georgina was pleased to see May go to work. It gave her chance to be alone with Johnny. She found him easy to talk to. Johnny also enjoyed talking to Georgina, especially about his experiences as a pilot. It seemed to give him confidence and, at the same time, buried the demons which had previously haunted him, especially at night. Now he could close his eyes and revel in the adulation he felt from the people in this community and from his friendly women, May and Georgina.

"Glass of beer, Johnny?" It was almost an evening ritual now.

"Thanks, Georgina, I'm parched," was Johnny's stock reply. A serene Georgina soon appeared with beer, bread, cheese, and a small sherry for herself, all neatly laid on a wicker-framed tray.

"Does May know you are swigging her sherry?" Johnny's voice was more teasing than remonstrative.

"It's either this or gin; but I can't drink that stuff without something to take away the smell. It reminds me of a surgery."

"Cheap gin. You need some good stuff," suggested Johnny. "I've some you should try." Johnny ran up to his room and returned with a small green bottle of Gordons. "This is the best. I've got a couple of limes I sneaked from the officer's mess. Gin and lime, you'll love it!" Georgina fondled the bottle of Gordons, and then grasped at the limes. "I've never seen these before."

"Here let me show you." Johnny took one of the limes and cut it in half with his pocketknife. He held the limes out to Georgina. "Smell these." Georgina cupped her hands around his and lifted the limes to her nose.

"Mmm...delicious." Johnny then sliced one half into a series of thin wafers. He dropped three of them into a glass and poured a liberal measure of Gordons over the green citrus.

"Leave it for a few moments, let the gin absorb the lime." Georgina picked up the taller glass, unscrewed the stopper from the brown bottle and poured out the beer for Johnny. They chinked glasses.

"Cheers." Johnny sprawled on the settee and took two large gulps of his brown ale. He eyed Georgina through the top of his froth-layered glass. Georgina returned his gaze, her eyes twinkling in the soft light. She sauntered over to the couch and sat on one armrest so that her feet faced Johnny. He let his hand fall onto her ankle and began caressing her lower calf.

"That's nice," Georgina said, softly.

"Just what I was thinking," replied Johnny. He slid his hand along her smooth, uncovered leg and over the under side of her knee. She giggled.

"That tickles," she laughed. Johnny moved his hand under her thigh. He could feel the warmth spreading down her leg. Georgina leaned forward to kiss Johnny, letting his hand caress the top of her leg as she did so. Her mouth opened and her lithe tongue explored his lips. Johnny slid his hand under her pants.

"No Johnny, don't." She pulled back until he removed his hand.

"That's better. You're too randy." She leaned forward to kiss him again.

Johnny leaned back on the couch as they kissed, lifting Georgina towards him, causing her to lean forward until her upper body was resting on his. He swung his legs under hers so that she was sprawled out on top of him. Georgina kissed him fiercely. Her small mouth engulfed his upper lips, sucking and kissing and occasionally using the tip of her tongue to explore his mouth. He tugged at the fold of her cream blouse, causing it to slip from the waistband at the rear of her skirt. His hands caressed the warm flesh in the middle of her back, gradually pushing at her small bodice until it was furled up against her breasts. Georgina shifted her weight, without letting her lips part from his, so that his right hand could slide under her bodice and over her breasts. She moaned in delight as his thumb slowly rubbed at her nipple. Johnny slipped both hands around her back and down over her upper thighs. He pulled her up against his groin and pushed her legs wide with his. His right hand stroked firmly at the base of her cotton pants.

"Oh, Johnny, don't," appealed Georgina, somewhat weakly.

May got in at about 6:30 am after a particularly long night shift and was feeling very tired. Johnny was sprawled out on the couch. He'd apparently been there all night.

"Where's Georgina?" asked May.

"Dunno...upstairs sleeping I expect." Johnny got up from the couch, grabbed the kettle from the stove and filled it with cold water from the kitchen tap.

"Tea?"

"Yes please, I need something to revive me after the night we had at the hospital." Johnny appeared disinterested. He was busying himself setting out two cups and saucers. He then proceeded to spoon liberal helpings of loose tea into the brown teapot.

"You should warm it first, it makes a better brew," May suggested. Johnny seemed to ignore her; he was entrenched in his own thoughts.

"May, I've got something to tell you." May turned, half-heartedly at first, but then she noticed the serious expression on his first.

"What is it Johnny, anything serious?"

"No, not really, it's just that I got the all clear from my doctor last week and yesterday I received a letter ordering me back to service."

May gasped. "Oh Johnny, I'd hoped you'd be here for a while. We were all starting to get along so well."

"I know, but all good things..." The high-pitched whistle from the kettle interrupted Johnny. "I'll get it, you sit back and relax." May flopped onto the couch, glad to be off her feet at last. She watched Johnny make the tea.

He slipped a woolen cozy over the teapot and joined her on the couch. May slipped her arm around his.

"It's been good having you here Johnny. I've enjoyed the company."

"Me to," replied Johnny. "You've been very good to me May. I'm glad I met you." He leaned over and kissed her cheek. May felt awkward. She knew he had to move on; but the unexpected news of his imminent departure had taken her by surprise. The patient who had needed her care so badly had provided her with a feeling of comfort and stability. She was also physically attracted to him. She'd nurtured him and seen him gain in strength and confidence. Her prize specimen was a source of pride. His heroics had elevated his stature and given him an exalted status in the disrupted, male afflicted world of this war. Johnny seemed to sense her feelings for him. He cupped May's chin in his hands and kissed her quickly on her mouth.

"Thanks May for all you've done for me." May moved closer to him and pulled his head towards hers. He kissed her passionately, slapping his lips against hers, drooling down her cheek. Their faces skidded against each other's as they searched for lips, ears, eyes and chin on the wet slippery surfaces.

"Oh Johnny, I've wanted you for so long." Johnny suddenly pulled away and held her at arms length. "Why didn't you say so earlier May? I needed to know."

"But I thought you did. I couldn't understand why you hadn't..." She broke off.

"Is something wrong Johnny?"

"No May. I wish I'd known earlier, that's all." He was starting to sulk, adolescent like. May pulled him towards her. Johnny kissed her, gliding his hands over her breasts as he did so. May didn't pull away. She seemed eager to have Johnny before he went for good. She lay back on the couch, pulling Johnny towards her. She seemed oblivious to anything else but Johnny. He tugged at her blouse, flipping open the buttons as he continued to kiss her. He pushed up her silk bodice and buried his face in her breasts. Her hands clasped the back of his head and her legs coiled around his waist, causing her skirt to slip high over her thighs. She groaned loudly as Johnny turned his attentions to her pelvic region, his face pushing hard against her groin as his hands fondled her breasts.

They didn't notice Georgina come into the room. She stood holding the door, her eyes transfixed on the writhing, groaning entanglement of arms, legs, hands, breasts, and lips. Only their eyes seemed inert. May's were rolled back in their sockets; Johnny's were almost hidden under closed lids. May saw Georgina first. She gasped, pushed hard at Johnny and then grabbed for her blouse, making futile attempts to cover her breasts as Johnny rolled off her. He propped himself up on one elbow.

"Oh God," moaned Johnny. May tried to speak. She couldn't. Words formed in her brain but lodged, inexplicably, in her throat. Georgina just stood by the door, staring hard, first at May, then at Johnny. She suddenly slammed the door and ran, whimpering as she did so.

"Georgina...Georgina!" May shrieked at the top of her lungs. She scrambled to her feet, snatching up and straightening her under-clothes as she made for the door. She ran up stairs to Georgina's room. The door was locked, but she could hear dressing table drawers being slammed. "Georgina," called May, "we need to talk..."

"Go away, just leave me alone." Her voice was crisp, hard and determined. May suddenly felt very frightened. She ran back downstairs to Johnny and implored him to help. He was cold and dispassionate.

"It's not my problem, May. It's obviously time I left."

"Johnny, don't go. I need you. Please help me with Georgina, she likes you, you can talk to her." May tugged at his arm, her eyes pleading with him for help.

"Leave me alone May. It's not my problem. I don't want to be involved." He pushed her arm from his. "I don't want to be caught in the middle of two women."

"What do you mean, Johnny? She's only a girl..." Before May had time to explore this any further, her attention turned to the hallway. She could hear Georgina opening the coat cupboard. She ran to the door, her heart beating wildly, her mind unable to comprehend what was happening. It was as if her world was unraveling before her and she was incapable of doing anything about it.

Chapter 12

Joe Jackson — Things Unravel

I watched the Australian Embassy man, Max Jordan, flip open two brass coloured buckles and reach into his mottled and well worn brown leather attaché case. He extracted a slim manila folder, which he held up as if displaying some key item of evidence to a jury.

"I can tell you exactly what the letter said," announced Max. "I've brought along a photocopy. It makes interesting reading."

"Let's hear it then," I said, my mouth suddenly very dry. My tongue felt like a piece of thick leather.

John Taylor, the official from the US State Department, slowly raised an arm as if directing traffic.

"Before we do that, I'm going to ask that we wait a few minutes. George Archer had a relative who must be present before we go any further." He glanced at his watch. "They should be here very soon."

The rap on the office door was as if on cue. I turned, intrigued, curious, and just a little nervous. The Coroner reached for the door and grasped its ornate brass handle.

"Come in, both of you." I felt my jaw drop; my mouth gaped in amazement. Emerging from behind the frame of the tall thin man who led the twosome into the office was the easily recognizable hair tuft and curvaceous figure of Tracy, the old man's 'assistant'.

"What on earth...What's going on now?" I asked, in an exasperated voice. Max Jordan intervened.

"Joe, let me introduce Dick Pruit; Tracy you know." Dick Pruit took one giant step, moving his thin frame quickly across the room to greet me.

"Hello Joe. I'm a lawyer representing Tracy. I'll be providing counsel on her behalf during this hearing."

"I don't understand what's going on," I protested.

"You will, bear with us, please," replied John Taylor. "Max and I have previously spoken with Tracy and Dick on several occasions. But I don't want to get into that just now, I think its time we asked Max to read the letter... Max..." Max Jordan unfolded the manila envelope and extracted the photocopy. The group waited anxiously for him to commence.

"The letter is dated May 20th, 1926. The address is 32 Gilbert Street, Earlsdon, near Coventry."

"The house was owned by a nurse, May Carter," interjected John Taylor. "We had the Brits dig up the information." Max ignored the interruption and continued.

'Dearest George,

Please forgive me for not writing to you earlier. It seems an eternity since we were last together and I've wanted so many times to write and tell you how much I miss you. I've delayed writing because I love you and because circumstances have changed so dramatically. There has been a very good reason for my not writing.

Let me get straight to the issue (Oh dear, that sounds terribly blunt – but blunt I must be).

What I've been putting off telling you, and what I'm desperately trying to put into words is that something wonderful and exciting is going to take place; and yet it fills me with dread!

The fact is that I am pregnant. And you, George, will soon be a father!

I'm so proud to be having your baby, but so disappointed at the circumstances. I feel guilty as if I've done something deliberate and cunning; something that would make you marry me. It's precisely because of this feeling that I haven't written, but I now know I must. You'll be a father by the time this reaches you.

I do hope you're not angry.

You'd better not bloody well mind, George. This baby is kicking me to death. He or she obviously has some of your adventurous streak. George, it's time we got together and planned for our future and for the future of our child.

I love you George. Please write soon.

Doris.

Max handed the second page for inspection.

"And the significance of this is one reason Tracy and I are here." It was Dick Pruit who now addressed the group. "Doris died giving birth to a daughter. That daughter was adopted by May, her Aunt, and raised by her as her own daughter. The daughter was named Georgina; Georgina Carter, which was her Aunt's surname. Georgina left home at the end of the war. She married an American

GI. We know she was pregnant when she married because her daughter, Tracy, was born about four months after the wedding."

"Tracy!" I groaned, "I might have guessed there was some ulterior reason for your closeness to the old man."

"I'm just here to protect my interests, Joe. I wouldn't want any outsider to move in unfairly." She gave me a look that suggested she was pleased at my surprise. Dick Pruit interjected to state the obvious:

"Tracy is in fact George Archer's grand daughter. She is, as far as we know, the only living legitimate heir to George Archer's estate." He emphasized the words 'living' and 'legitimate' as if implying that I was obviously not an 'Archer', and had no reason for being at this hearing. There was a strange, sudden pause in the conversation. No one seemed prepared to violate the sanctuary of this lull; they simply looked blankly at one another as if pleading for an end to this increasingly uncomfortable silence.

It was Max Jordan whose loud, crackling voice pierced their thoughts. They all turned and flinched, as if startled by his interjection.

"There is something you should all know about this case. A body was recently found at the base of an old dam in Western Australia. We'd like to clear up this case and we believe George Archer was involved. A murder was committed. The body we found was stuck at a grotesque angle in the mud at the base of the dam. It had a seriously fractured skull. It looks as if it had been struck by an iron bar." There was a stunned look from Tracy and I heard myself utter an involuntary gasp.

"Couldn't it have been a rock that crushed his head?" I asked.

"Possibly, but unlikely. Our boys are sure the size and shape of the damage to the skull matches an iron bar we uncovered a few metres from the body. This fellow was murdered; he was hit on the side of the head with a savage blow." My stomach turned as I listened to the Australian's twang. The old man had lied to me. Simply an accident, he'd claimed; he'd only taken advantage of the situation.

Charlie had neglected to mention that he'd created the situation in the first place.

"So what happened, have you any idea?" I asked.

"Ideas yes," replied Max, "in fact we are fairly confident we know what happened." Tracy was leaning so far forward she almost slipped out of her chair. "Go on," implored Tracy. Max paused, glanced at John Taylor, who gave a nod of approval, and then continued.

"We think that George Archer committed the crime. The dead man was his partner, Charles Watson. Charlie Watson came out from England a few years earlier. He got into some trouble when he first arrived and he may have been embezzling money from George Archer...sorry Joe."

"Sorry Joe. What the hell has Joe got to do with this?" demanded Tracy.

"Charlie Watson was Joe's Uncle," replied Max.

"We suspect that George Archer called on Joe so he could make a confession before he died," interjected John Taylor.

"Is that right, Joe?" asked Max Jordan.

"Sort of," I replied.

Max continued with his assessment of what had happened.

"We think Charlie had set up a scheme to establish a separate account for himself in Perth. We found evidence of an old account supposedly established by George Archer, but we suspect Charlie used it stash money away. He must have also stolen some letters and personal belongings from George Archer. Our belief is that Mr. Archer found out about it and challenged Charlie. They probably had a fight. George Archer must have hit him hard with the iron bar and left him nearly dead at the foot of the dam. The dam burst shortly after by all accounts, trapping Charlie and covering him with tons of mud and clay. We think he was still alive when the dam burst. From the position of the body, it looks as though he made some futile attempt to climb out."

"Oh my god," exclaimed Tracy. "My grandfather was a murderer. It's amazing the lengths some people will go to. But then again, that's probably why he's done so well and also got so many enemies. He was ruthless in his business dealings. I've seen him operate..." She paused as if suddenly confronting some imagined hurdle. "Will this affect my inheritance? Can a murderer be made to pay now that he's dead?"

"Probably not," offered Dick Pruit. "The case against your grandfather is largely circumstantial; it would be difficult to prove."

"Unless he made a confession." My clear voice seemed to startle them all.

"If he did make a confession, that might establish a claim against the estate. Is that why you're here Mr. Jackson, to claim against George Archer's estate on behalf of your uncle's family?" asked Dick Pruit, his voice shrill and icy.

"Perhaps," I replied. It was my turn to be obtuse.

Dick Pruit coughed.

"My client is the only living relative of George Archer. She therefore stands to inherit the Archer estate. However," he continued, "I think I can see a case for exploring a conclusion which recompenses your family for any alleged misdeeds involving Mr. Archer. Before I discuss this more fully with my client, I want to know if this is something you might agree to as a final claim on any of the Archer estate?"

"It depends very much on the settlement," I said, rather boldly.

"You bloody gold digger!" Tracy suddenly lunged her little frame and loud voice into the fray. "You are scum! No wonder my grandfather topped your Uncle. You're just like him; just a scumbag jumping at a chance to get money for nothing!"

Dick Pruit coughed again. This time it was a loud and practiced cough that caused Tracy to turn immediately in his direction. "Tracy, we need to talk." His voice was stern and commanding. Tracy meekly obliged and followed him through to an adjacent office. Dick Pruit quietly closed the door. He motioned as if instructing Tracy to sit down and calm herself.

"Look Tracy, you ... we need to be very careful in handling this situation. You need to bear in mind several important facts. Firstly, you have told me just how close and secretive the old man and Joe had become just before he died. God knows what he confided to Joe. I know, and you know, that George Archer hasn't been squeaky clean over the years. His reputation was as a maverick – someone who was quite prepared to trample on people who got in his way and pay those that could help. And then there are his political links. He gave significant donations to both the Democrats and the Republicans. He also funded an array of lobbyists when it suited his cause. I don't suppose you remember all the controversy over the money that went to Archer's firm when they won a huge government contract to relocate and rebuild a small township for the Ogalala Sioux. They were displaced by a major hydro-electric scheme on the Missouri River near Pierre in South Dakota. And guess whose lobbyists were pushing the scheme? – Archer's. And guess whose firm specializing in native Indian affairs recommended the resettlement programme? – one set up by Archer. And guess whose company got the entire contract – houses, roads, transportation, the lot? – Archer's. And just who do you think was employed as legal counsel by Archer? Why none other than the firm of solicitors in Sioux Falls which also had the then Governor of the State as one of its senior partners. And that's just one of many examples lurking in the woodpile. Archer had powerful friends and also some powerful enemies, many of whom will by delighted at any opportunity to put the company under investigation and file law suit after lawsuit. You don't want any hint of publicity from past misdeeds. Get this guy off our backs; pay him off, and make it a settlement he'll appreciate." Dick Pruit finally turned to Tracy, inviting her to speak.

"What do you suggest?" she asked, her tone suddenly very conciliatory.

"That's better," retorted Pruit in a manner that admonished his client. "We need to agree that this is the only strategy we can pursue – and then we need to agree how it will be implemented. We don't have much time. I want to get this settled now – the longer it drags out the greater the chance of a serious slip up."

"OK," said Tracy, slowly. "Just how much are you suggesting?"

"Well let's put it in perspective first," said Pruit. "Archer's empire includes real estate in Washington and Florida, his transport business, which is the main part of his organisation, and a number of small firms many of which he acquired or set up over the years to support some business deal or other he was involved in. Most of these are small; many in fact are dormant or continue to run at a small loss. They are there just in case they might be needed, or to hide the fact they were rogue companies in the first place. The bottom line, however, is that the company is potentially worth millions"

"Potentially?" remarked Tracy, "what's this 'potentially' shit?"

"What I mean is, that until we get into the books, who knows what might be in waiting. There could be all kinds of creditors and bad debts waiting to be paid – there's bound to be a few; but my guess is that the firm is very sound. Archer was a very shrewd operator. I think you are about to inherit a gold mine. But you'll need good professional help."

"And that's where you come in?" commented Tracy in a cynical voice.

"Dead right," replied Pruit. "If you want this deal, I want in. I worked for Archers for years – now it's my turn. I want a directorship and 25 percent of the company."

"What?" screamed Tracy.

"Shush," implored Pruit, putting his finger across his lips. "Look, you need me to make this work, and you'll need me to get things rolling. Remember, the old man is gone now – and just who do you think you can trust?"

Tracy gave a hollow laugh. "Guess I've no option. I think I'm going to need a slime ball like you Pruit," she commented.

Dick Pruit smiled. "Thanks for that vote of confidence," he said.

"Now, about Joe Jackson, I suggest we offer $100,000 in cash and be prepared to go to $150,000 if necessary."

"Hell," retorted Tracy, "just who is getting the deal here?"

Dick Pruit frowned at her.

"Ok, ok," uttered Tracy, "I have no choice, I can see that. Let's get on with it."

"Good," replied Pruit. "I'm glad that's settled." He picked up his large brief case; it was a bit like a leather box, full of compartments and manila folders. "This is my traveling office," he commented. "I've got a standard form we can use. It will prevent Jackson from making any comments about this settlement or giving any information that could prejudice the good name of the Archer company."

"Let's hope he agrees," commented Tracy.

"Oh he will," said Dick Pruit. "I don't think he's interested in the Company. I'll bet the old man has left him some money in his will; this will be a real bonus."

"He's making more money by the minute!" exclaimed Tracy. "Let's get this over with before he ends up with anymore!"

Pruit laughed. "Just remember what I told you about the value of the company."

Dick Pruit pulled out the document he was looking for. Tracy could see that much of it had been already prepared.

"You knew something like this was going to happen," said Tracy.

"Let's just say I was given some good advice," replied Dick Pruit.

"I'm beginning to appreciate your talents," commented Tracy.

Dick Pruit quickly completed his work on the settlement document. He then ushered Tracy into the room to join the others.

Pruit looked over in my direction.

"My client and I had anticipated a possible outcome of this nature. She is prepared to enter in to an arrangement."

"What sort of arrangement do you propose, Mr. Pruit?" I was amazed at myself; it was as if someone else had taken control of my voice. I had nothing to loose; I knew that. I reasoned I might as well stretch this thing as far as they would go before the bubble burst. Besides, I didn't much care for Dick Pruit, or Tracy. Pruit turned and smiled at me as if welcoming me into his web.

"I've advised my client to seek some form of settlement. Naturally we'd want you to sign a document that prevents you, or your family, from having any claim to the Archer estate. We would also insist that you make no attempt to reveal what happened in Australia. I presume you're willing to enter into such an agreement?"

"It seems reasonable to me. After all, this all happened a long time ago and I've no real desire to drag this thing through the courts. What sort of settlement arrangement have you in mind?" I asked, my heart beating wildly.

"I've already discussed this at length with Tracy, my client. She is in agreement with an arrangement that will provide you with a cash settlement of $100,000 in exchange for your signing a release against any further claims on the estate, beyond those that might be specified in the old man's will. Both parties will also be required to sign a statement barring either party from releasing information as to the alleged murder in Australia. Are you in agreement with this Mr. Jackson?"

I paused as if considering the proposal at length.

"$100,000, that's a lot of money – but not in comparison to the size of the Archer estate. It's got to be worth millions," I replied. It was a game now, and I loved a game. They were suddenly in my territory.

"I'll agree to a settlement, but it needs to be a reasonable figure – something that befits my uncle." I paused before declaring my position.

"I think when all said and done, a figure of $200,000 is more appropriate. I've no wish to drag this through the courts...or to raise the spectre of someone being murdered."

Dick Pruit started to answer, and then turned to Tracy. They walked to the corner of the room and huddled in hushed conversation. Dick Pruit appeared to do most of the talking. Tracy seemed to nod in agreement to all he said.

Dick Pruit turned to address Max Jordan and John Taylor.

"If you don't mind gentlemen, I'd like to settle this as quickly as possible. I have the necessary documents prepared for signature, I can type in the settlement amount and you could assist by serving as witnesses."

"Fine with me," replied Max Jordan, "John?"

"Ok, I suppose. I won't pretend I'm enthused about being entrapped to be a witness on your behalf, Dick." Pruit shrugged his shoulders.

"You both make respectable witnesses," he smirked.

"OK, let's get on with it," snapped John Taylor. "We need to discuss Mr. Archer's confession with Joe anyway so that the Aussies can tie up their loose ends." I was amazed at the speed with which Dick Pruit acted. He'd previously prepared a document containing the outline of an agreement. He'd obviously anticipated this outcome, or perhaps decided to direct it to this end. He fed the draft into a typewriter and proceeded to thump on the keys, adding sentences and deleting others. Within ten minutes he had a finished agreement. Pruit turned to the Coroner.

"Mind if I make copies?" He strode towards the Xerox machine without waiting for the Coroner's reply. He then Xeroxed the agreement and circulated it for all signatories to read.

"Is this a legally binding document?" I asked.

"It will be once you and Tracy sign it and we witness it," replied John Taylor. "You will need a copy for your files, and have your lawyer read it," advised Taylor. "You'll have thirty days to issue a challenge if there are some legal problems."

"Sounds alright to me," I offered. Dick Pruit jumped in, as if wanting to bring the discussion to an end.

"Pass the copies to me; I'll organise them for your signatures." The copies were dutifully passed to Dick Pruit, who spread them out on the office table and handed a pen to Tracy. "You'll need to sign each of the copies here, here and here. I also need you to initial the changes I've made, here and here." He pointed his long, manicured forefinger to the relevant sections. With the signatures in place, they shook hands in turn. Dick Pruit collected the copies for his client, carefully placed them in his black shiny briefcase and turned to escort Tracy from the office suite. Tracy turned to me.

"Bye Joe." She looked pleased with herself. I reached out to shake her hand. She ignored my polite gesture and moved closer to me. I felt her warm body against mine; she was almost tingling with excitement. She cupped my face in her hands, gently pulling my lips to hers. She gave me a long slow kiss as if oblivious to, or perhaps for the benefit of, the others in the room. "Bye Joe," she repeated. And then they were gone. Dick Pruit held the door for his client as if wanting to usher her from the room as quickly as possible. He closed the door as the sound of Tracy's heels clicking off the tiles echoed along the corridor.

John Taylor addressed the remaining group.

"Max and I need to discuss some issues with Joe for about thirty minutes or so." The Chaplain and the Coroner took the hint. The Chaplain announced he would return to his office and wait for further instructions. The Coroner decided he would pop next door to grab a coffee and doughnut, and wrestle with the crossword.

John Taylor turned to address Joe.

"There's one scenario we neglected to explore."

"Oh, what's that?" I replied, tensing myself for what I knew was coming.

"That the man who was killed in Australia was not your Uncle Charlie; it could have been George Archer." I tried to appear surprised and shocked.

"But that would mean that the man who just died could not have been George Archer."

"Exactly. The man whose body was nearly cremated could have been that of your Uncle Charlie. We believe he may have killed George Archer and then assumed his identity. How does that sound as a possibility?"

"I suppose it's possible," I offered, reluctantly. "It seems a bit implausible to have Uncle Charlie masquerade as George Archer for all these years."

"By today's standards, yes," replied John Taylor. "But pre-war..."

"...and in Australia," added Max Jordan.

"It seems a perfectly reasonable possibility," continued John Taylor. "The body was found with George Archer's wallet and with some of his personal effects. Your Uncle could simply have murdered George Archer and taken the opportunity to assume his identity. They were similar in age, both from England and both in the same business."

"What if this scenario is accepted," I posed, "what happens, what happens now?"

"Well, that depends on you to some extent."

"Let me try and explain," said John Taylor. "If you had decided to claim you were the heir to the Archer estate, we would then have proceeded to establish just who it is waiting to be cremated. You see, it seemed far more likely to Max and me that George Archer was the man who died in Australia, and that your Uncle has been living as in imposter. We reckon the old man told you who he was before he died. You could then have tried to establish a claim to his estate."

"Had you done that," interjected Max Jordan, "it would have forced us to try and make an accurate determination of exactly who the old man was. That's why we prevented the cremation from taking place. We met with Dick Pruit and suggested he attempt to reach a settlement with you. He seemed convinced that George Archer, as he knew him, must have killed your Uncle, so it wasn't difficult to assure him that this would be in his client's best interests."

"Fortunately, you were willing to accept this idea. A shrewd move on your part," offered John Taylor.

"As far as the Australian Government is concerned, this result effectively closes the case." Max Jordan turned to John Taylor as he spoke.

"The United States Government will also close the case," responded John Taylor. The cremation can now take place and the body can be buried as George Archer. Is that arrangement acceptable to you Mr. Jackson?"

"Perfectly," I replied, "I'm just glad it's all over."

"So are we," commented John Taylor. "I take it you will be heading home some time after the cremation?"

"The reading of the will is tomorrow afternoon, at George Archer's apartment. I intend leaving as soon as possible after that, probably in a few days," I replied. Max Jordan and John Taylor gave each other a conspiratorial smile at the mention of George Archer's name.

"Good," said John Taylor, in an emphatic tone. "We'd expect nothing less. There is one small thing we need you to do."

"What's that?" I asked.

"We want you to sign documents from both our governments stating that you will never discuss this case, the outcomes or mention the involvement of our governments to anyone."

"We'd hate this to become public," added Max, reinforcing Taylor's comments.

The reading of the Will took place at 11:00am two days later. The firm's lawyers were hovering over a sealed envelope. Tracy was seated on small couch near the window, looking very pleased with herself. Dick Pruit had squeezed his lanky frame in next to her. She gave a half smile, almost a smirk, when I entered through the glass doors leading to the main drawing room.

Max Jordan and John Taylor arrived shortly after me and took up defensive positions on either side of the glass doors.

The will was extremely brief; however, it did have some interesting wording.

The old man simply left his estate to his legitimate next of kin. It didn't specifically identify Tracy, nor did it identify me. There was a second element to the will which then left $100,000 to Joe Jackson, nephew of his former partner, Charlie Watson. It was made clear that this had been added recently, just prior to his death.

It left me slightly breathless and tantalized. Should I now declare that the dead man whose will we were reading was my Uncle Charlie? How could I prove this; he'd now been cremated? The further $100,000 was beyond my wildest expectations. Should I shut up and play along with the charade as I was expected to? What about the documents I had signed?

As if sensing my dilemma, I suddenly found myself being gently escorted by Max Jordan and John Taylor to a small ante-room, with Dick Pruit in tow.

It was John Taylor who spoke. "Can we assume there isn't going to be a challenge in terms of probate?" It took me a while to answer; I was trying to marshal my thoughts.

"My only wish is to abide by the terms of the will," I replied, somewhat obliquely.

"And just where does this leave my client?" roared Dick Pruit.

"She's Archer's granddaughter isn't she?" I replied.

"Of course she is," countered Pruit. "But the question we can ask in this room is – who was George Archer?"

"Oh, I'm sure he was a grandfather to some and an uncle to others," I suggested.

"Don't get smart with me," shouted Pruit. "What I want to know is – which of those relationships is my client to be aware of?"

"And don't forget, "interjected Max Jordan, "you've signed documents essentially protecting Tracy's interests."

"I'm well aware of that," I replied, "and I have absolutely no problem in asserting that Tracy is George Archer's grand-daughter."

"… and legitimate heir," added Pruit.

"Let's not get too hung up on the word 'legitimate'," I replied. "Heir will do."

"That's what I want to here," replied Pruit, staring at me with a stern look.

Chapter 13

THE FIRM

The company known as 'Archer Transportation' had flourished in the United States. George Archer had established the headquarters for his trucking and shipping business in northern New Jersey, close to docks of New York and New Jersey. It was also convenient to the main highways that moved southward to the established cities along the eastern seaboard, and westerly, to the steel towns of Pennsylvania and the rapidly expanding industrial base in the mid-west.

In the 1950's there were only a handful of interstate truckers. Rail was still the primary means of getting materials from city to city. George Archer was quick to capitalize on the weaknesses of the rail system. It was inflexible. Goods had to be transported to and from rail destination points, whereas road haulers could take materials directly from the source right to the destination. He could never understand why the rail companies hadn't implemented their own road haulage system to augment the efficient interstate system of transport, which they had dominated and monopolized for so long. The other advantage of road haulage was, of course, that you could use the existing system of roads, which the government was willing to build, develop and maintain.

George Archer foresaw that state governments would be ever keener to ensure the development of excellent roads, often at the expense of rail systems. Detroit wanted everyone to own a car and that inevitably meant the further development of large and elaborate road systems, roads that could support his vision of a major interstate trucking company. He bought out two smaller trucking businesses, giving him control of deliveries to and from several major companies in the eastern states, including General Electric Corporation (GEC) in Erie, Pennsylvania. GEC had a number of defence contracts and George Archer benefited from the large shipments of materials that resulted.

He'd hired Dick Pruit as the company lawyer in the early 1960's. Regulations were becoming increasingly complex. States were starting to infringe on his business. They were starting to charge higher road taxes on truckers, limiting the axle loads and Congress was investigating the extended driving hours that were part and parcel of profitable trucking concerns. George Archer needed legal counsel and political clout. He hired Pruit to provide both. Dick had graduated from The University of Pittsburgh and went on to Penn State to complete his law degree. He had many contacts in Trenton, New Jersey, Philadelphia and even Washington, DC. He quickly became an indispensable part of George Archer's organisation. Contracts were becoming more complex with casualty, loss and time clauses interwoven in the legal jargon of contract law. Dick Pruit was a master in phrasing contracts so as to establish the best terms for Archer's firm.

Things started to go wrong in the late 1960s. Dick Pruit convinced George Archer to diversify by investing in barge traffic.

"I think this is a tremendous opportunity, Mr. Archer," insisted Dick Pruit. He never ventured anything more personal than 'Mr. Archer' and George Archer never encouraged anything other than the formal form of address, despite working in adjacent offices for almost a decade.

"I'm not sure Dick. In the past I've always had a gut feeling about what will work and what won't. This does nothing for me. It doesn't excite me...that's when I get worried. Why change what's worked well for our business?"

Dick Pruit responded patiently to George Archer's concerns.

"We're coming under more and more competition from other truckers. We're having to make substantial under the table payments just to maintain our existing contracts."

"I know, I know. It annoys the hell out of me to make payments to crooked officials just so that they'll see our bids get through."

"It's how business is done these days."

"I don't like it!" thundered George Archer. "Those bastards are cutting into our margins. I wish we'd never started this payment racket. It just raises the costs of doing business."

"That's why we need to diversify," said Pruit with a sigh, as if trying to explain to a child.

"Don't patronize me Dick," shouted George Archer. "I know our profit margins have slipped; but I also know where the bulk of our profits are going."

"But it's only going to get worse," continued Pruit, "we can either accept these payments and operate with shrinking margins, or look for other opportunities which will give us alternative income opportunities."

"What the hell do I know about barge traffic, I'm comfortable with what we do now, I just don't see any long-term future in this barge idea."

"Look at New York, Philadelphia, Camden…these are cities that need help. Landfills are overflowing. People are upset about unsightly smelly heaps of trash. Dumping at sea is the only viable answer. And it's easy money. Just simple contracts with city officials. Barges loaded by city employees with city equipment. All we have to do is get these barges at least three miles out, and then dump. It's dead simple."

What Dick Pruit failed to mention was that the Mafia issued these contracts. The contracts were already "owned", in the sense that no one else could touch them. The only way to get in on the business was to sub-contract with the Mafia. Dick Pruit had been paying small time Mafia operators in New Jersey for some time. They controlled much of the local trucking business and had a powerful influence with the truckers union, the Teamsters. To Dick Pruit's way of thinking, you either cooperated with the Mafia or got out of the big time. He was also feathering his own nest by a series of payments he received from the Mafia to maintain the business connection with George Archer's firm. But that was all small in scale compared with the ocean dumping contracts that were now being offered.

The contract for ocean dumping of refuse and sludge was just as profitable as Dick Pruit had predicted. So much so that George Archer was easily persuaded to buy additional barges and take out further contracts. It was the increasing political influence of the environmentalists that worried Dick Pruit. Their agenda was to put an end to any further dumping at sea, and they appeared to be gaining political support, especially with the Democrats. He even tried to warn George Archer. But George was not easily convinced. Although he'd been against the barge idea in the first place, he was now stubbornly convinced that it would be the salvation of his company. For a couple of years, things went along very nicely; and then the bombshell hit. Congress passed a bill preventing further dumping of sludge and refuse at sea. It was just what Dick Pruit had expected.

"Explain it to me again," insisted George Archer, as if not convinced by the detailed account Dick Pruit had given him.

"Look Mr. Archer, we're in trouble if this bill is signed into law. If they prevent ocean dumping, our barge trade is ruined."

"I know that; it's those damned clauses that result in our barges being sold for almost nothing. I'd no idea we had an arrangement like this. Why the hell didn't you keep me better informed Dick? How the hell did I know what I was signing? I pay you to keep a handle on these things."

"We had to offer collateral in order to get those contracts; there was a lot of competition," replied Dick Pruit, defensively.

"But we bought the damn things from a group I subsequently learned was Mafia owned; I signed a contract to dump sludge with a second Mafia owned group, and now we are having to sell the damn barges because they have a clause which protects their investment in the event the contract cannot be completed. It's bloody robbery. What the hell am I paying you for Pruit, didn't you read these damn contracts?"

"Of course I did," replied Dick Pruit. "I told you about the pitfalls; I just didn't think this was a serious risk. We did discuss each of the penalty clauses, if you remember." Of course George Archer remembered, but he didn't want to admit he might have made a mistake. After all, it was Dick Pruit who got him into this business in the first place. "What the hell do we do now?" asked George in a soft voice, as if talking to himself.

"We should pay the penalty and get out of this business; the boom days are over; it's time to look for something else," suggested Dick Pruit. "For once," replied Archer, "we're in complete agreement. We'll cut our losses and get back into something we're good at...trucking. What's it going to cost us to get out of this contract?"

"Quite a lot, I'm afraid. But I agree it's our only option, short of selling up."

"What!" screamed George Archer, "are you telling me that this is nearly costing me my business; that I might have to sell up?"

"It's an option to be considered Mr. Archer, that's all. But it's an option you should be aware of. I'll put together some numbers for you to look at."

"You do that Dick, you do just that. I've no intention of giving in to crooks or incompetent lawyers," blasted George, his voice rising in anger and frustration.

Dick Pruit toyed with the familiar looking long white envelope on his desk. He knew what was in it. It always came on the fifth or sixth of each month. It was always in a similar envelope, there was never any return address and it was always marked, 'Personal and Confidential'. It was his regular payment from the New Jersey Mafia. He'd looked forward to receiving these envelopes at first; but he now felt trapped. He knew that George Archer's firm was too deeply involved with contracts which were essentially owned by the Mafia. There were also the extensive payments to ensure the trucking business would not be interfered with. The Mafia was only too keen to involve Dick Pruit. It was their way of ensuring that a business such as Archer's would become increasingly dependent on the Mafia. Infiltration was so much more sophisticated and ultimately safer and more effective than intimidation.

Dick Pruit felt himself getting hotter and uncomfortable as he looked at the envelope. He opened his right-hand desk drawer and tossed in the offending example of modern origami. He locked the drawer with a single key on a thin gold chain that was attached to his belt loop. He sat for several minutes with his hands folded and resting on the desk blotter pad, his thin fingers intertwined as if to hold in check the nervous spasms that twitched beneath the skin on the back of his right hand.

He slowly stretched the gold chain in front of him and then proceeded to reopen the desk drawer. He slipped his dagger shaped silver letter opener into the end of the envelope and quickly slit the flap. Attached to his usual money order was a letter written in a strangely familiar deep red ink. The note thanked Dick, politely, for his 'dedicated and loyal work'. It ended with a chilling footnote:

'In case you're wondering; yes, this is written in blood, it's your blood. We got this without spilling a drop or harming a hair of your head. Clever, don't you think? Unfortunately, we cannot always guarantee that our supply will be so simply obtained.'

The blood drained from Dick Pruit's face. He was white and sweating. His thin arms began to tremble. "Oh my God," muttered Pruit to himself, "what have I done; what have I got myself into?" He suddenly realized where they must have got his blood. He'd been for a medical two weeks earlier and had three samples taken by a bright, smiling nurse. They have their tentacles everywhere, thought Pruit. He sighed a weary, resigned and tired sigh. He stared again at the cream coloured writing paper. His sweating palms smudged the red, cursive, letters. The red smears looked more blood like than ever. He carefully placed the stained letter and the envelope in his empty trashcan and ignited the edge of the envelope with his lighter. He watched as the flame spread slowly changing the cream paper to shades of brown before it suddenly burst into a ball of yellow flame. Dick Pruit sat for several minutes staring at the charred ashes in the trashcan. He felt a little better now that the blood evidence had been destroyed. He tried to get up from his chair to open a window. The room felt very stuffy and he was hot and clammy. He only managed to take a couple of steps before having to sit back down on his chair. His legs were weak and wobbly, refusing to comply with his need for fresh air. He sat at his desk for almost fifteen minutes, trying to breath deeply and slowly to counter the twitching nervousness he felt.

George Archer leafed through the report that Dick Pruit had prepared. His company's net worth was still impressive, despite having to consider selling off his barges at salvage prices to get out of the dumping contracts. What irked George Archer the most was the feeling he had been 'had'. The only company able, or willing, to buy his barges was obviously owned by the Mafia. And they were then taking that as partial payment against his penalty clauses. The very thought of being tricked so blatantly, so legally, annoyed him intensely. He had his suspicions that somehow Pruit was involved in all of this. "If I find out he's in on this, I'll string him by the balls," George Archer told himself.

The document was sufficiently detailed and clearly explained. Dick Pruit had done an excellent job, thought George Archer. The "Executive Summary" on the second page really said it all. It was obvious that the company was in fairly sound financial health, but that the payment to the Mafia over the barge contracts would have to come, in part, from their sale. Archer could elect to sell out; however, the financial losses over the ocean dumping contracts would only serve to depress the value of Archer's holdings. Pruit's recommendation was to absorb the losses and to put greater emphasis on the interstate trucking, which was, pointed out the ever-clever Pruit, the bread and butter of Archer Enterprises. George Archer nodded in agreement as he read this section. It felt good to read that his very smart lawyer was concluding that the company's strengths lay in the very enterprises Archer had built up over the years. He smiled to himself in self-satisfaction, just as Dick Pruit knew he would. Dick Pruit was at his best when it came to exploiting George Archer's vanities and weaknesses.

George Archer went on what amounted to an industrial rampage. He bought out three small trucking companies in the southeast, who between them covered areas around Memphis and Tennessee. It stretched his finances to the limit, but he prided himself on knowing the trucking business and on being able to spot profitable concerns. He was right. Within six months, each division, as he now called them, was making tremendous profits, in part because of the extra long driving hours that he insisted on.

Dick Pruit called him at home at about nine in the evening. That was unusual, and George Archer knew to expect trouble as soon as he heard Pruit's voice.

"I received a call from a friend of mine in the Department of Commerce. They've received a complaint from one of our drivers about the twelve-hour shifts we've been insisting on. They're going to investigate..."

"Shit," interrupted George Archer, "who the hell...?"

"It's Eddy Reynolds."

"Eddy, Eddy fucking Reynolds, he's the last driver I would have expected; he's been with us what, ten, fifteen years."

"Eighteen," replied Dick.

"Then why the hell has he done this?" asked George, angrily.

"He's complained a couple of times, but what got him really upset was that crash two months ago."

"We lost an expensive rig," commented George. It was out before he had time to think.

"And a young driver, Rodgers, Jeff Rodgers," replied Pruit. "He had a wife and two young children," he added. This man's an absolute bastard, Pruit thought to himself. He's forgotten about Rodgers already. He's forgotten that these drivers are human beings. George Archer hadn't seen it necessary to attend the funeral. He'd told Dick Pruit to send a wreath and a card – "nothing too expensive". Dick had enclosed a cheque for $500 – he thought it was the very least the firm should do, and it gave him a smug feeling of being one step higher on the moral ladder than Archer.

The sound of George Archer's voice booming at him over the phone intercom interrupted his thoughts.

"We need to get rid of Reynolds," thundered Archer.

"What the hell do you mean?" asked Pruit, fearing the worst.

"Fire the bastard. I don't want him in my firm."

"But we can't just fire him. He's got eighteen years of unblemished service, he's never put a foot wrong."

"Then we'll just have to see he does," replied Archer.

"How?" enquired Pruit. "It's impossible."

"It's not a word I like to use," sneered Archer.

* * *

Eddy Reynolds slowed as he approached the truck stop. He had been driving for eight hours straight and badly needed a break. It was late afternoon, almost dusk. It was a time he hated. The fading light made him more tired and he had difficulty in clearly picking out small cars in the dim, diffuse light. He'd rather get off the road for an hour or so and wait until it was dark. He skillfully slipped into lower gears, slowly bringing his eighteen-wheel rig to a slower speed as he approached the turn off ramp. He liked this particular truck stop. They served thick, black coffee in oversized chipped mugs. The menu hadn't changed for years, not since that Italian had taken over. They served hamburgers of course, but these were special. They were hand-made; each scoop of ground beef was rolled into a sticky ball by two or three waitresses with pink, greasy hands. The balls of meat were laid by the side of a black hot plate while the waitresses turned to take customer orders. Change was returned with bits of raw hamburger meat that had managed to escape the single, abrasive, swipe of slick hands against once-white nylon coats. The black hot plate had a two-inch lip, which served to hold in the one-inch lake of hot, bubbling fat. The balls of meat were allowed to swim in the spitting liquid, before being flattened to shape with a well used metal spatula. The man wielding the spatula was the architect of these culinary delights, a large, sweating Italian named Luigi.

"Eddy, welcome back; it's a while since we've seen you in here." The friendly waitress poured him a full mug of the steaming, black, coffee. "What'll it be, the usual?" Eddy stopped in here about once a month, yet she always remembered his name, and his order. Maybe everyone ordered the same, thought Eddy.

"Sure."

"Three burgers with the works," she screamed in Luigi's direction by distorting her mouth. Her eyes remained fixed on Eddy.

"Why-a you shout-a. I have-a the ears." Luigi had a comic like Italian accent, despite having lived in the US for over thirty years. His wife was Italian and they had lived with both sets of parents ever since taking over this truck stop eleven years ago. One of the older Italians was usually helping out, rolling those meatballs, or picking off the cooked burgers and slipping them into white bread rolls. The burger juices stained the bread, edging the cut rim with a thin black line of fat. Eddy sat at the counter, sipping his coffee, and watching as Luigi forcefully coaxed the meatballs to resemble burgers. Relish, onions and pickles were added to each roll and the three splendid burgers were laid out before him on greaseproof paper. It was the ritual, as much as the smells and the taste, that made these the best hamburgers that he'd ever found. Nobody said a word when a customer was taking his first bite. He was left to savour the delight for himself without interruption.

The phone booth was at the far end of the room on a small length of flat wall between the entrances to the male and female bathrooms. The receiver was stained with grease from the hands of long distance truckers and the wall in and around the booth was scratched with quickly jotted phone numbers, doodles and some quite skillful art depicting trucks, motorbikes and portraits of full busted women. Eddy called the dispatch number collect. Five years ago he could chat to one of the dispatchers, but most of them were gone now. In the interests of efficiency, an answering system had been installed. He hated the idea of taking directions from a machine. The connection was made and a voice asked him to punch in his four-digit ID code. The same mindless voice issued a couple of instructions about how to replay the taped message and how to sign off.

"Yea, yea," said Eddy, speaking to the receiver in an irritated tone, "get to the message will ya." The machine continued.

'Order change, please note new delivery address.' The taped message proceeded to give a town in Tennessee as the destination, about two hundred miles away from his original unloading point.

"Hell," muttered Eddy, "I hate these damn order changes." He replayed the tape to make sure he had the correct address for the new destination. This kind of thing happened occasionally, particularly with electronic components, which he knew he was carrying. It usually meant the original buyer had sold the truckload to someone else and contracted with Archer's to redirect the shipment.

Eddy could see the flashing lights of two state patrol cars speeding toward him in his wing mirror. They were moving at a very fast pace and he could hear their sirens wailing. They've spotted some poor sucker, though Eddy. He slowed slightly as the first car neared. To his surprise, it veered directly in front of him. The second car pulled along side and signaled Eddy to pull over. Must be a taillight, thought Eddy. Two troopers got out of the first car. One held a flashlight; the other walked with his hand on his gun butt. These guys mean business, what the hell is going on, Eddy thought to himself.

"Eddy, Eddy Reynolds?"

"Yea, that's me. What's up?"

"This rig was reported missing. Climb down, we've some questions to ask."

"I don't believe this," muttered Eddy, under his breath.

"Explain it to me again," demanded the Station Captain in a slow, pedantic manner.

"There was a taped message...it told me to deliver to an address in Tennessee..."

"Not to Beta Electronics in Bristol?" interjected the Captain.

"I've told you, that was the original shipping address; check with Archer's."

"We did. They say the only instruction they issued was the one you were given when you left. There was no order change, no taped message from dispatch."

"What the hell's going on?" demanded Eddy.

"You tell me," replied the Captain. "Beta Electronics called Archer's when you didn't arrive as scheduled. Archer's called us. They were worried you might have had an accident, or even been hi-jacked."

"I'll bet they were," replied Eddy.

"What's that supposed to mean?" asked the Captain.

"I've been set up." Eddy suddenly realised what was going on. "They want rid of me."

It was the first police report against Eddy in twenty years of driving on the interstates. 'Held for questioning under suspicion of stealing electronic components which were the property of Beta Electronics.' That's what the Captain had put in his report. Mr. Pruit, the lawyer for Archer's, had been very helpful, so the Captain had told him. He'd persuaded Beta to drop any charges; there wasn't any evidence to hold him and he'd promised that Archer's would keep a close eye on him. Eddy was just relieved it was all over. He called Pruit to thank him for his help, at the same time, he wondered who'd gone to all this trouble to set him up. Someone in Dispatch? Must have been. Archer's Transportation Manager? He'd argued a lot with him recently over the extended hours, especially after the death of the young driver, Jeff Rodgers. Nice kid, that Rodgers, Eddy thought to himself.

A couple of months passed without incident. Eddy was very nervous whenever the dispatch message told him there was an order change. The first time it happened, he called Pruit at the office and demanded that someone call him back to confirm the change. Pruit was very understanding. He had the Transportation Manager make a call back to Eddy. The Manager was obviously not pleased at being summonsed in the evening to give Eddy assurances which he really knew nothing about. That was Dispatch's job. He did it anyway; Pruit had insisted. He took the opportunity to rail on Eddy, telling him that this had better not get to be a habit; and why didn't he get a job elsewhere if he couldn't cope with Archer's procedures? He's the boy, he's the one who's got it in for me, Eddy told himself.

"Damn," Eddy muttered to himself, "another order change." He replayed the taped message. It simply confirmed what he didn't want to hear. It was 3am. There was no point in trying to call. Pruit had an ex-directory number, and the Transportation Manager would only deny any knowledge of orders issued by the Dispatch Office. He didn't trust the Transportation Manager anyway. He'd convinced himself that the Manager was the one out to get him. For thirty minutes or so, Eddy kept a wary eye on his wing mirror. He began to relax, telling himself not to be so paranoid. It was making him ill. He flicked on the radio. Country music blared from every station in this region, and the light, catchy tunes made him feel at ease.

Eddy became so engrossed in the country music that he only spotted the State Trooper's vehicle when it was almost on his tail. It was as if they had stealthily crept up and surprised him. To some extent, this was true. The State Troopers spotted Eddy's truck about fifteen miles back. They'd received a report of a missing rig in the early hours of the morning. The report said the vehicle was owned by Archer trucking and was headed for Savannah, Georgia. This was an Archer vehicle, but it was heading in the opposite direction. There were so many Archer Trucks these days that this was not that unusual. They radioed in for further details. As they approached, they could see that the license number checked with that of the missing rig. They radioed in for assistance, and simply sat on Eddy's tail without giving any hint of an emergency. Eddy could see them in his mirror, sitting in the inside lane, about a mile or so from his truck. Relax, he told himself; there's nothing unusual about a State Trooper car cruising along the interstate highway.

He spotted another cop car sitting on the next overpass. He began to feel tense. His worst fears were realised. As he moved from under the overpass, he could see the cop car speeding down the ramp, its lights flashing. The other cars had also turned on their blue and white flashing lights. Eddy could see two of the cars, which were now driving two abreast in the outer lanes. The trooper in the nearest car signaled him to pull over as they drew level.

"Look, this happened to me before..."

"We know that," replied the trooper.

"You don't understand, I've been set up. It's the transportation manager, he wants rid of me."

"Look buddy, all we know is that this rig was reported missing. You were supposed to be heading for Savannah in Georgia."

"I got an order change from Dispatch."

"Not the way we hear it. The only order Archers know of is the one for you to go with this load to Savannah. What are you carrying anyway?"

"Electronic stuff."

"Just like last time, eh?"

"Oh hell," muttered Eddy.

Dick Pruit got Eddy out after he had spent most of the day held in the County Jail. Nothing was missing, he had explained to the Station Sergeant. The Savannah Company wasn't interested in pressing charges; they just wanted their shipment to be delivered as quickly as possible.

"We'll be handling it Sergeant. Eddy Reynolds will never drive for us again."

"Or for any other trucking company, I hope," added the Sergeant.

"Don't worry Sergeant, we'll make sure he never gets behind the wheel of a commercial vehicle again."

"It's a pity, but I've seen it before," continued the Sergeant. "A man is straight all his life and then suddenly decides he wants a couple of big payoffs. They're the worst kind, difficult to trace. You were lucky he got caught."

"He's just lucky not to be in prison," commented Dick Pruit, "but he's got a wife, and a couple of kids."

"Maybe he should have thought of that," suggested the Sergeant.

Chapter 14

THE PRICE OF FORTUNE

Tracy was ecstatic. She could hardly believe it was true. She was rich beyond her wildest dreams; she was sure of that. She now owned Archer Transport Inc., not to mention a very smart town house, which was rented to Dick Pruit, and the very spacious apartment in the Watergate building. Her first job would be to redecorate the apartment and get rid of the hospital-like smell that seemed to pervade every room. She decided to collect some essential things from her room, check into the Hyatt hotel and then arrange for a firm of decorators to start on the apartment. It took a couple of days to locate a suitable firm. Once that project was underway, her next task was to tackle Dick Pruit. She'd heard all the rumours about how the firm had lost its edge once the old man had become too ill to be involved in its day-to-day affairs. Dick Pruit had taken over as CEO, but he'd always seemed weak and ineffectual to Tracy. She was determined to do two things; first, find out all she could about the financial status of her company, and then to sack Dick Pruit as soon as possible.

She would bring in her own legal advisor and her own CEO; people she could trust.

Dick Pruit was becoming concerned. He hadn't expected Tracy to take such a strong interest in the firm. He'd assumed she would be just concerned with money. He hadn't reckoned on her almost zealous interest in the running of the company. Now that she had been established as a relative of Archer's, it seemed as if she wanted to emulate him in some way. And then he got really worried; Tracy announced that she was bringing in a firm of auditors to review the accounts. Not the firm they usually used, but a reputable and very independent firm from New York. They were renowned for their thoroughness and honesty; two qualities that Dick Pruit knew would only lead to trouble.

"Why on earth do you want to bring in Marks and Coleman to look at our books? They're far too expensive for this size of company."

"And far too reputable," retorted Tracy.

"What does that mean?" snapped Pruit, in a defensive manner.

"Just that I want to know how this firm stands financially, and I don't trust that firm Archers have used for years. I've heard the rumours about how they have Mafia connections."

"That's nonsense. We are very sound financially. Why don't you let me worry about the finances for you? I can get you a full report in a couple of weeks."

"Don't you patronise me," thundered Tracy. Her voice was shrill and angry and her blue eyes stared coldly at Dick Pruit. Her voice changed, becoming lower and more pedantic, but it still conveyed a dogged determination and intensity. "I will not be fobbed off by you or anyone else. I want to know how this company runs, where it makes a profit, where it is losing money and where its money goes." Dick Pruit felt himself retreating under the onslaught. It was similar to the berating he had received from the old man.

"But Tracy," he protested, "the Archer Company is in fine shape. It went through a difficult period several years ago..."

"The barge contracts" interrupted Tracy, "I heard about those."

"Who told you?" queried Dick Pruit. She seemed to know too much and she wanted to know even more. The thought of Tracy continually digging out information that wasn't supposed to surface worried him.

"Mr. Archer... George, who do you think?" replied Tracy, cockily. Pruit looked concerned, almost worried. It only made her more determined than ever to take a closer look at Archer's accounts.

"That was several years ago. Archers are much stronger now. We control most of the trucking contracts on the east coast."

"Control, control, what does that mean?" asked Tracy. "It sounds as if we are coercing companies to use our trucks." Dick Pruit looked strangely at Tracy and then laughed. It was a forced and nervous laugh, which caused the ever-alert Tracy to eye Pruit with even greater intrigue. I've hit a nerve; I know it, thought Tracy. We're either using some illegal practices or we're mixed up with some shady outfit acting on our behalf. Her mind continued to race and consider a myriad of imagined scenarios. Her eyes remained fixed on the puzzled and shuffling Pruit throughout her deliberations.

The financial auditors from Marks and Coleman gave her a preliminary assessment, based on materials compiled by Dick Pruit. Three auditors from the firm met with Tracy in her private office. The lead auditor was Michael Klingman, a small dapper man with bright blue eyes and a shiny bald pate. He talked in short, rapid sentences and spoke intently about auditing as if it were a major science. He was very serious about his work and proud of his ability to be probing, efficient and exact. His assistant, Jonathan Scott, was a quieter man of medium build with a brooding, worried expression. He dealt with the details, the infinite minutiae that an ordinary accountant might overlook. He had the habit of staring at the floor for long periods with his head bent forward and his eyes fixed on some imagined blemish on the carpet that no one else had noticed. The third member of the audit team was a woman; tall and slim wearing a well cut business suit and a pair of rimmed glasses that made her look rather serious. Ingrid Klosterman explained that her role was to bring together the two areas of work covered by Mr. Klingman and Mr. Scott. Her expertise in business management and finance would enable the team to probe areas that a simple process audit might miss. Following these introductions, it was Michael Klingman who outlined the work to be undertaken.

"Archers is in sound financial shape, as far as we can tell. We've only been given selected information to work with. We would need at least a month to thoroughly examine the accounts in detail. There are a couple of points we found interesting."

"Go on," urged Tracy.

"Archers has a substantial share of the trucking business along the eastern sea board, and into the Midwest. These contracts are very profitable. Yet Archer's rates are among the highest in the business. We fully expected that Archer's rates would be very competitive, given the volume of business they handle."

"Is that cause for concern?" asked Tracy.

"Not really," replied Klingman, "in fact it's good business sense ... charging whatever the market will bear. It's just odd that others haven't managed to move in with lower bids. Could be all sorts of reasons...reputation, effectiveness, capacity, insurance rates...we'd need to do more work...need to contact the companies."

"What else seemed unusual?"

"We would have expected greater quarterly profits. Not that the firm isn't doing well...but given the contracts, the high rates, the volume of business, we'd have expected greater returns on capital."

"Any ideas?" asked Tracy.

"Jonathan spotted a couple of things." Tracy and Klingman turned to Jonathan, who continued his intense interest in the carpet. Klingman apparently realized that he would have to do the explaining.

"There have been some substantial payments to a small New Jersey firm; another trucking company we think." Klingman waited briefly for Jonathan, and then continued. "Jonathan has come across them before, trucking, barge traffic, that sort of thing."

"Barge traffic," exclaimed Tracy. "I'm not sure I like the sound of this."

"Oh, it's probably some sub-contracting. Archers have arranged for this firm to handle smaller local haulage," replied Jonathon.

"We'll be doing further checks," Ingrid Klosterman added, somewhat forcefully. "We will of course let you know immediately if we have any other causes for concern."

Later that week, Tracy received an urgent memo from the audit team. She read it, slowly and carefully, absorbing every word.

Over the days following the memo from the auditors, Tracy had the sense that she was being watched. She'd seen the same navy blue Lincoln in her rear view mirror for the fifth day in a row. It wasn't that unusual to see the same vehicles and the same faces as she traveled to work; but this vehicle never got any closer no matter how much she consciously varied her speed. She had also caught a glimpse of the same vehicle when she took a trip to the hairdresser, and again when she took a quick dash to a local drug store one evening after work. She was now convinced she was being followed. She thought there were two men in the Lincoln, but they never got close enough for her to see their faces, and besides, the windows were heavily tinted. She tried to read the licence plate, but the letters were just an annoying blur. She began to dread pulling into the underground car park and began using the valet service to have her car parked. She could then slip into her apartment building through the main security doors and be greeted by a friendly grunt from old Jack, the rather elderly bellhop. Tracy felt herself becoming more nervous, and almost paranoid about strangers she encountered. She began looking intently into the faces of people she met, looking for some sign of hostility, or at least, unfriendliness. She made a mental note of any level of discomfort she felt with those she regularly encountered.

The parking valet, Richard, opened her door as she pulled up to the service area reserved for residents at the front of her building. There was a sense of security and comfort in having the car door opened by the same shiny black shoes, stiff blue trousers with their familiar yellow stripe, and matching jacket trimmed with yellow braid. Tracy handed the keys to the outstretched hand.

"Thank you Richard. I'll need it..." Tracy froze. Cold chills formed on her shoulders and neck causing her to shiver. It wasn't Richard; it was some other valet. Someone dressed in Richard's clothes. The face seemed to leer at her, as if sensing her discomfort. She dropped the keys, missing the outstretched hand, and ran inside the building. She was breathless. She was engulfed in a feeling of relief when she spotted Jack, the concierge, patrolling the lobby.

"Jack, Jack, where's Richard?"

"He took off Miss. You know what these young ones are like, unreliable. The building manager got a call from Richard's brother. Something about a job offer in California. Funny thing though, I never heard him mention his brother before. But he was always dreaming about making it big in California. Sounds just like Richard."

"Thanks Jack," muttered Tracy, although she was feeling distinctly uncomfortable. She felt nauseous, cold clammy and frightened. She ran to the elevator. I'm going to call the police, she told herself. There is just too much going on that I don't like.

Tracy's heart was pounding in the elevator. Images were swirling in her mind: the new valet, Richard, Jack, the blue Lincoln, and Dick Pruit. She felt claustrophobic in the metallic box with its rows of numbered brass buttons. The elevator seemed to take an unusually long time to reach her floor. The doors slowly opened and Tracy raced to her own apartment. She fumbled with her keys, taking longer than she wanted to open her door. She slammed the door behind her and slipped the dead bolt in place. Tracy lay back against the comfort of the solid and locked door, taking a deep breath and mopping the clammy sweat from her brow as she did so. A drink, I need a drink, she told herself. Tracy flung her keys onto the kitchen counter top and headed for the living room. She poured herself a liberal measure of Scotch whisky. She added a splash of soda, and then found she needed both hands to steady the glass as she raised it to her lips. Tracy needed only three attempts to drain the glass completely. She wasn't used to its strong effect. It burned in the back of her throat and felt hot in her stomach. Her face became flushed and her head seemed light and detached. But she felt better. The cold fear, and the weak feeling she had felt in her legs were gone. Tracy glanced in the direction of the telephone. The phone, must phone the police, she told herself.

As Tracy moved to the telephone, she just caught sight of a crouching figure, kneeling behind the couch. She gasped, and tried to cry out. Her scream was stifled by the suede glove of a second man who caught her from behind. She could taste the fine-grained chamois leather as the huge palm engulfed her open mouth. Tracy struggled violently. She could smell the chloroform. The gloved hand was replaced in an instant by a white muslin cloth. The vapours penetrated her mouth and nasal passages. Her head began to swim violently. The images she had encountered in the elevator returned in distorted and contorted forms. Spinning coloured lights swirled in her brain, carried by the noxious penetrating fumes. Blackness followed and she felt herself slump in the arms of her faceless attackers.

Tracy's lifeless body was found at the foot of her third floor balcony window. Her neck was broken.

Dick Pruit took no notice of the navy blue Lincoln as he quickly crossed the street to a news stand. He wanted to get a copy of the morning paper to read the account of Tracy's death. His mind was filled with fear, fear at what might happen to him. He'd warned his Mafia connections to expect trouble. He'd told them that Tracy was having the accounts audited; but he hadn't expected this. He'd received a call from the police department about three this morning and he hadn't slept a wink since. He tried to call his Mafia connection, but to no avail. The number had been disconnected. Dick bought a copy of the *Morning Post* and immediately turned to the local news section. Tracy's photograph stared back at him. It was a poor photograph; about three years old, but it captured her spunky independence. He turned away from the news stand, forgetting about change from his ten-dollar bill. The vendor made a half-hearted attempt to call after him. Dick was engrossed in the article. How had she died? Did they suspect foul play?

The Lincoln car hit him just as his foot stepped off the sidewalk. His body splattered against the right headlight sending a shower of glass and blood over the news stand, staining the morning copies. He was dragged about a hundred yards before his clothing tore away from the front fender. The body slipped under the front and rear tyres. The double bump crushed his skull, leaving the newspaper seller to stare in horror at the blooded and battered body of Pruit and the navy blue Lincoln speeding away.

* * *

It was in a single column in the 'World News' section of the newspaper, but it caught my immediate attention. *'Archer Heiress Killed – Police suspect foul play.'* The article summarised the deaths of both Tracy and Dick Pruit. It described in sufficiently graphic detail how Tracy's body contained traces of chloroform and that marks on her neck led police to conclude her neck had been broken prior to her body being pushed over the balcony of her apartment. Dick Pruit's death was described in even more grisly detail. The company director had been struck by a navy blue Lincoln. A shocked newspaper vendor had reported that it appeared the driver deliberately drove to hit Pruit as he slowly crossed the road at a very quiet time of the day. No other cars were involved. The article described how Pruit had been dragged along before falling under the wheels of the heavy car. His skull had been crushed and his internal organs ruptured by the impact. It seemed to the newspaper seller that the driver briefly slowed afterwards, as if checking to see if Pruit was dead. He then sped off in the direction of the city. There were no other witnesses although the police had suspicions of

Mafia involvement. The newspaper seller was reported to be in protective custody.

I felt the muscles in my arm twitch involuntarily. My mouth went very dry and I suddenly felt very cold, despite the beads of sweat I could feel gathering on my forehead. It was as if the available moisture in my mouth was subject to some sudden and intense capillary action direct to the pores on my brow. I tried to read the article again, but now I was shaking quite violently. I threw the paper onto the chair and poured myself a substantial whisky. Its scented aromatics filled my nostrils and I felt the warming liquid slipping down my throat, steadying my heaving stomach. Within minutes, I felt warmer; my arms stopped twitching and my attack of paranoia began to subside. I tried to make myself be rational and logical about these ghastly events. I wasn't linked to Tracy or to Dick Pruit – or was I? I had no involvement in the running of the Archer empire – I had a document that severed my connection with the firm. I imagined myself waving it in front of the hit men, trying to persuade them that it offered me absolution from Archer's affairs, even protection. I felt reasonably safe and untroubled in the daytime; however, at night, my fertile imagination persisted in destroying all my attempts at rational thought.

It had just started to get a bit easier. A month had passed since I read of the deaths of Tracy and Dick Pruit. And then I received a letter from a firm of lawyers in Washington DC. I recognised their name. It was the same firm who had been hired to deal with the old man's estate. Their names were embossed in black on the back of the cream-coloured envelope. I sat staring at the envelope turning it over in my hands as if inspecting it for evidence that might reveal its purpose. I grabbed a knife from the kitchen and carefully slit the envelope along its longer side. The folded letter was in the same cream coloured paper. I unfolded the letter, focusing initially on the same embossed black lettering on the left hand side of the paper. I forced myself to read the letter slowly and carefully.

Dear Mr. Jackson,

As you may have heard, Tracy Ivers, who only recently inherited the Archer estate, was killed by persons as yet unknown. You may also be aware that the firm's lawyer, Dick Pruit, was also killed in a hit and run incident. Police are investigating both incidents and are hopeful that the perpetrators of these crimes will be apprehended shortly.

My purpose in writing is to ascertain if there is any link between you and Mr Archer that might enable you to lay claim to the Archer estate. Mr Archer's will simply left his estate to his next of kin. We have not been able to establish any family connections. We know, however, that you had some connection with Mr Archer. It has also come to light that contained in Dick Pruit's papers was a document you signed essentially preventing you from making any claim on the Archer estate. The deaths of both Ms Ivers and Mr Pruit means that this document is no longer relevant. I am therefore writing to ascertain if you are in any way related to Mr. Archer and if you intend registering any claim to the Archer estate?

I look forward to hearing from you.
Sincerely,
Darryl E. Keogh
Attorney at Law.

I felt as though I was being engulfed by a potentially life threatening situation from which there seemed little chance of escape. I could make a very strong case to inherit the Archer empire; however, the overriding fear was that I would end up the same way as Tracy and Dick Pruit. Somehow they had pissed off some very powerful and nasty people and I could only assume that whoever they were they would continue to target the head of the Archer organization. I felt weak and sick to my stomach just thinking about the situation. How the hell had I landed in this mess?

The next day I received a letter from the London firm of solicitors who had contacted me in the first place; Vietch, Leonard and Wilcox.

Dear Mr. Jackson,

We have been instructed by a New York firm of solicitors to enquire as to any possible claim you may have to the Archer estate. We will not, of course, divulge any client information to any party without clear instructions; and given the recent deaths and ensuing press coverage, we are reluctant for this firm to have further involvement. We do recognise, however, that we have a duty to act in the best interests of our client and we await your instructions on this matter. I must remind you that we reserve the right to withdraw our services at any time should our senior partners consider the work might in any way jeopordise the reputation of this firm.

I look forward to hearing from you.
Sincerely,
Geoffrey Leonard
Partner

Vietch, Wilcox and Leonard.

Slippery bugger, I said to myself. But at least it sounded as though he was on my side, or at least, not the enemy. I slipped a glass alongside the whisky bottle and poured a substantial draft. The single malt, and its friends and relatives, had become quite a companion to me in recent weeks. I sometimes worried that I was becoming a little too attached to the warmth and comfort they offered.

At first, the whisky had helped me to relax and to consider things in a logical light. Now it was becoming an essential part of my daily routine. It was only a fleeting thought …

I phoned Mr. Leonard of Vietch, Leonard and Wilcox. He seemed a bit distant with me, rather off-hand I thought.

"I got your letter earlier this morning," I told him.

"Er … yes, Mr Jackson. Have you had some time to give it any thought?" he asked.

Is he mad? I thought to myself. I've obviously thought of little else, actually nothing else. No that isn't true, I also thought about having a drink – an expensive single malt, or something a little more prosaic? I had wrestled with this dilemma throughout the morning. I had resolved it by sampling both the single malt and the blended bottle of Bells. I'm not too sure how many I had consumed – I was hoping it was an equal number of each; it seemed somehow quite important. This all flashed through my brain in micro seconds; no, make that pico seconds. Anyhow, it was too fast for Mr Leonard. I could hear him stammering at the other end of the line.

"Mr. Jackson, are you still there? Is this an inconvenient time to discuss this?"

"Of course not," I said. My voice didn't sound like mine. It echoed in the phone as if I was repeating myself. I sounded a bit odd if you ask me.

"Look," I said, "I want you to let them know in no uncertain terms that I am not an Archer, that I have no claim on the estate and that quite frankly I'm not interested."

"You're absolutely sure that's what you want me to convey?" asked Mr. Leonard.

"Look," I said, my voice rising to an uncharacteristic pitch, "that is exactly what I want you to tell whoever is asking. So please write to Mr. Keogh and make this absolutely clear." I'm sure I sounded a bit desperate. My whining voice sounded like a pathetic plea rather than an instruction.

"I'll do my best to stifle Mr Keogh's concern as to any possible claim on your behalf," replied Mr. Leonard.

"And for that I'll be eternally grateful," I replied, somewhat condescendingly.

This conversation with Mr. Leonard had quite exhausted me. I was glad to put the receiver down; however, no sooner had I done so than I felt incredibly lonely. I'd resigned from my job and told Mr Wilson where to stick his parcels and bits of string. He'd been quite offended and at the time I'd been quite delighted at his reaction. Now how I wished I had some of the old routine; its dullness was quite appealing.

I peeked at the clock – 11:30. Good, I thought, the day is at least underway. What I needed was company, and what better place than the local pub? I found myself a relatively quiet corner where I could sip my whisky and water, and observe the comings and goings. It got busier as lunch time approached. Soon there was quite a buzz in the place and my once quiet corner was now delightfully noisy. I felt quite at home listening to their chatter about work, football, partners, infidelities, office politics, gossip, holidays, families – the stuff that lives are made of. It was as if I'd been given a chance to glance at the mundane side of life and to admire and value it for all its pretensions, its vagaries and inconsistencies. The perils of office politics, the repetitiveness of daily routines and the stresses of suburbia were, I'd now decided, the admirable elements of stability. I envied those who thought they had no right to be envied. Their lives were the embodiment of predictability. Mine seemed frighteningly fragile and unstable. I noticed one or two in the corner looking at me and whispering to each other. I must have been staring in their direction. My hands were sweaty and my eyes felt as though they were on stalks, searching the room like giant antennae. The room began to thin as my companions drifted away, back to their neat desks, decorated with family photographs and littered with the detritus of office life; plastic coffee cups, a flask of coffee, doodling pads, perhaps a desk toy or two. I consoled myself with another drink. I quickly became annoyed, however, at their unwillingness to engage me in the group. Who did they think they were? Snotty clerks, office underlings, adventureless soles, shitty shirkers (I liked that, it made me smile). I glared at those of them who dared glance in my direction as they exited noisily from the bar. Was I like them before all this happened, I wondered?

The rest of the day was a bit of a blur. I wandered from pub to pub, adding a few more whiskies to the tally, I felt I wanted company; normal everyday chat, but I had no such luck. The most I got were the usual few words from the bar; "I think you've had enough, sir. Why not make that your last, eh?"

I didn't feel like going back to my flat. I walked aimlessly towards the centre of town, drawn by the flickering neon signs pitching their illuminating light into the dark sky and the shop windows smearing the pavements in diffuse yellow puddles of light. There was a well-lit hotel on a corner; I'd passed it many times but never been inside. On a whim, I decided I'd book a room for the night. It had steps leading to a big set of revolving doors with large off-white pillars giving further definition and some splendour to the entrance. I stumbled a bit going through the revolving doors and encountered the critical gaze of the doorman. No, I didn't have any bags, I told him, but yes, I did want a room for the night, in fact the best room available. I paid the receptionist in cash while the doorman hovered as if waiting to get the nod to have me ejected.

I liked the room. It was long and narrow and had a large double bed at one end that was separated from a sitting and working area by a large couch across the centre of the room. In front of the couch was an oval shaped coffee table and against the back wall was a large television sitting on a cabinet, the doors of which had been strategically left ajar to reveal a tea service, a small kettle, some fruit and some biscuits. A door adjacent to the head of the bed led to a large bathroom with black and white floor tiles. A very large old-fashioned bath with centre taps and ornate legs dominated the room. The lighting was subtle and soft, complimenting the decor and giving a warm and comfortable feel to the room. On the back of the door hung a large white dressing gown and a row of heavy white towels. It was lovely, I thought, and I gazed dreamily around at the enchantment before me.

I took great pleasure in running the bath. I liked the way the heavy brass plug fitted so neatly and the large brass taps gave just a squeak of resistance when I opened the taps to fill the bath.

I went for a long soak. The water was deliciously warm and there was a sponge headrest that invited me to stretch and wallow in this bed of water.

I must have dozed off. The next thing I remembered was feeling a bit chilly in the now tepid bath water. The skin of my hands and toes were wrinkled and bleached white at the tips. They looked as though they should belong to some person considerably older who could lay claim to such wrinkly skin. I pulled myself out of the bath, grabbed a large fluffy towel and rubbed vigorously across my back and then my chest and legs. I felt better – now considerably warmer and deliciously clean. I rewarded my endeavours with four aspirins from the medical cabinet above the sink followed by a miniature whisky filched from the bar cabinet. I reasoned to myself that they might stave off an incipient headache. I now had a dull aching thud pulsing from somewhere on the left side of my head. So much for the home cure, I thought.

It suddenly occurred to me that what I needed was food. I dressed quickly and smoothed my still damp hair. My reflection gave me a bit of a shock. I looked old. My eyes were bleary and encircled by dark rings. I hadn't shaved properly for days and several creases in my face were amplified by lines, and a few tufts of dark stubble. I stuck out my tongue – it was coated in a thick white fuzz. I gazed in disbelief at this abhorrent reflection. I splashed my face with handfuls of icy cold water from the tap in the sink and plunged my face into the hand towel. I found a toothbrush and a small tube of toothpaste in the wicker basket that contained toiletries, a sewing kit and a shoe polishing cloth. I also found, much to my delight, a phial of mouthwash in the toiletries. I scrubbed my teeth and brushed my tongue and then rinsed the mouthwash around my gums, holding it in my mouth until my gums started to tingle. I felt refreshed; I even looked more like the reflection I cared for. I got dressed in my rather dishevelled clothes, smoothing down my shirt and trousers trying to make them and me somewhat presentable. I was not entirely satisfied with the result, but sufficiently assured that my grooming had produced a substantial improvement in my appearance. The old doorman gave a double take as I strode past him into the dining room.

Dinner was a wonderful experience. It wasn't the food, which was passable, it was the sense of stillness and security it gave me; I could relax and think. By the time I had been served coffee, I had decided that I had two options. The first, and most dangerous, was to make claim to the Archer estate. I would need to surround myself with the best lawyers and the most reliable protection service. The second, and surely the most logical, was to deny any association with the Archer estate. This was surely the easiest course to follow; but would I be believed? Would I be left alone? This option wasn't quite without some risk, I reasoned.

I looked around the dining room as I sipped my coffee. It was very small and intimate. There was a middle-aged couple who, I noticed, hardly spoke. Bored with each other and nothing to talk about, now the kids were gone. The only other person dining that evening was an American woman, I'd heard her order from the menu, late thirties I guessed. Attractive and a good figure from what I could see. To my complete surprise, she leaned over in my direction.

"Mind if I join you over coffee? Having no one to talk to gives me the creeps." She got up carrying her cup of coffee and stood poised over the seat at my table.

"Er ... er ... yes," I stuttered, motioning her to sit down.

"Thanks."

She smiled at me and slid onto the seat opposite mine. She ignored her coffee and just played with the spoon, tapping it against the saucer.

"Where are you from?" I asked.

"Oh ... hear and there, but mostly New York." She had a clipped accent with a hint of something akin to an Irish brogue. "Brooklyn, originally; how about you?"

"Me, oh, I live here, in this town. I've a flat down near the river."

"Is that an invitation?" she teased.

I felt myself blushing. "No, it wasn't ..."

She held up her hand, "Whoa, only kidding." We looked at each other and laughed. I was enjoying her company; it was good to feel normal again.

She picked up her cup and sipped her coffee. It was as if we had broken the ice.

"It's Joe isn't it; Joe Jackson."

I coughed and spluttered on a half downed gulp of my coffee. My paranoia returned immediately. I suddenly felt cold, clammy and breathless. I gasped trying to suck some air into my lungs.

"Sorry, I shouldn't have just sprung that on you."

"Who the hell are you?" I hissed, leaning forward in her direction.

"Look Joe, you don't mind me calling you Joe do you?" She continued before I had a chance to reply. "I'm a lawyer, I was working with Tracy in sorting out the Archer's mess before she was killed. She told me all about you, old Charlie and her connections to George Archer."

Hmm, I thought, I wonder which George Archer she means?

"How do I know you are telling the truth?" I asked, "and what is it you want with me anyway?"

"This isn't going to be easy," she replied. "but maybe this will help."

She produced her passport and her business card.

I read her name from the passport and checked it against her card.

"Ingrid Klosterman … that's unusual …"

"My Dad was from South Dakota; a big German colony not to mention the Norwegians and the Dutch," she replied. "Too many Lutherans was my Dad's excuse for moving to New York."

"But all this shows me is that you have a business card and a passport with the same name. It doesn't tell me anything about who you are. You might be a lawyer working for Keogh and his cronies."

"I know all about Darryl Keogh and his connections – believe me, I don't work for Mr. Keogh."

"I'm listening because I want to believe you," I replied. "But how can I?"

"Look," said Ingrid in a firm voice that gave a hint of a strong personality, "as I see it, you don't have many options. I can leave you to stew in your own misery or you can hear me out and then decide if I'm friend or foe. So, I can leave right now, or you can listen to what I have to say ... and then decide."

I sat and looked into her eyes. They were a deep blue colour and had become vibrant and shiny as she spoke. She gave the impression of being very bright, alert and seemed full of energy. I felt strangely comfortable and reassured by what she was saying – I also knew it was what I wanted to hear – and there was danger in that. Ingrid seemed to just assume that my stares were a signal of acquiescence; perhaps they were.

"Let me tell you about Tracy. We met at a party shortly after she took control at Archers. She was worried about Dick Pruit, and as it turned out, she had every reason to do so. I hadn't exactly run into her by accident. I had been working with the FBI investigating the Mafia connections to Dick Pruit in particular."

"You seem to be very effective at making acquaintances," I added. Ingrid laughed. I suddenly realised what she had said ...

"The FBI?" I said, in a startled voice.

"Yes, the FBI," she replied in a quite matter-of-fact way. "I'm seconded to work on projects that involve legal problems; especially those related to large businesses – hence my interest in Archers."

"A sort of special agent," I quipped.

"If you like," she replied, brusquely. "By the time Tracy took over Archers, we had been monitoring the company's activities for some time. Too many large contracts with organisations we suspected or knew had links with the Mafia. We also knew that Dick Pruit was the main connection, but we couldn't pin anything on him, so we just monitored and waited."

"For what?" I asked.

"For some turn of events. The death of the old man and the transfer of ownership to Tracy was just such an event."

"How did that help?" I said.

"Oh, well Tracy began to suspect Dick Pruit was up to something right from the start. Her decision to call in auditors is what triggered everything. Pruit panicked, the Mafia bosses got nervous and then these 'accidents' started happening."

"Murders you mean," I corrected. She ignored my remark and went on.

"We've got these guys rattled, they know we are getting close," she added.

"And in the meantime they are committing murders to make sure you don't get close enough," I remarked.

"Look," she said in stern tones, "we think the game has changed."

"Oh yeah, you're not going to tell me you've got them on the run?" I replied.

"No, but we believe that at first they were trying to protect their interests in Archers. They wanted Archers to continue operating as before, with Pruit ensuring they got their slice of the cake. Their first instinct has, predictably, been to save their own skins, and stop the further investigation of Archers. They didn't want a connection to their operations to be established. We think they were worried that their connections to Pruit would be exposed as soon as the auditors start to pour over the accounts and Pruit's files in particular. The problem for them is that the Archer connection has been very profitable, something they would like to continue."

"But why kill Pruit?" I asked. "I can see why Tracy … but Pruit?"

"He was weak. They think he would squeal if any pressure was brought to bear. The threat of a long prison sentence in a tough penitentiary would make Pruit do anything to get a plea bargain." Her eyes scanned my face as she spoke as if looking for signs of weakness on my part. I could have assured her that there was no need to peer too intently. My instincts were only too clear.

I took a final gulp of my now cold coffee.

"I'm not sure I like any of this," I remarked.

"We didn't think you would. But like I said, the way we see it, you don't have many options other than to listen to us …"

"… and agree to do what you want?" I added. Ingrid gave a big smile, as if welcoming me into her den.

"Tracy told us this incredible story … about how your Uncle Charlie was killed by George Archer when they were both working in Australia. But when we checked with our Australian colleagues, we got a slightly different scenario; that it was more likely that your Uncle Charlie killed George Archer and then assumed his identity. We also looked at his cleverly worded will, leaving his estate to his legitimate next of kin – which would be you Joe. But you'd elected to keep it to yourself and sell out to Tracy. It would have all finished there if Tracy and Pruit hadn't been killed. As it is, you are now the only heir to the estate – the true next of kin to the man who claimed to be George Archer."

"But I don't want any of this," I protested.

"Look," replied Ingrid in an emphatic manner, "the Mafia will do anything, and I mean anything, to protect their business interests, especially the lucrative line they seem to have had with Pruit and Archers. They want Archers to remain in business; it helps them launder money as well as providing a legitimate front for insurance scams, protection rackets, and access to government contracts. They thought Tracy was safe in Pruit's hands. They hadn't reckoned on her taking such a keen interest in the firm. Having to kill Tracy wasn't in their original plan. Now they have a problem. They can't get control of Archers, and having it sold off and broken up doesn't serve their needs. They need the legitimate side of Archers to continue … and that's where you come in."

"What do you mean?" I asked.

"We want you to claim the Archer estate."

"What…?" I hissed. "You must be mad. You are asking me to commit suicide."

"Not quite," replied Ingrid, "but we have a plan."

"I'm glad to hear it … no, on second thoughts, I don't want to hear about any crazy scheme that puts my life in danger," I retorted.

Ingrid was quick to reply. "On the contrary, we want to get you to a safe place as quickly as possible."

Chapter 15

THE MEETING

It all happened so quickly; just as well because I'm not sure I could have dealt with a protracted affair. I can only marvel at the way the FBI executed their plan of action. And me? Well, I'm in a witness protection programme, somewhere in England. I can't tell you where, that's part of the deal. I will say that it's near the sea in a picturesque town large enough to absorb me virtually unnoticed into the community. I've a new name; not one I care for, but I had no choice in that matter. As far as my neighbours are concerned, they have been fed the rumour that I'm an ex city trader, a bit of a wide boy who made a lot of money but also made a few enemies and that I decided to get out before things got nasty. Not a million miles from the truth.

That's the easy bit. The difficulty is getting close to people. I can't afford to let my guard down. I wondered, was it like this for my Uncle Charles in the first years of his deception? The fear that hearing your real first name brings and the instinct to respond; a glance from someone you don't know that suggests they know who you are;

the fear of meeting someone who knows you from your past life; the worry, the intense sense of paranoia; all this precedes the sense that you really are someone new, a different person, a different persona.

Ingrid began a series of visits as soon as I was provided with my new home. She steered me away from talking about the Archers and the Mafia. She wanted to discuss what I felt about my new role – was it a deception I could live with? Was I comfortable playing the part? This eventually led to discussions along the lines of 'Did I see any benefit in being someone else?' Was there a distinction between playing the role and actually being a new and possibly different person?

At first, I had no idea what she was driving at.

"Look," I said in fit of exasperation, "I've entered this protection programme at your suggestion. I feel strangely safe and even comfortable, but I don't know yet how you think you can persuade me to help you fight the Mafia. I just want to curl up inside this comfortable house and be as anonymous as I possibly can."

"Sounds awful," replied Ingrid. "You might as well be dead." She laughed, as if finding this fittingly funny. There was a pause, as if we were both reflecting on the forbidden word – 'dead'.

"I'm sorry, that was uncalled for," added Ingrid. "I've been involved in a number of witness protection schemes, most of which have involved a change of identity. Some have been successful, some have been unmitigated disasters." She sounded like a professor giving a tutorial to her prize student. It was her stance as much as her words, poised and reflective, occasionally stroking her forehead with the tips of her fingers. She went on; "those that were most successful seemed to have worked out what it takes to make yourself someone else – you need the fear of being identified to be replaced by a sense of belief in the new person you must create. The name change, the hair style, the tinted contact lenses are all part of the cosmetic and superficial adjustment. The real change is in accepting and believing that you can create a new person, a new character; someone whose traits and mannerisms will, overtime, become quite separate and distinct from those you previously cultivated. It is not that your inherited characteristics are altered, it is as if a series of profound external influences impact quite dramatically on your personality to create a radical change, a mix which results in a whole new identity."

I was enthralled. This beautiful, forceful and intelligent agent was opening up something I hadn't expected. I just looked at her and nodded, as if coming to a sudden cerebral awakening.

"Uncle Charlie…" I mumbled, "he made it work. You know, when I first learned of his deception, I was simply angry … at the audacity, the secrecy, and the enforced separation from the rest of his family. Then I began to feel sorry for him and eventually to even respect and admire the old bugger. I think I can see now that he had to create a new and different George Archer who was also fundamentally different from Uncle Charlie."

"Yes," interjected Ingrid. "And your Uncle could not have replaced George Archer without creating something different, something that was more than just a blending of two individuals. His strength, as the new George Archer, was that he knew he had to adopt a strong personality; a personality that slowly but surely engulfed and eventually obliterated the old self."

"I suppose that explained why he couldn't contact his sister – he no longer had a sister – he was a different person," I added. "The old Uncle Charlie only reappeared when he knew he was dying, that's why he had to contact me – and he nearly broke his cover to attend my mother's funeral. In both cases he was regressing back to his former self – and finally he needed to contact all that was left of the family he had largely forgotten."

My epiphany came with this realisation; this awakening to my new identity. I had been given a chance at being a different and stronger character. I could grasp it with both hands and build a new 'me' ... a better person, someone with a real sense of purpose.

Ingrid came to see me more frequently. She seemed to sense that a change was taking place and she was using all her subtle skills to encourage my new-found determination.

It all came to a head over dinner at my flat. She had suggested we have something special to celebrate. It was two months since I had moved in to the protection programme. I had rather jumped at her suggestion and had gone to some lengths to prepare an intimate dinner. I'd settled on the things I knew she liked; slivers of salmon with brown bread and wedges of lemon and lime followed by grilled fish, thin white sauce, peas and spring onions, and new potatoes – and finally my favourite, dark chocolate mousse. And to drink? I couldn't decide; but after trawling the supermarket I came across a New Zealand white wine that I'd read about in the *Sunday Observer*.

"Tell me Joe, how do you feel about the programme? Do you feel comfortable, safe?" White sauce oozed from the corner of her mouth. She wiped it away with the back of her hand. Quite uncharacteristic I thought.

"Safe – no, I don't think I'll ever feel really safe," I replied. "But bored, empty, unfulfilled - those are words I'd use." Ingrid exhaled slowly and pushed her plate to one side. "It's as if I'm an object in a private collection, well-protected and most people don't know I'm hear," I added.

We exchanged long looks as if not daring to break some sort of precious moment. Ingrid broke the spell of silence that had rendered us inanimate.

"I think it's time," Ingrid said.

"Time for what?" I asked.

"For you to decide – do you stay in your present state, occasionally peering over the parapet, or do you do something constructive, something that will give you a life."

"Redeem myself," I suggested.

"If you like."

"And that means helping you?" I replied.

"It is the only way," added Ingrid.

I got up and walked to the window and peered out. A deer suddenly ran out of the wood a couple of fields away. It ran skittishly, diving back into the undergrowth only seconds after its brief foray into the open space.

"It's the only way," I repeated, still gazing out of the window.

• •

It was clear to me that Ingrid was more than just a lawyer. Her first degree in psychology was obtained at Rutgers University in New Jersey. It was the home of the Scarlet Nights she would say with a smile, admitting with feigned reluctance, that it referred to the University's football team. After graduating *magna cum laude*, she studied law at the University of Chicago School, specialising in commercial and international law. She was recruited by the FBI in her final year at Law School. There was nothing secretive about it; the FBI recruited openly at many of the major campuses around the country. However, it soon became clear that the FBI regarded her as someone who may have the qualities they were looking for.

Over a period of months, Ingrid went through a series of assessments in addition to the extensive background checks the agency made. At first, the assessments focussed on logic, speed of thought and physical endurance. This led to more complex assessments which tested her resolve in situations that subjected her body and her mind to the effects of disorientation and hardship. She received training in the use of firearms and explosives. Ingrid acquired skills in interrogation, persuasion and applied her skills in psychology to profiling of individuals. She produced a manual detailing the information required and procedures to follow in building up a complete psychological and emotional profile of an individual. She was able to demonstrate the effectiveness of her methods in the field and it was quickly adopted by the FBI as one of its standard procedures.

Ingrid was brought in to work on the 'Archer Case' soon after the death of the old man. The FBI's interest in the Archer empire was heightened when it became clear that Tracy was intent on bringing a new approach to management at Archers. It was a break they hadn't expected and they hadn't any background on Tracy Ivers. Ingrid's job was to get involved when and where possible and to get to know Tracy. They wanted to know about her mental toughness, her motivation for taking on the firm and to support her where possible if it could give them a lead to the Mafia connections they were chasing. Tracy's decision to bring in auditors was a lucky break. Ingrid was able to add herself to the team which not only gave her access to a potentially important document trail, but also closer contact with both Tracy and Dick Pruit.

There was already a comprehensive file on Pruit. Tracy simply confirmed what was already known. He was a manipulative operator with a liking for an expensive lifestyle. He was quite prepared to sell his next of kin if required. People were expendable and were there to be used wherever and whenever possible. 'A user and an abuser of people' was how the report in his file had neatly summarised Pruit. Ingrid could find no reason to quarrel with this succinct assessment. But the file was less clear in its assessment of his involvement with corruption on a major scale. 'We suspect Pruit has links with the Mafia. A number of business transactions …'

Ingrid decided to focus her attention on Pruit as much as she could. It was patently obvious that Pruit didn't like the presence of the audit team. She overheard Pruit and Tracy arguing on their purpose on a number of occasions. It was clear that Pruit was very uncomfortable with the questions they were asking and with the information they were requesting. Ingrid decided to tighten the screw by sending an urgent memo ostensibly from the auditors to Tracy with a copy to Pruit.

Memo To: Ms Tracy Ivers, Managing Director
Cc: Dick Pruit, Financial Director
Memo Subject: Missing documentation
Status: Confidential
Level: High importance.

We are at a very early stage in our audit of the company and it is unusual for us to identify specific concerns in advance of the full report. However, we have some significant concerns that we feel represent a high risk to the firm of Archers. We feel it necessary, therefore, to draw the following to your attention.

A large number of payments have been made over a period of at least five years, it may be longer, to a series of companies. This in itself is not unusual, given the scale of Archer's business interests, however, almost all of these companies appear to be shell organisations with no reported business transactions other than to serve as conduits for financial transactions. The structure of shell companies can make it very difficult to determine who the directors are and the purpose of the company. Most are entirely legitimate, however, a growing number have been set up specifically to hide illegal transactions and payments, or to launder money. They are therefore quite popular tools of Mafia related organisations.

We would appreciate your fullest cooperation in determining the reasons for these payments.

Ingrid saw Pruit rush from his office shortly after he received his copy of the memo. Her eyes locked on his as he turned to move down the corridor. He froze for an instant like an animal caught in the glare of headlights. He looked ashen. And then he fled, slamming every door on his way to the elevator. She could see him from the second floor window. He was heading for the carpark, a large brief case wobbling at his side and banging into his legs as he tried to break into a run. He stumbled a couple of times and opted to try a fast walk, his arm held rigidly to keep the brief case as stable as possible. The animal was wounded and very frightened.

* * *

I had two days to pack. I had a passport registered in my new name, however, Ingrid insisted I use my old passport and travel as Joe Jackson. It felt strange to be back in my old 'skin' – not quite as comfortable as I had assumed. Seats had been booked on a British Airways flight from London to JFK for Ingrid and me. The seats were in business class which was only half full. Ingrid had told me that another agent would be accompanying us on the flight. I assumed he, or she, would also be in business class. I tried to get a look at each of the other dozen or so business class passengers to see if any of them looked 'agent material'. But all I could see were 'suits', the perfect business camouflage.

'Base camp' was Ingrid's term for the hotel suite in which we were ensconced. It was an old hotel in New York, just off 42nd Street. It had seen better days judging by the décor in the lobby which had worn carpets and large red drapes that were faded and dusty. The rooms, however, conveyed something of its former splendour. They had large sash windows, almost from floor to ceiling, and a splendid chandelier. The main room had a very large bed, an old-fashioned writing desk, four easy chairs and an oval-shaped coffee table which was stained with the splashes and half circles left by cups of coffee. Two large oak panelled doors led to adjoining rooms. One was for Ingrid's use and the second was home for the agent who had accompanied us on the plane.

Ingrid had arranged for a law firm to write on my behalf to explain that I would be making claim to the Archer estate. In the meantime, she put in place a 'management team' to continue running the company. All contracts remained in place, including payments to those companies suspected of being Mafia fronts. Some business had been lost, but the Mafia was still getting their slice – however, they were obviously nervous about the new arrangement.

"The first nibble!" exclaimed Ingrid, waving a piece of paper excitedly. "Listen to this." She motioned for me to sit down opposite her.

"Darrell Keogh's law firm has written – on behalf of his clients. They want to meet with you to discuss their continued good working partnership with Archers." My heart started racing a little faster.

"So, what happens now," I asked.

"You'll go and meet them, accompanied by Bill here," she nodded in the direction of her agent who seemed suddenly interested in what up until now had been, for him, a rather dull affair. "Bill is one of the best – he also has a law degree as well as being an expert with firearms. He'll provide you with all the support you need. Oh, and just so you know, he'll be wired. It's a bit of a risk – but hey, that's what this business is about." Ingrid gave a smile and Bill added a snorting laugh. He had a lazy eye that was only slightly out of alignment, but it was enough to be disconcerting. It seemed to give him the ability to look almost sideways with his lazy eye and at the same time, focus straight ahead with his other eye. He looked at me and then turned his head ever so slightly as if giving the lazy eye an opportunity to assess me from its unique angle. His face hardened and he slowly squeezed his errant eye in a threatening squint. Quite frankly, Bill scared me.

"Are you sure about that?" I asked, feeling distinctly uncomfortable with the thought of putting my life in Bill's hands.

"Just stay calm and remember, make sure you answer any of their questions briefly and succinctly – just sufficient to be plausible. Oh, and watch out for long silent pauses – it's a classic way of embarrassing someone to fill the void and say something they wish they hadn't."

"Yea," grunted Bill, "keep it brief. Don't say anymore than you have to and refer questions through me. Just remember, I'm your lawyer."

"And don't whatever you do call him Bill. From now on, his name is the name on the card you are holding in your hand," added Ingrid.

I glanced down at the card in my hand, even though I had memorised this over the last two days. "Yes," I said, "it's Steve, Steve Bulley." The trouble was he didn't look to me like a 'Steve', although I could certainly go along with 'Bulley'.

"Shit," said Bill, "if you ever glance at that card again as if you've just seen it for the first time, I swear I'll stuff it down your throat."

"Now Bill," intervened Ingrid in her best soothing voice, "I'm sure Joe will get it right and heed your little warning. You know what they say about rehearsals."

Bill ignored her. "Get it wrong you dickhead and we both could end up dead in the bottom of some slimy landfill." He glared hard at me, making the hairs stand on the back of my neck. I suddenly felt angry. I pushed my whole body towards his, as if squaring up for a fight. "I'm doing this," I blurted, my voice rising as I shook my finger in his face, "because I want to help get these bastards and I don't need any threats from you or anyone else."

The room was silent after my outburst. I looked from one to the other, my face flushed with anger.

"I think we've got a real player," said Bill quietly, his face breaking into a smile.

Ingrid joined in. "That's good – shows commitment. We've been waiting to see if you are really up for this. I think we can count on you."

We met in Darryl Keogh's office. Bill and I were ushered upstairs from the lobby into a small room with a leather inlayed table and matching chairs. The secretary poured us coffee and left us to help ourselves to cream and sugar. Bill spooned in three sugars and whisked vigorously with his spoon. I settled for a half spoonful. I could hear Darryl Keogh laughing and chattering as he walked up the stairs from the lobby. He was accompanied by two other men: one looked just like another lawyer, well dressed in a dark suit, white shirt and red silk tie. The other was older and stouter with close cut and thinning grey hair. It was brushed back and shone with hair cream. He had a camel coat worn like a cape over his shoulders. It flapped open as he climbed the stairs revealing a shiny grey suit and white shirt, open at the neck. He was the quintessential Mafia man. I couldn't help stare at him. I was transfixed by the likeness to the supposed Mafia type that I had created in my mind. It was as if he had stepped off the set of a 1930's gangster movie.

He shrugged his shoulders and his companion caught his expensive camel coat as it slid from his shoulders.

Darryl Keogh nodded in my direction.

"Nice to see you again, Mr. Jackson." He reached out and shook my hand. Bill quickly intervened. He leaned over and shook hands with Darryl Keogh as he introduced himself. "Bulley, Steve Bulley. Mr. Jackson is my client." He slid his card in Darrell Keogh's direction. Keogh picked it up and casually inspected it.

"And these gentlemen are your clients ..." Bill nodded in their direction.

"Very astute," replied Keogh with a smug grin. "I'll speak on their behalf."

"Mutes are they?" said Bill, fixing his eyes on those of Keogh.

The 'Camel Coat' took out a set of nail clippers, sending the nail ends flying in the direction of Bill and me like tiny pieces of shrapnel. A couple of pieces bounced off Bill's lapel and landed on the table. I could feel the tension rising in the room. It was as if the air was becoming electrically charged. Keogh turned in my direction.

"Let me explain why my clients are interested in meeting with you, Mr. Jackson."

"I'd prefer you addressed all your questions to my lawyer," I replied, surprising myself with my confident response. I felt on edge and I could sense my heart beating at an abnormally high rate.

"You mean Mr. Bulley here," replied Keogh as if baiting both me and 'Steve Bulley'.

"Who else?" I replied.

Steve Bulley gave a little cough and smiled at Keogh. "Now that we have established that, perhaps you would care to continue?"

Keogh suddenly looked annoyed. It was as if he sensed he was losing the upper hand in controlling the conversation.

A further volley of nail clippings rained in from across the table. It seemed it was Camel Coat's way of expressing his annoyance. His 'Slick Friend' began drumming on the table with his fingers with barely audible taps.

"My clients," said Keogh, addressing Steve Bulley directly, "are interested in discussing their existing contracts with Archers. They are aware that Mr Jackson is the hot favourite to inherit …"

"He's the only runner," interjected Bulley.

The 'Slick Friend' grunted. "Hope he's quick," he remarked. Camel Coat's face creased into a smile.

"… to inherit Archers," continued Keogh. "My clients want to assure Mr. Jackson of their continuing support for Archers and would be keen to continue the existing business arrangements." I looked over at Steve Bulley as if wanting a word. He ignored me and continued.

"Mr. Jackson is of course here to consider any reasonable business proposals; and I think I can speak for Mr. Jackson in saying we are pleased at your offer of continuing support for Archers …"

"Yes," I interjected, "particularly in regard to business you have put in our direction in the past. I've discussed Archer's performance with my financial advisors and it's clear that our trucking along the east coast is one of the most profitable areas." Steve Bulley gave me a quick glance of disapproval.

"We know the east coast business like no one else Mr. Jackson," said The Slick Friend. His perfectly even white teeth were displayed as his upper lip curled upwards into what might have been a smile. His teeth glistened like porcelain and seemed to fill his mouth like dinner plates. His lip unfurled and the dinner plates disappeared into his black cavernous mouth. "You can count on us to keep business moving your way. We have our fee structure of course, but I think you will find that we can't be beat."

It was the Camel Coat's turn to raise a lip in a semblance of a smile.

Darrell Keogh was fidgeting with his pen, screwing and unscrewing the top and finally tapping it several times on the table. Everyone turned in his direction. He looked nervous; I sensed this conversation wasn't to his liking.

He leaned in towards his clients and whispered. "Gentlemen," he said, turning his back to Bulley and me, "I think we need to pause here and have a discussion." I could hear his whispers quite clearly, despite his attempts to lower his voice.

"Hell no," said Camel Coat, in full voice, looking directly at me. "I like these guys. We're hear to do business and I like what I'm hearing."

"But …," protested Keogh. Camel Coat lifted his hand, silencing Keogh in mid-sentence.

The Slick Friend took over from Camel Coat.

"We want things to work out for both of us. You get something, we get something." He gestured with his hands as he spoke. There was something a bit threatening in his manner. There was a smirk and a definite emphasis on the 'we' as he pointed to himself and his partner.

"We can guarantee contracts. In return, we need guarantees that you'll only work through us … and we want ten percent of the contract value." He paused, sipped from his cup of black coffee and then held it deftly. "Oh, and we want our payment up front," he added.

Bulley feigned exasperation, emitting a pronounced sigh, shaking his head as he did so.

"Gentlemen, I can't recommend these terms to my clients, they're simply not acceptable," Bulley announced. I nodded in agreement. Camel Coat fidgeted momentarily in his seat before slapping his hand hard on the table.

"Not acceptable … not acceptable … what the fuck's not acceptable?" His voice rose to a crescendo.

Keogh interjected quickly.

"What my clients would like to know is what terms do you propose?"

"Well," said Bulley, "there are two issues to be resolved. Firstly, does Archers wish to continue doing business with your clients – how do we know that you can continue to deliver the contracts?" He paused as if waiting for a reaction from Camel Coat or his Slick Friend. Neither of them rose to the bait, although they looked anxious to do so. It appeared to me that they wouldn't need too much more goading before they would be brandishing weapons in our faces.

"And the second?" asked Keogh, looking distinctly uncomfortable at the agitated state of his clients.

"And secondly," replied Bulley, "are your terms acceptable to my client?"

Camel Coat looked ready to blow a fuse. His face turned red and ugly. He motioned as if about to get up from his seat, but his Slick Friend placed an arm out as if encouraging him to remain calm. It was the Slick Friend who now spoke:

"Let me deal with your first question, Mr. Bulley. There is nobody else who can deliver what we can. We have very loyal clients who look to us to ensure that all their freight needs are handled by Archers. They trust us."

"Why won't they come direct to Archers, why do they want to deal through you?" asked Bulley, pushing the issue further.

"We support them, make sure they understand where they can get a good deal," replied the Slick Friend. Camel Coat chuckled into his cupped hands.

"I don't want Archers to be involved in anything illegal," I added.

Darryl Keogh almost leapt out of his chair. "Illegal …ILLEGAL … who mentioned anything about being illegal? Certainly not my clients. They are simply offering excellent business terms which they can provide because of their extensive network of connections and loyalties, loyalties that they have built up over the years. You would do well to remember that Mr. Jackson. You would do well to remember the value of loyalty. My clients have helped Archers obtain massive contracts up and down the east coast. They are simply offering to maintain that very successful relationship. If you don't regard that as deserving your loyalty, I don't know what does."

Bully intervened. "Ok … we're not here to sling any accusations. What my client wants is proof you can deliver. This is a new team at Archers and my client and his team need convincing that working with you is going to be profitable."

Keogh glanced nervously at his two clients. He wasn't sure if they would go berserk or jump in with some crazy scheme. It was their unpredictability that he feared most.

The pause that followed was dense with silence. Keogh became increasingly uncomfortable. He could feel his heart banging against his sternum. His chest felt tight and his throat felt dry and constricted. His two clients simply stared across the table at me and Bulley.

Eventually The Slick Friend spoke.

"I think we can help you there. There are a few new transport outfits operating in the area – they moved in to fill the void as Archers lost its way a little. We can get you some of that business back. We know that a few of the suppliers are unhappy with the reliability of these new guys. Take that new outfit that's started moving steel from Phili down to Tucson. Nice contract that. But they're a small outfit, breakdowns are a real problem for these guys – no backup. I reckon the steel suppliers would be only too happy to deal with a firm like Archers. A word in the right ear and the contract is yours."

Bully leaned over to me and whispered in my ear. "Just nod, I'm recommending we go for this."

I pushed my chair back from the table and waited until they were all staring intently in my direction. I nodded in Bully's direction. "Sounds good to me," I said.

"Ok," said Bully. "We'll wait for Mr. Keogh to come to us with a contract."

"Good doing business with you guys," said Camel Coat as he grabbed his coat. Keogh exhaled audibly as his two clients made their exit.

"I think that concludes the meeting gentlemen," offered Keogh, somewhat breathlessly. "You'll be hearing from me in due course."

Bulley rose to go and I followed his lead.

Bully turned to Keogh. "You sure you're up to this stuff?" he said with a smirk. We didn't wait. It was obvious Keogh just wanted the office to himself.

We caught a cab back to the hotel. Bill appeared to remain in character throughout the journey. I wasn't sure whether to call him Bill or Steve, so I opted for silence.

Ingrid wanted to know every detail of the meeting, despite having the tape of the meeting which Bill produced from somewhere below his waistband. What the office was like, how they were dressed, where we were seated and the movements and inflections of our two 'clients' as well as the lawyer, Darrell Keogh. She was particularly interested in Keogh. Bill gave her a good sense of Keogh's initial attempts at being officious and in control, followed by his obvious rising level of anxiety as the meeting progressed.

"I think we can get to him," commented Bill. Rather stating the obvious I felt.

"Maybe," responded Ingrid, "but I think he's too scared of his clients to compare any pressure we could bring with a death sentence. Maybe later … he must be regretting ever getting involved in that lot."

"Not for the prestige, anyway," commented Bill, with a smile.

Chapter 16
THE BAIT

The call came out of the blue to one of Ingrid's operatives in Archer's office. Ingrid replayed the taped conversation for the third time. Neither Bill nor I had commented, we simply listened as intently as Irene, cloaking the room in the kind of silence that makes you hold your breath in case you disturb the karma. The caller had requested to speak with the 'Head Guy'. Another of Ingrid's team posing as a PA had instinctively nudged the 'record' button as she switched the caller through.

"You the Chief?"

"How can I help?"

"I'm gonna keep this short - my trucks are gettin' sabotaged, my drivers are shit scared and I don't like it. I think you bastards have something to do with it. I got a letter here – says we aint deliverin' and our contract might not get renewed. I called a guy I know … he says the contract's going to Archers. I want you to back off ya hear…"

"Look, we've not been involved in any intimidation …"

The caller interjected quickly and angrily. "Don't shit me! I know youz are behind this …somebody's goin' to get hurt … and it aint us. We pay our dues, if you get my drift, and the boys we pay aint gonna take this kindly – so watch your backs."

"Are you threatening me?"

"Yeh, and just make sure there's no more accidents – just remember, I'll be speaking to the boys." The click signalled the end of the conversation.

"What do you think?" asked Ingrid, turning to Bill.

"It's obvious," replied Bill. "He's paying protection money to the Mafia hoods we are dealing with and they've now decided that Archers are going to take over his contract. They have him both ways. They'll squeeze more protection money out of him at the same time as they're sabotaging his trucks. I reckon Archers will get a call within a few days confirming they have the contract."

I could see that Ingrid was hatching something in that sharp brain of hers. Her eyes were sparkling like glitter on rouged cheeks. She started stabbing the air with her fingers. She turned to Bill, "see if you can find out who the caller was – or at least, the name of his trucking company."

"Shouldn't be too difficult," replied Bill. "There are only a few serious players left."

Bill didn't have to do too much digging. It was a fairly small outfit operating from Newark, New Jersey. It was owned and run by Tom Konofski, a member of the tight knit Polish community in Newark, New Jersey. He had a number of contracts in the area and his company appeared to have grown quickly in the last five years. He had about twenty rigs operating entirely along the east coast. He also had one big contract trucking steel to Tucson.

"OK Bill, it's time we put things in motion," said Ingrid. "Go and see our trucking friend. I want him to understand the situation. Get him to realise that the Mafia only want one thing – to get him out. Make him know that the Mafia hoods he thinks are protecting him are working for Archers. They'll play with him like a cat playing with a bird. He's got one chance to save his skin … and that's working with us."

Bill nodded in agreement. "What's the bait; what do we use to get him on board?" he asked.

Ingrid looked at him sternly. Her square jaw jutted in his direction.

"His life … isn't that enough?"

"I don't know," replied Bill in a slow drone, "it might not be that easy. He's going to be pretty hard to convince, especially if he thinks he's got their protection."

"Take him some photos of the other killings," replied Ingrid. "Let him get a good look at the most gruesome shots we have – it shouldn't be too difficult, Pruit's skull was smashed like a cardboard box and his brains were dripping down the windscreen.

Oh, and get the media men to knock up a replica of the front page of the *New York Times* with the photo and headline of Pruit's murder, but change it a little – I want the headline to read '*Trucking Boss Killed in Freak Accident*' and I want his name in place of Pruits. Get a lead story written to go with it. I want this character to be staining his underpants."

"Ok," replied Bill, "want me to send it to him in the post?"

"No," replied Ingrid, very emphatically. "He'll probably go to see his minders if you do that. I want you to slap it on the table when you visit him. It'll help our case."

The trucker's office was littered with the detritus of his business. Bill glanced quickly at the piles of papers and several well thumbed telephone directories perched precariously on the corner of a large wooden desk. The rest of the room consisted of a couple of chairs and a battered green filing cabinet standing in the corner of the room. Tom Konofski was stooped over the upper drawer of the filing cabinet, impatiently thumbing through manila files. His squeaky asthmatic voice surprised Bill; it seemed unsuited to the large frame that hulked over the cabinet.

"Take a seat – I'll be right with you," he wheezed, nodding in the direction of the chair furthest away from the desk. He turned back to the cabinet and tugged out a file. His big greasy hands added to the smeared stains on the cover. He slapped it on the desk, slammed in the filing cabinet draw and eased his big frame into an oak office chair. The curved back of the chair extended on either side to form two large arm rests which were scrubbed to the bare wood where arms and elbows had rubbed over the years. The legs of the chair creaked as he leant back to allow his considerable girth to nestle against the desk.

"What can I do for you – got some work for us? You want it delivered, we'll get it there – it's our motto."

Bill shifted in his chair and leaned back to pick up his briefcase.

"Not exactly; I'd like to discuss these with you…" He reached into his case, fingering the envelope containing the pictures he wanted to lay out in front of Konofski.

"Hey … are you some kind of fucking insurance investigator?" Konofski looked suddenly very angry. He slapped his hand down on the desk. "Get the fuck out of here – while you can still walk." There was a base ball bat in the corner of the room and Konofski was nodding in its direction.

Bill gave a half smile. "Nothing like that – it's business – so sit back on your fat ass and listen."

A bead of sweat trickled down Konofski's forehead. He looked nervous. His voice lost some of its edge.

"Ok, I'm listening – but it better be good – I've got friends …"

"Oh, but that's why I'm here," replied Bill, "to talk about your friends." He put extra emphasis on the word 'friends'.

"Those friends of yours are going to get you killed – and I'm here to help."

"Oh yeah," replied an obviously nervous Konofski, "and who the fuck are you, the FBI?"

"Something like that," replied Bill. He moved on quickly. He sensed Konofski was getting nervous and he wanted to press home his advantage.

"Those Mafia minders are using you to get at Archers. Once they've got what they want, you are dead meat … maggot bait. Look at these." Bill shoved the coloured photos of Pruit in front of Konofski. They were as graphic and ugly as it gets. The close up of Pruit's head showed the battered and crushed skull. One eye had been partially dislodged from its socket.

"Jesus ..." breathed Konofski. He stared intently at the photograph. "Poor bastard – who is he? Nothing to do with me."

"Not directly – but he was involved with the same hoods you're with."

Konofski looked startled. His wheezing got louder. He was gripped by a fit of coughing. His chest rattled like the shaking of a dice. Bill pressed on. He produced a copy of the mocked up newspaper with the story of Pruit's death on the front page.

"Hit and run," said Bill. "It's their preferred style. Can always claim it was an accident, if they get caught."

Konofski now had the photograph in one hand and was intently reading the article. His sausage like fingers were holding the paper firmly in place against the desk.

"What do you want anyway?" asked Konofski.

"To save your skin," replied Bill. "You help us get these scum. We want you to help set them up."

"Oh yeah – get me killed you mean." He wheezed loudly and grabbed his inhaler from his top pocket. Bill paused as Konofski sucked on the mouthpiece and squeezed the button. The spray pulsed into Konofski's throat. His watery eyes were less bulging and his wheezing eased.

"It's your choice. Help us and you'll be free of them; most importantly, you'll still be alive. Stay with them and you'll be killed as soon as they've finished with you – just like that poor sod." Bill traced his finger along the photograph in Konofski's trembling hand. Bill produced a hand written card and pressed it against the newspaper, directly in front of the transfixed Konofski. It simply said 'BILL' in capital letters with a phone number underneath.

"You call me on this number by tomorrow at 6:00."

Bill stabbed a finger at the mock up newspaper as he turned to leave. It had the headlines, *'Truck Owner Tom Konofski Killed in Hit and Run.'*

"Read the article – it's not every day you get a chance to read your own obituary." The mock-up article went on to describe a 'witnesses account' of how Konofski had been hit by a first car and then crushed by a following second vehicle that appeared to deliberately run over his head.

He glanced back to see Konofski transfixed by the photographs and the press article. His attention seemed firmly riveted on the mock-up article.

Bill stretched out on the couch, a cold cup of coffee on the table next to the telephone. Irene was unusually fidgety. It was now late afternoon and no call from Konofski.

"Bill, are you sure you got to him? The way you described his reactions I thought he would have seen sense by now."

"Look, Ingrid," replied Bill, "this is a big step for him. He's really under the cosh whichever way he goes. He's scared witless. The biggest danger to him and to us is that he goes running back to the boys from the Mafia. Let's hope he sees sense."

The sudden ringing of the telephone startled Bill. He had drifted off into a light sleep. His body twitched into life as he flung his arm in the direction of the phone, knocking over his half full cup of coffee as he did so.

"Shit," muttered Bill, reaching for the receiver. His eye caught the spilled coffee running off the table onto the carpet. He ignored the sudden urge to clean up the mess and grabbed the phone. He knew who it was. He could hear Konofski's rasping gasps. Bill signalled to Irene to pick up the extension.

"Bill?" squeaked Konofski. "That you?"

"Yea," grunted Bill.

"This line ok?"

"Yea," replied Bill, "it's a secure line. Are you going to work with us?"

There was a sniffle from Konofski followed by a resigned sigh. "What do you want me to do?"

"We'll meet and I'll explain. There's a Ramada Inn off 95 from Philli – it's on Bristol Pike."

"Yea, I know it," replied Konofski. "I used it a couple of times."

"We know, that's why we're using it – avoids suspicion. I booked a room for Wednesday night. Just ask for the key at the desk. Stay in your room – use room service for food. We'll meet in your room - I've got the other room key."

"What time?" asked Konofski.

"I'll decide," replied Bill. "I want to make sure you haven't done anything stupid."

Bill glanced at his watch as he moved along the corridor towards Konofski's room. It was 2:00 am. There were still a few revellers. A trio of what appeared to be salesmen were vacantly propping themselves against the wall as if too drunk to risk moving any further. Bill slid quickly passed, ignoring the half empty bottle of bourbon that was thrust towards him as he did so. There was a half-hearted call for him to join them which trailed off into a slur of obscenity.

"Well fuck you buddy ..."

Fortunately the section of the corridor leading to Konofski's room was deserted. The corridor lights had also been dimmed to prevent light seeping in under the doors. Bill slipped his room key into the lock and eased the door open. The room was lit only by the television screen. The images reflected from the shiny surfaces on the veneered dressing table and on the glass of a half empty bottle of whisky and an ashtray brimming with cigarette stubs. Tom Konofski was sprawled on the bed, snoring loudly. Judging by the way his large frame twitched and shuddered, his wasn't a relaxed sleep. The light from the television splashed onto his face adding different colours and hues with every scene change. It made his face look ghoulish. Cigarette smoke hung in the air. Its acidic tang caught the back of Bill's throat causing him to cough. There were also unpleasant body odours, whiskey breath and the smell of cheap vinyl. Bill flicked on the standard lamp. Tom Konofski immediately snapped into life, sitting bolt upright in a wide eyed stare. He looked relieved to see it was Bill.

"Oh, it's you. What time is it?" He rubbed his eyes vigorously distorting his podgy cheeks.

"Ok", said Bill, ignoring Konofski's question, "let's get down to business. Are you definitely in?"

"Got no choice, have I?" replied Konofski with a shrug of his shoulders.

"Glad you see it that way. Just make sure you keep that thought in that brain of yours – that's if you want to keep those grey cells." Bill motioned to the two chairs in the room.

"Get you pants on. I want you sitting in front of me so I can look into those blood-shot eyes of yours. I want to make sure you are taking in what I'm about to tell you." Konofski rolled off the bed and shoved a leg into his pants. Bill kept his eyes glued on the lumbering frame. "No privacy is there?" said Konofski as he jerked up his pants and pulled his belt.

"That's the least of your worries," replied Bill. He had a 35mm Smith and Weston in a shoulder holster. He loosened his jacket letting Konofski catch sight of the gun. Konofski glanced at the gun and quickly finished cinching his belt. He sat on the upright chair like a school boy waiting to be reprimanded by the teacher.

"That's better," commented Bill. He pulled the other chair round so he could sit facing Konofski. He angled the standard lamp so that it shone mainly on Konofski's face while he remained in the shadow.

"Ok," said Bill, looking intently at Konofski, "here's what you have to do. You have that big shipment to make down to that mining company in Bristol, West Virginia…"

"Yeah," interrupted Konofski, "batteries for mining trucks. Real big suckers – heavy too…" Bill's stare caused Konofski to abruptly halt. Bill continued;

"It's the shipment due out next Wednesday. I don't want you driving; use one of your drivers…"

"Larry's scheduled for that trip," interjected Konofski. "That ok?" He coughed several times, clutching at his throat as his wheezing returned. He instinctively reached for his inhaler and ingested the spray of the atomised analgesic.

"Yeah," replied Bill, as if ignoring Konofski's asthmatic attack. "Just make sure there aren't any last minute changes. I want him to stop at the truck stop off 81, near Staunton, Virginia."

"Doesn't use that one, he uses the one 10 miles further down," added Konofski.

"Not this time he doesn't," said Bill, firmly. "You make sure this is the one he stops at. Tell him to pick up an important package at the counter. That way he won't forget to stop."

Larry Wesser cursed again at having to leave the main highway to find the truck stop. He liked a regular routine and this didn't fit with his normal arrangements. He'd complained as soon as Konofski had told him he'd have to pull over at the Staunton stop. It was much smaller than his usual rest stop. It didn't have much of a turning circle and there weren't any showers. He'd used it a couple of times a few years ago when the regular place was being refurbished. Larry decided he'd make it a quick stop. Grab the all important package, a quick cup of coffee, and get back onto route 81. "Hell, I might even go on and stop at my usual," he thought. It brought a smile to his sullen face.

Larry swung the rig around the bend onto the exit ramp and headed towards Staunton. The sign indicating the truck stop came into view as he rounded the bend. He pulled off onto the small road that led to the café truck park. His rig virtually filled the road. Larry shifted down the gears to slow the rig at the entrance to the truck park. The inertia of the heavy load made turning treacherous.

The truck shuddered violently and its brakes squealed as Larry fought to slow the truck and keep it on the entrance road. He punched at the air brakes bringing the big rig to a stop in the car park. He was a bit further from the café than he would have liked, but he was relieved that the truck had come to a halt. He sat for a moment or so with white knuckled hands refusing to let go of the wheel. The engine droned on as he sat and stared out of the cab window. He caught sight of his wide-eyed reflection in the side window. It gave him quite a shock. "Shit," said Larry, out loud, "let me out of this damn rig."

"Think I need a drink," muttered Larry as he switched off the engine and began climbing down from the cab steps. It was several years since Larry had touched alcohol. He'd had a long and hideous relationship with the bottle in what now seemed another life. At certain times the pull of booze returned, but he'd managed to resist the temptation for a long time. Sometimes, when he was alone at a motel, he'd chain smoke half the night and swig at cans of coke to fight of the overwhelming urge to sink into the haze of a drink. The thought of a drink could make his hands damp and his forehead glisten with tiny beads of sweat. He'd try to think of something else, watch a football game or a movie; anything to distract his mind from the illicit substance, this toxin that prostituted itself in such tempting displays.

There were no lights in the truck park, unlike the well-lit facility he usually used. He stumbled in the darkness and moved cautiously towards the pools of light spilling onto the tarmac from the bright neon tubes inside the truck stop. Larry eased himself onto one of the bar stools at the counter. The waitress slid the menu down the countertop.

"Here's what's on offer." She motioned to the kitchen over her shoulder, "Al does a great ham and eggs – not great on steaks though."

"That'll do, ham and eggs," replied Larry, grateful for the chirpy voice.

"Say, you look bushed. Get you some coffee or something?"

Larry was staring at the bottles of Jack Daniels sitting on a glass shelf behind the waitress. He felt his pulse quicken with excitement at the prospect. Seeing his focus on the whiskey bottle, the waitress moved to lift a shot glass. Larry put up his hand, "No, not for me. Make it a black coffee." His hands were shaking as he lifted the cup of hot coffee she had poured. He held it with both hands, sniffed hard at the burnt aroma and sipped on the scolding brew.

The waitress came over, set out a place mat in front of Larry and pulled a knife and fork from her top pocket. A few minutes later she slid a shot of Jack Daniels in front of him.

"What's this," demanded Larry, pushing himself away from the bar.

"Hey, don't shout at me, it's from that guy at the end – thought you could do with a drink." Larry looked along the bar counter. A large man with his backside spread all over the stool raised his glass to Larry as he looked down the counter. Looked like a regular trucker, thought Larry.

"It's on me, just goin' and I seen you there looking beat. Didn't need another anyway. Thought you could use it." He hoisted his frame of the stool and headed for the door.

"Thanks," stammered Larry, staring at the shimmering amber fluid in the thick glass. He slid his finger slowly along the counter top and touched the glass. He flinched as if encountering something slightly alarming and almost repulsive. This was the point, he knew, of no return. Another push, another prod of the glass and his reasoning would be increasingly biased in favour of consumption and his right to have a drink. Recriminations and guilt would be dealt with on another day. He pushed again at the glass and smiled to himself at the prospect.

Larry was very drunk by the time he emerged from the truck stop diner. He'd forgotten to ask about the package he was supposed to collect. The light from the diner contrasted starkly with the pitch black darkness of the parking lot. He staggered forward, his arm outstretched reaching into the blackness. He sweated profusely, despite the coolness of the evening. He felt sick. He leant on the side of the nearest rig and vomited heavily. Larry stood with his feet straddling the murky pool, his head bent forward and his hand gripping one of the chrome bars on the truck's radiator. After gently swaying in this position for several minutes, he set off in the darkness wandering among the rigs until he spotted the familiar colours of his own truck. Larry let out a little chuckle; he looked forward to his comfortable cab and the cot bed behind the front seats. He managed to get his foot up on the front step and lunged forward to grab the door handle.

The explosion shook the truck park and shattered the rear windows of the diner sending a shower of razor sharp shards of glass towards the truckers and waitresses in the diner. Barely before they had time to scream, a second explosion ripped through the air as the adjacent rig caught fire.

"You bastard," screamed Konofski down the phone, his voice shaking with a rage that transcended any sense of fear and subdued his normally asthmatic wheeze. "You fucking bastards … you fucking, fucking bastards…"

Tom Konofski was breathing very heavily, trying to compose himself. Bill could almost feel Konofski's shuddering sobs. "Larry – he was no angel, but you bastards had no right …"

Bill interjected, "Pull yourself together. Larry was a drunk – he beat his wife on a regular basis, pissed away their home and whatever money they had."

"He didn't deserve this," hissed Konofski.

"It's his life for yours, just remember that," said Bill, calmly. He replaced the receiver, ending the call.

Chapter 17
The Plan

Ingrid gave me one of her uncompromising stares. "Look Joe, this is not a game. You think we can just ask them to be nice boys and cooperate? Not a chance. We've got to do some nasty things to get their attention – make them worried – that's how it works – and just remember that if we don't make this work your life will be in constant danger. You'll never know when or how – it'll be a miserable existence."

"And that means murder? You are no different from them. You want to get them no matter what the cost. I can't believe I'm mixed up in this shit."

"And that's the point, you're in it up to your elbows – but there is a way out – if you keep your nerve." Ingrid maintained her steely stare, fixing mine with a seemingly hypnotic intensity.

"What, more murder, more mayhem?" My voice quivered part in rage and part in fear.

"I hope not," replied Ingrid, tersely. "For what it's worth, I wasn't comfortable with the plan to blow up the truck driver. I got overruled from above – probably with a bit of encouragement from Bill," she added, ruefully. "He can be extremely ruthless – a real mean streak."

"So I've noticed," I replied. There was a hint of acknowledgement from Ingrid; however, it was clear that she was keen I understood the situation.

"Despite any reservations you may have on the methods employed, we now have Konofski where we want him."

"On our side?" I asked.

"Not exactly," replied Ingrid, "let's just say he's no longer convinced his Mafia friends are acting in his best interests."

"Oh, and we are?" Ingrid ignored my remark, perhaps because Bill had slipped into the room. She spun on her heels and glowered at Bill. "Bill, where've you been? This is not the time to be going AWOL – and I don't like you going behind my back. In future, you discuss things with me – I'll decide if anything needs to be referred."

"Oh, you mean the truck ...?" replied Bill, obviously not enjoying this dressing down from Ingrid. Far from relishing their spat, it made me nervous. I dreaded the thought of Bill taking over the operation.

"Exactly," replied Ingrid. "I'll say no more on this Bill; we've other matters to attend to."

Bill grunted in acknowledgement. As Ingrid turned away and moved sharply across the room to the desk, Bill's lazy eye wandered in my direction and for a moment there was a hint of a smirk on his hard-edged features.

Ingrid poured coffee and beckoned us to join her at the small oval table by the window. Bill suddenly regained his enthusiasm as if he'd been waiting for this stage to commence. He thrust himself into one of the chairs, his lazy eye dancing erratically and flashing like a pinball machine racking up the points. I somehow found myself seated opposite Bill and Ingrid as if I was being interviewed. It was as if they were testing my resolve at every critical stage and this, quite clearly, was to be an explanation of my role in the next crucial part of their plan. Whatever animosity there was between them had gone as quickly as it had surfaced. Despite, or perhaps because of, their obvious differences in personality and style, they were an effective pairing. Ingrid was elegant, attractive, polished and as smooth as silk, but with a determined steely edge. Bill seemed to delight in making me, and probably all he encountered, uncomfortable. I never felt quite comfortable with either Ingrid or Bill; however, Ingrid had a softer touch which she used to great effect. Bill, on the other hand, was ugly and unpredictable. He could switch instantly from being a suave lawyer to that of a tough and dirty street fighter. He had developed carefully crafted mood swings which he used to intimidate, even threaten. He also used his ugly looks and lazy eye for added effect. I always felt a sigh of relief when Bill left the room and an anxious foreboding whenever he entered.

Neither of them spoke for what seemed a considerable time. I shifted in my chair under Ingrid's steady penetrating stare, made barely less threatening by the hint of a smile and the sparkle in her eyes. Bill allowed his lazy eye to wander as if trying to fix on some object that was flitting about behind me while his 'good' eye fixed on a spot between my eyes.

Ingrid spoke, her clear voice shattering the silence with shards of penetrating sound.

"You'll be involved in the next part of the operation." She paused and let the silence reclaim its previous territory. Bill continued to let his lazy eye rove over the top of my head. I had to consciously resist the urge to turn my head and follow its erratic gaze. He leaned forward, his good eye staring directly into mine, his lazy eye dancing ever more erratically, sweeping across my face. "No fuck ups – it's not just your life; it'll be mine as well." He pushed his big face further towards mine. He was only inches away. "Get this wrong and we're all screwed." I could feel the heat of his breath and the unpleasant flicks of his spittle hitting my face.

It was Ingrid who intervened. "What Bill is saying is that we're counting on you – relying on you - to enact our instructions to the letter." She smiled and added, "no matter how uncomfortable you may feel."

"That was my point exactly," added Bill, leaning back on his chair and sneering in my direction. "My point exactly."

I phoned Konofski the following morning at 6:00am. My hand was trembling as I dialled and my heart was racing. I wasn't sure I could pull this off. After several rings, a bleary voice answered.

"Konofski?" I asked.

"Yea, who's this?" I could here him stifle a yawn.

"This is Joe Jackson from Archer Transport." I tried to sound confident and in control. I feared the pounding in my chest would be heard down the phone. Konofski's early morning brain was now quickly slipping into gear. There was a clunk as if the receiver had slipped or a chair been knocked over.

"Archer, Archer Transport?"

"Yes," I replied.

"Are you the new er …?"

"That's right," I replied, feigning a sigh. "I'm the one who inherited Archers."

Konofski had now shed his early morning blurriness. "What the hell do you want? I've no dealings with you and don't want any."

"You're operating in my territory, stealing my contracts." I was beginning to get more comfortable with my role.

"Your territory!" replied Konofski, his voice rising to a barely audible squeak. "Just because you're the big boy on the block don't give you the right to accuse me of muscling in. And talking of muscle, I've got plenty. One word from me and …" I jumped in before he could finish his threat. "That's not what I hear. The word is that your so called protection is worthless. That was your rig that got blown up, wasn't it? I'd say the Mafia boys have another client who wants you out." There was no reply; the only sound I heard was that of short heavy breaths. I visualised Konofski clutching the phone in a state of near panic. I continued; "I also hear that the FBI are on your case. Bet that would please your Mafia friends if they heard?"

Konofski coughed and spluttered, struggling to speak. "Where did you hear that shit," exclaimed Konofski.

"It's surprising what you hear in our business. We're a small tight-knit family, us truckers. No secrets."

There was another long pause as Konofski wrestled with what I was saying. I heard the whish from his inhaler.

"What the hell do you want?" asked Konofski. "You want me to quit so you can take over. You're scum, you Archers. Always were, always will be."

Konofski's remark jarred a nerve. It was as if Konofski had delivered a low blow. It was my turn to pause.

"You there?" Konofski's voice got me back on track.

"Look Konofski, I want your company to join the Archer family of truckers. Simple as that. It's a friendly gesture. I hate to see a fellow trucker in so much…er…trouble."

"FRIENDLY GESTURE," screamed Konofski. "You want me to join you and you call that a FRIENDLY GESTURE? Who the fuck do you think you are?"

"A business man Mr. Konofski. Simply a business man. I'll get right to it; Archers are willing to make you a serious offer – a substantial offer for your business. It'll be enough for you to get out of the business and go where ever you please. You'll have no money problems, no more deals with the Mafia and no more involvement with the FBI."

There was another long pause as Konofski pondered on what he was hearing.

"Look Mr. Jackson, this is a lot to take in. I need time to think this over. Just how much are you talking about?"

"Quarter of a million dollars," I replied, following the script.

"That's serious money," replied Konofski.

"When it comes to business dealing, I'm a serious man. You've got five days to think about it. I'll call you – and I'll need an answer, just yes or no, got that?"

"Er, yes, thanks. And I'm sorry for getting mad."

I ignored his change of tone.

"I'll call on Friday." With that I replaced the receiver.

"Excellent," said Ingrid, who'd been standing in the room with Bill, listening on a phone extension.

"Couldn't have done it any better," added Bill. His face distorted into what I took for a smile.

Bill got the call he was expecting. It was Konofski.

"Don't know what's going on, but I got a call from Archers."

"Oh yea," said Bill, dryly, "tell me about it."

"This new guy, the new owner, Joe Jackson. He offered me money, big money, to buy me out. He seems to know a lot about what's been going on – he even mentioned the FBI."

"That's a new twist," replied Bill, following the well rehearsed script, "what is he suggesting?"

Konofski replied slowly and deliberately. "He's offering two hundred and fifty thousand dollars." The excitement in his voice suggested he was pleased with the offer.

Bill let out a low whistle, "It's a lot of money; it'd set you up for life, what do you think?"

"I've got to give a decision on Friday; but what about the boys in the Mafia? It scares me to hell to think what they might do once they get to know. I'm paying them a lot to keep me in business. They'd loose that – and then they'd come after me for a slice of whatever I get from Archers. I'd be worse off – they'd come for me, that's for sure." He was beginning to sound less confident about the offer. His wheezing got louder.

"Maybe, but I think the Mafia hoods are going to turn their attention to Archers and Mr. Jackson in particular. After all, he's the one causing the problem."

"What do you reckon I should do?"

"Tell Jackson you want more time – in the meantime, let your Mafia contacts know you've had this offer."

Konofski breathed heavily into the phone. It sounded like a low growl.

Konofski called his 'minder' shortly after the talk with Bill. He'd smoked two cigarettes, lighting his second with the stub of his first. The nicotine hit steadied his fraying nerves but tightened his asthmatic chest like a vice. He felt ambushed from all sides.

"That Tony?" asked a nervous Konofski.

"Yeah, whose this?"

"Konofski, Tom Konofski. Look, I need to talk. Some things have come up."

"Hang on." Konofski could here Tony barking at others to get out. No pleasantries, simply instructions.

"We can talk. What's up?"

Konofski swallowed hard. He was having difficulty in getting words together. Tony began to sound irritated.

"Come on, talk you fat bastard." Konofski pushed a large sweaty hand against his cheek. He wished he hadn't made this call. It was too late now.

"It's the trucking business …"

"Didn't think it was your sister's virginity," came the sarcastic reply. Konofski hunted for his breath and continued.

"I've been approached by the new head guy at Archers – Joe Jackson. Wants to buy me out … he's made an offer." Tony grabbed at the table and pulled his chair upright. This sounded like trouble. "He did what, made you an offer?"

"Yea, that's what I said."

"Don't get smart with me Konofski," replied Tony. "I'll need to talk to the boss. I'll get back to you soon. Meanwhile, don't do anything stupid like taking up Mr. Jackson's offer. Stall him." With that he slammed down the receiver.

"Oh shit," Konofski muttered to himself, burying his head in his hands.

I called Konofski early on Friday, following a briefing meeting with Bill and Irene. They were still trying to predict the next moves with what Irene called 'a reasonable level of certainty'. That very phrase had me worried.

It took several rings before the phone was answered. I almost gave up. A wheezing voice answered. Konofski was breathing hard. "Konofski? It's Joe Jackson from Archers."

"Yea, it's me ... caught me in the men's room."

"Hope I didn't interrupt anything?" I asked. Konofski grunted.

"You know why I'm calling - I want a decision," I said as forcefully as I could. Konofski didn't reply; there was just the sound of his wheezing and a raspy rattle from his throat.

"Look Konofski," I said, after listening like a doctor on the end of a stethoscope, "I'm making an offer, a good offer, to take you over. Take it or leave it. And for what it's worth, I'm sorry about the accident." I immediately regretted departing from the agreed script.

"It was no accident," replied Konofski in a slow and deliberate voice.

"Sounds like I'm buying trouble," I said. "You're in worse shape than I thought."

"I need more time," replied Konofski, "...another week."

I tried to sound reluctant. "I told you I need a decision today. I'll tell you what I'll do, you can have five days, that's next Wednesday. I'll call then."

It was Bill who finally convinced Konofski.

"Remember our little chat at the motel?" Konofski replied quickly. "Yea – so ...?"

"We want you to take the offer from Archers."

Konofski protested. "Why? My Mafia friend wants me to buy more time."

"It's important," emphasised Bill. "I'll be in touch," he added. A personal visit would be needed he'd decided. He didn't want Konofski to buckle completely.

Daryll Keogh called Bill on the line he had been given. It was a separate line, reserved for Bill's role as Steve Bulley, my lawyer.

"That Steve Bulley?" Bill paused long enough to get in character.

"Yeah, whose calling?"

"It's Darryl Keogh. Your Mr Jackson has been doing things my clients are very unhappy about. They want a meeting – urgently."

"Is that so," replied Bill. He was enjoying himself, tugging first at Konofski and now at Keogh.

"Yes, it is so," replied Keogh with more than a hint of exasperation creeping into his voice. "You've met my clients, and you're probably aware of their … er … reputation."

"Nicely put Darryl," replied Bill, in what he felt was a soothing tone, "and of course we'd like to meet them again."

Keogh sounded relieved. "I'm glad you see it like that. Can we fix a date and time?"

"How about next Tuesday at ten in your office," replied Bill. "I'll expect coffee and cookies – I'm assuming it's a sociable meeting."

"My clients have indicated that they will adjust their schedules to suit," replied Keogh, not rising to the bait.

"Then unless I hear differently, we'll be at your office on Tuesday morning around ten."

"Er … at ten," replied Darryl Keogh.

Ingrid was pleased and obviously nervous about the meeting.

"This it," she stressed to Bill and me. "We've got them where we want them. The next part is entirely up to Bill and to you Joe." They were both staring directly at me. "You up for this Joe?" asked Ingrid. I grunted a sort of affirmation which didn't please Bill. He scowled at me and his lazy eye wobbled crazily in its socket.

I expected a roasting and felt myself shrinking into a protective curl. He was surprisingly sympathetic.

"Look Joe, you played a blinder last time, and your work with Konofski was better that we could have hoped." I glanced at Ingrid, but she had chosen to fix her gaze as if expecting to see someone out of the window.

"We need you to get this right one last time. OK?" He looked up at me with his sympathetic good eye. His lazy eye was half closed as if it had been reprimanded and only allowed to peep at the proceedings from under the lid.

"Thanks Bill," I muttered. "I'm sure I'll be fine."

Ingrid smiled benevolently at her two children, as if pleased that they were now getting on so well.

I think I caught Bill's lazy eye wink at Ingrid. She certainly gave a knowing nod to Bill. I felt for a moment as if I were being excluded from the inner sanctum of some secret society. In a way I was.

Bill drove us round to Keogh's office in a large silver Mercedes he had rented. He looked every inch the city lawyer, dressed in a smart grey pinstripe suit and equipped with a battered legal attaché case embossed on the side with the letters 'SB'. Bill had assumed the identity of Steve Bulley over the past three days. Bill became 'Steve Bulley' in the course of all our conversations. It was, insisted Irene, essential we get into character and ensure that using the name Steve Bulley is as natural as possible. I made a couple of slip ups late on the first day. Bill scowled viciously the second time I made a mistake.

"Just think that there is a gun at your head that is fired the instant you get it wrong and that in the instant before you pass out you can see your brains splattered against the wall," he hissed.

"Sorry, Bill."

"STEVE!! You useless bastard."

Bill parked the car on a parking lot across from Keogh's office. He patted his 'wire' one last time to check it wasn't visible. I had a small brief case which contained a note pad and a couple of manila folders. It also had a second 'wire' in case Bill's should fail. Ingrid was leaving nothing to chance.

Keogh greeted us at the door. His secretary had been keeping a look out. She stood hovering in the background, ironing the sides of her blue skirt with her hands.

"Mr. Bulley, Mr. Jackson, you're bang on time. My clients are waiting to see you. Coffee?" We both nodded. His secretary moved quickly to the coffee machine.

"She'll bring them up," said Keogh, as if she was as inanimate as the white china cups stacked adjacent to the coffee machine. He ushered us upstairs to his office. Unsurprisingly, Camel Coat and his Slick Friend were already seated. They offered no formal greeting other than to shift in our direction and grunt in acknowledgement.

"Good morning gentlemen," said Bill in a bright and breezy tone. Keogh took the initiative.

"Welcome Mr Bulley and Mr Jackson. Thank you for agreeing to meet with my clients. Oh, and let me introduce Tony, an associate of my clients." Tony was dark, swarthy, thickset and mean looking. He grunted in our direction, only slightly louder than the muffled acknowledgements we had received from Camel Coat and his Slick Friend.

"I didn't catch your second name?" asked Bill, staring at our new friend.

"Tony, Tony Mascopelli …"

"Tony will do," interjected the Slick Friend, obviously annoyed at Tony's unnecessary additional elaboration.

The rap on the door silenced any further preliminaries. Keogh's secretary entered carrying a silver tray with coffee cups, biscuits, a milk jug and sugar. She placed them next to Keogh, hesitated an instant in case Keogh had any further instructions, and left the room. Keogh handed out the cups and saucers and invited us all to help ourselves to cream and sugar. He then passed round the plate of biscuits. Tony struggled with the wafer thin saucer and matching cup with its delicate handle. For a few moments, everyone's eyes were fixed on Tony watching his thick clumsy fingers engulf the delicate porcelain. His hands circled the cup and his fingers reached around just below the rim as if he was attempting a slow strangulation. Darryl Keogh interrupted the embarrassing performance; "Tony, try a biscuit." Tony's face lit up at the sight of the expensive chocolate covered wafers. He slid a handful onto the palm of his hand and proceeded to devour one, spilling and spitting crumbs over the table.

"Tony, for fuck's sake." The Slick Friend was annoyed at his associate's lack of refinement. "Sorry," mumbled Tony, spitting yet more crumbs in an even wider arc onto the table.

"Enough of this shit," exclaimed Camel Coat, "we've got business to attend to. Mister Keogh (he emphasised 'Mister'); I don't pay you to lay on coffee and biscuits."

"Yes, yes of course," replied Keogh, cautiously. "I'll get straight to the point."

"You do that, Mr. Keogh," replied Camel Coat in an aggressive tone. Darryl Keogh coughed to clear his throat.

"Mr. Jackson …"

"You address all your comments to me," interjected Bill. "I'm Mr. Jackson's representative, in case you've forgotten."

"Yes, I added, "I'd prefer you addressed all your comments through Mr. Bully, my legal representative."

Keogh started again, in a somewhat exasperated tone. "OK … Mr. Bully," he paused as if waiting to see if there were any further comments, "my clients are led to believe that Mr. Jackson is no longer acting in the spirit of our previous arrangement. There was an understanding that my clients would help Archer Transport secure contracts and this they have done in good faith. We believe that Mr Jackson has taken actions that are in direct violation of that understanding."

"Just what are you implying?" asked Bill, nudging things along. Camel Coat had resorted to clipping his nails in a tacit sign of frustration and impending anger. Keogh turned as the clippings flew across the table, looking extremely uncomfortable.

"My clients are of the opinion, an opinion I share I must add, that Mr. Jackson, we presume in his capacity as the new owner of Archers, has been acting to circumvent our agreement."

Camel Coat slammed a fist on the table. "Would you cut the legal bullshit Keogh. Mister Jackson here has made an offer to Tom Konofski. He runs a trucking company that's one of ours …"

The Slick Friend quickly interjected. "One we support and advise."

Camel Coat examined his nails, "yea, support and advise." Tony chuckled.

"Look," said Bill, turning to Keogh, "my client has done nothing more than take actions to support his company and looks forward to continuing to work with your clients."

The Slick Friend leaned forward towards Bill. "That may be your opinion Mr. Bully. But we know differently."

He held his finger out like the barrel of a gun and pointed it directly at me. "You've made an offer to buy out Tom Konofski. He went to Tony here. Tony's one of our field workers. Mr Konofski said you'd made an offer to buy him out – given him a deadline."

"It was a sound business proposition," commented Bill. "After all, we're all working in the best interests of Archers, isn't that so?" Bill looked directly at Keogh who gave a brief nod as if in agreement. It was an involuntary reflex that caught Keogh off guard.

"Look Mister Bully, does your client, Mister Jackson here, know who he's messing with?" asked the Slick Friend. I felt distinctly uncomfortable. Sweat was dripping from my armpits and yet I felt cold and clammy.

"Is that a threat?" asked Bill. I was in no doubt as to the implication in his remark.

"You interpret it how you like, Mr. Bulley," replied the Slick Friend.

"Look, I don't think this is getting us anywhere," I added, bravely. "I want Archers to be successful, and that may or may not involve working with your clients Mr. Keogh." I hoped the quaver in my voice was not as apparent as I thought it was.

Bill intervened. "What Mr. Jackson is making plain is we don't expect you to interfere with Archer's plans for expansion – and this involves them absorbing Konofski's business, if he's willing to sell."

Camel Coat slapped his palm on the table. His face was flushed and angry.

"I can't believe what I'm hearing. You just want us to hand over Konofski's business to you? You must be fucking crazy."

"I didn't know it was your business," replied Bill, calmly.

"What my client means," said Keogh, "is that he has given substantial professional support to Mr. Konofski's business, and this has involved considerable financial outlay."

Bill decided it was time to push things along.

"We are confident that Mr. Konofski will sell his business to Archers. As you know, there has already been a discussion between Mr Jackson and Mr Konokski which is progressing amicably." Bill kept his good eye on Camel Coat and seemed to let his lazy eye flick between Keogh, Tony and the Slick Friend.

"That's not what we hear," replied Camel Coat, "'ain't that right Tony?" Tony duly grunted and nodded in agreement.

Bill introduced his *coup de grace.*

"I have a letter here from Mr Konofski, addressed to Mr. Jackson, accepting the terms offered and agreeing to the sale of his trucking company to Archers." He slid three copies onto the table. No one touched them. No one moved. The silence sucked the oxygen from the room. I felt my neck redden and swell against my collar. Darryl Keogh looked ashen. He hiccupped and emitted a foul smelling draft in my direction. I thought he was going to be sick.

Camel Coat sprang to his feet. He leaned forward and glared at Bill, not quite sure which eye to focus on. "MISTER BULLY that was your client's biggest mistake." He pointed angrily at me. "YOU," he balled, spitting across the table, "are finished." His expensive coat slipped off one shoulder. His Slick Friend made a vain attempt to rescue the garment. It would have been rather comical had the air not been so charged with aggression.

Bill remained calm. He half turned away from Camel Coat and appeared to address Darryl Keogh. "Of course, Konofski finally wanted out because of what happened to his rig and his driver. He thinks you boys were responsible." The three hoods looked at one another in genuine surprise.

"We had nothing to do with that," hissed Camel Coat. "If I knew who was responsible, I'd cut off his balls."

Tony felt emboldened. "Yeah, and maybe a serious accident …"

"Shut the fuck up, Tony," said The Slick Friend halting the hood from any further remarks.

"For once," remarked Bill, turning to Camel Coat, "I believe you."

"And you know who …" Camel Coat stopped in mid sentence. He shot to his feet, his expensive coat slipping from his shoulders. He pointed directly at me. "Mister Jackson," he hissed. "You are finished, dead meat …"

The Slick Friend grabbed his arm. Camel Coat jerked his arm away as if resenting being touched. The Slick Friend glanced at Keogh and flashed his teeth in a menacing grimace. Keogh got the signal.

His voice crackled as if absorbing all the static in the room.

"What my client is implying is that he wishes to terminate his arrangement with you Mr. Jackson, forthwith, and with Archer Enterprises."

Camel Coat couldn't resist. "What I mean Mister Jackson, is that you are dead, kaput!"

Chapter 18
Arrests

The Police report from the Trentham homicide squad was stark and factual. It simply reported that a badly decomposed body of a caucasian male, between thirty and forty years old, had been found in a skip in an alley at the rear of Ming's Chinese Restaurant off Brunswick Avenue. The deceased's hands had been cut off and had not been recovered. The pathology report established that the individual had suffered a severely fractured skull from a metal bar also found in the skip. The report concluded that the badly decomposed state of the body meant that identification would be difficult. There were no finger prints. A report provided to the press contained similar information. It also stated that the police were following up a significant lead and that they were cooperating on the investigation with the FBI. The press immediately suspected that there was a Mafia connection. The discovery of a body on the streets of Trentham was not an unusual event. What was unusual was for the FBI to have such a significant involvement. The clothes on the body were of good quality. There was a Weiss watch and a monogrammed shirt with the initials JJ. More important were the documents in the inner pockets of the suit jacket. There were memos on good quality paper headed with the address of Archer Enterprises. Others were letters addressed to Joseph Jackson, or marked for his attention.

The FBI provided copies of the recordings of the meeting at Keogh's office to the State of New Jersey Attorney General's Office. The Special Investigations Division of the New Jersey Police Force had been thwarted in their attempts to indict local Mafia chiefs and this was a major breakthrough. Camel Coat, Slick Friend and Tony Mascopelli were each arrested in dawn raids. *The New York Post* had been tipped off. Splashed on the front page of the late morning edition was the headline, *Mafia Arrests in Dawn Raids*. The accompanying photograph showed three men, one wearing an expensive looking camel coat, being led handcuffed into a side entrance of the New Jersey Police Headquarters. Their attorney was feigning surprise at their arrests and protesting innocence in regard to the charges against them. Almost in rebuttal, the Chief Prosecutor read out the charges to the gathered press in a hail of flashing cameras and a squall of microphones grasping at the sound bites in a feeding frenzy. He read from a prepared statement.

"The arrests have been made in connection with the recently discovered body of a person we believe was the new owner of Archer Enterprises."

"Is this a murder charge?" screamed a female reporter, thrusting her microphone at the Prosecutor.

The Prosecutor nodded. "They have been indicted on charges of murder. I will also add that we expect to be making further arrests."

"Does this have any connection with the other Archer murders?" asked a reporter from the pack, shouting to be heard.

"No comment," was the stoical reply.

Darryl Keogh answered the call on his office phone. He'd just got into work and was waiting expectantly for his secretary to bring him a cup of black coffee and a bagel with cream cheese. It was a ritual that he savoured and looked forward to. It briefly annoyed him that he'd have to take a business call before he'd enjoyed his morning treat. He took his gold ball point pen from the inner pocket of his jacket, slid a yellow legal pad onto the blotting pad and instinctively clicked open his pen. He lifted the receiver.

"Darryl Keogh …"

"Darryl, this is Jim." Jim Stanton was one of the junior partners in the firm.

"Yes Jim," replied Keogh, abruptly.

"Have you seen the *Post*?" Stanton had an urgent note in his voice.

"Why, what's up?" asked Keogh, cautiously. He had the feeling this was news he wouldn't particularly enjoy.

"Looks like a couple of your clients have been arrested on a murder charge, something to do with Archers I think. I'll leave this copy in the front office."

"Er … thanks, thanks Jim," stumbled Keogh in reply. He replaced the receiver slowly and carefully, as if handling the most delicate of crystal. He sat staring at the receiver. His body sagged and he slumped forward leaning on his elbows. Those meetings with Joe Jackson and Steve

Bully hadn't gone well. His Mafia clients had handled themselves badly; they simply weren't used to being on the back foot, and he'd been powerless to get a control of the agenda. What was he involved in? He needed to get a copy of the paper. He lurched towards the door and rushed down the corridor. The paper was lying neatly on a tray next to his cup of coffee and plate with a bagel and cream cheese. His secretary looked up.

"Oh, I was just going to bring this in, Mr Keogh. Mr Stanton dropped off …" Before she could go any further, Keogh grabbed the paper and rushed back to his office. He spread the broadsheet on his desk:

'Mafia Arrests in Dawn Raids.'

He stared at the photographs, there was no mistaking his two clients and the henchman that had accompanied them on the recent meeting.

He flicked on the TV set in the corner of his office. The NBC news was in full swing –

"… and this just in from New Jersey," read the anchorman in smooth dulcet tones, "three men, allegedly members of the Mafia, have been arrested in connection with the possible murder of a businessman. We can take you now to outside New Jersey State Police Headquarters where a statement is being read by the Attorney General's Office."

The building so familiar to Keogh flashed onto the screen. The press were in a melee in front of the spokesman from the Attorney General's Office; baying for information, manoeuvering for position, shouting questions, heaving heavy cameras dangerously aloft, and jostling unapologetically with fellow journalists.

There were the dangerously familiar still pictures of his clients, of course. However, the words that lodged in Darrel Keogh's brain were 'indicted on murder charges' and 'we expect to make further arrests.' He flicked off the television and turned to read the lead article, looking for information about the further arrests that were impending. He felt vulnerable and exposed. He started to contemplate the likely scenario; he was sure to be to be under suspicion, but why hadn't he been arrested? He tried to make a list of his options but he felt exhausted. Things jumped around in his head; meetings with Mafia bosses – what a greedy idiot he had been. Murders – Tracy Archer, Dick Pruit, Joe Jackson, the truck driver; why the hell had he got involved? Money of course; and then there was no way out. Once you were in the Mafia circle, you couldn't simply decide they were no longer suitable clients. There were the implied threats to his business, his family and most importantly, to himself. They could be as smooth and polished as any Wall Street banker and at first he had been encouraged by their professional approach. He'd enjoyed showing off; pleased at their obvious appreciation at his clever skills. But they could be rough, coarse and vulgar when it suited. The smooth operators would always be led by the dirty mob; ones who didn't mind having blood on their hands. He shuddered at the thought of what they could do.

He could run. Grab a bag, money, some clothes, passport and fly – somewhere – Mexico? He dismissed the idea almost immediately. It would be almost an admission of guilt; besides, he hadn't any money in other banks, he didn't speak Spanish, he'd stick out like a sore thumb. He scribbled angrily on the blank legal pad as if scratching out this option. He could give himself up? He could … go to prison? The thought repulsed him. He was smart, slim, urbane and good looking. He dreaded the thought of how he might be treated – but think about it he did. What about the ultimate – suicide? He knew of a lawyer who'd committed the unthinkable act when he lost everything in some land investments. He reasoned he was too rational to contemplate suicide. Besides, he was too frightened by the thought of death. Maybe he'd get off – a plea bargain? He was one of the best lawyers in town, he had friends who – who – would probably desert him. They wouldn't want to be mixed up in this.

The arrest came at about 4:30 in the afternoon, just as he was preparing to leave. Not that he'd accomplished much during the day but it had at least provided a distraction of sorts to the gloom that had dogged him most of the morning. As they day wore on he'd even convinced himself that he wouldn't be implicated. He didn't even suspect anything when the two well dressed men were ushered into his office on the pretext of seeking legal advice on business taxes – a speciality of his. It was only when they refused the invitation to sit down and then produced identification cards that he realised he was being arrested, albeit in a very discrete manner. He was at least grateful for that.

"On what charge?" he vainly asked.

The reply of 'accessory to murder' was not what he'd expected. At worst, Keogh had thought he'd be charged with illegal practices, assisting in tax evasion, setting up bogus companies, money laundering; but this, accessory to murder …his knees buckled and he had to be supported by the two detectives as he was read his rights. They manoeuvred a stunned and silent Keogh past his loyal secretary and into the back seat of a car waiting right outside the office. One of the officers slipped into the seat next to him. "I need you to put these on Mr. Keogh." He clipped the steel handcuffs firmly around Keogh's wrists.

Darryl Keogh spent the night in the jail at Police Headquarters. He'd been allowed to make three phone calls to get legal representation. His first two choices, people he counted as 'friends', were not available. In each case it was their wives who answered the 'phone and both gave similar orchestrated replies. His 'friends' didn't want to be involved. His third choice was a young lawyer, Don Pohl, who'd done an internship at Keogh's office about five years previously. Don Pohl was somewhat hesitant, but after Darryl Keogh had reminded him of the help he had provided to get Don started as a lawyer, Don reluctantly agreed. He would make an application for bail first thing in the morning and meet with him later in the day.

The cell door was closed by a large unsmiling police officer with a truncheon dangling from his hip. He looked as though he would enjoy using it at the slightest provocation. He kept toying with the polished handle as if longing for the chance to demonstrate his skills with his head cracking weapon. Fear of what was to come and, in particular, fear of an impending prison sentence, left Keogh feeling vulnerable and impotent. For the first time in his adult life his future was in the hands of others. He shivered as cold seemed to penetrate his body. His skin felt unusually tingly and sensitive as if his nerves were bare, raw and exposed. He wrapped himself in the blanket and tried to sleep on the hard cot bed. He eventually managed a fitful sleep despite the constant glare of the single bulb in the ceiling and being periodically woken by a metallic screech as the duty officer slid open the small observation window in the door of the cell.

The morning light coming through the small cell window caused him to stir. His intermittent sleep had induced a sort of mild narcosis and for a moment or two he didn't realise where he was. The amplified sound of a key being inserted into the door brought him quickly back to reality. He was relieved to see it was a different police officer from the one whose sullen look and aggressive posturing had scared him the previous night. This one was all smiles.

"Coffee Mr. Keogh? I'll get you some breakfast. Ham and eggs ok?"

Darryl was so taken aback by the polite and softly spoken officer that he could only nod. The coffee tasted awful. It smelled faintly of urine. The ham was smothered in salt and the eggs were greasy and rubbery. His stomach heaved at the smell so much so that he banged on the door wanting the breakfast tray removed. The officer returned, but his demeanour was different. He spoke slowly and menacingly. "I'm having MY breakfast – don't interfere again, otherwise I'll find it necessary to conduct an intimate strip search. Just in case you have any concealed weapons, or drugs." He slammed the cell door leaving Darryl Keogh numb with fear. He curled up in a foetal position on his cot bed and pulled the blanket over his head.

At 10:30 he was taken to a small interview room and greeted rather coolly by Don Pohl. They were both given a mug of coffee – it tasted distinctly better than the coffee in the cell.

"It's not good," started Don, hesitating as he saw the look of utter dismay on Darrell Keogh's face. "Bail wasn't allowed. The basis of the District Attorney's argument was that as a major suspect there is a risk of you fleeing and, because of the involvement of the Mafia, a potential risk to your well being."

"Nice of them to show such concern," commented Keogh. Don gave a half smile and continued. "I'm afraid it's very serious. The DA's office is going for accessory to murder and will ask for five to ten."

"Five to ten years, inside! I'll be either dead or wish I was within six months." He chocked back the tears. "I'm sorry, this …"

"I fully understand," replied Pohl, "you're in one hell of a predicament. There is one option, and I think it's the only chance you've got to avoid a jail sentence."

"What's that?" asked Keogh, regaining a degree of composure.

"A plea bargain – in return for evidence against your Mafia clients."

"They'd kill me," replied Keogh.

"Not if they're inside."

"But they have contacts, they'd put out a contract, I know they would."

"That's a risk you'd have to take. Testify against them, leave New Jersey, get out of the country. It's either that or face a living hell in prison."

"I'd rather die than go to prison," came the terse reply.

Don Pohl looked squarely at Keogh. "Your only option is to agree to testify in return for a reduced charge."

"What's the best you can get," asked Keogh.

"Well," replied Pohl, "I had breakfast with the Assistant DA this morning …" "Hmmph," interrupted Keogh, "I'll bet it was better than the slop I got."

Pohl smiled. "… he says that if you give a deposition and answer their questions in full, and if you go on the stand, they are willing to push for a charge of malpractice. If they can swing that, it'll mean a suspended sentence."

"Hell," replied Keogh, sounding a bit more optimistic, "that's a long way from doing five years in the State Pen."

"That's the bait they're willing to dangle to get these guys," replied Pohl. "There is one other factor," he continued, "you'll be barred from practising in the United States. But if you'll take my advice, you should get out of the country. Try South America, or even Australia. What you need is a new start …"

"… a new identity," added Keogh. "What about bail? I couldn't spend another night in this place."

"You could," replied Pohl. "But I reckon you won't. I'm pretty sure I can get you out on bail if I can tell them you'll agree to a plea bargain."

"Thank God!" replied Keogh with a huge sigh. "It's been a fucking nightmare."

"So, I take it you want to give evidence and go for a plea bargain?" asked Pohl.

"I don't want to," replied Keogh. "I have no choice."

Darryl Keogh was the prosecution's star witness. He stooped uncharacteristically, as he walked into the witness box. He kept his eyes fixed on his hands, which trembled ever so slightly as they rested on the polished front edge of the box. The only times he deviated from this position was to answer questions put to him by the prosecuting attorney and the lawyers for the defence. He then turned directly to the jury, avoiding any chance of eye contact with his former clients. It gave him credibility with the members of the jury. Not only did they have sympathy with anyone who dared to testify against the Mafia, but his answers came across as genuine. Every member of the jury was convinced of the veracity of Keogh's testimony. He was able to corroborate the tape recordings as being an accurate record of their meeting. But he added much more. He testified about the bogus businesses he had established on their behalf which were used to launder money from drugs and prostitution. He gave evidence about the large sums of money that resulted from coercion and protection. In particular, he testified about his knowledge of skimming funds from large organisations, including Archer Enterprises, and the link between Dick Pruit and the Mafia. He was able to produce records of many of the business dealings he referred to, including payments to Pruit, and large 'contracts' between Archer Enterprises and one of the bogus companies he had set up on their behalf. He also informed the jury that his Mafia clients spoke cockily about having taken care of Tracy Archer and Dick Pruit. Most damning of all, he confirmed that he was sure the threat to kill Joe Jackson heard on the tape was meant and that after the meeting they had told him Jackson would be a dead man by the end of the week. His overriding fear about the possibility of ending up in prison had given him the necessary confidence to speak out to protect his own skin. He was smart enough to realise that the stronger the evidence against his former clients, the greater the likelihood of their being imprisoned for a substantial period of time.

Konofski was a different witness altogether. It was as if he had lost all fear of what the Mafia might do to him or his business. His bravado was evident from the minute he was called to testify. He gripped the edge of the witness box with both hands, kneading the rim as if attempting to tear off the mottled plank on which so many previous witnesses had raised their right hand, placed their left on the bible and sworn as to the truth of the evidence they would give. He answered the questions put to him in a loud voice – almost shouting – and he glared at the defendants, as if daring them to react. Over the days preceding the trial, Konofski had become more and more angered by what had happened to him, his business and to his driver. His anger became focussed on only one thing; to get back at the Mafia, no matter what the consequences.

He was a difficult witness. His answers were often based on emotion fuelled by his anger rather than fact. The prosecuting attorney had a difficult time in keeping Konofski on track. Konofski didn't care. He was more concerned with telling the assembled press about what had happened and what he thought of the Mafia than in assisting the District Attorney to get factual evidence to support the case against the defendants. The lawyers for the defence were on their feet, objecting to Konofski's evidence at every opportunity, so much so that the judge displayed his anger and exasperation by summoning both lead lawyers to his bench.

He leaned forward and hissed sternly in a low gravelly voice.

"I'm warning both of you – this is MY courtroom – I will not tolerate this behaviour. The prosecution will ensure that questions to this witness are phrased in such a way to encourage factual answers – and the lawyers for the defence will attempt to get their bums reacquainted with their seats. Do I make myself clear?" There were mumbled apologies as they both returned to their tables and conferred briefly with their teams.

The jury seemed to warm to Konofski. They appeared to be more interested in his angry outbursts than his nuggets of factual evidence. It was obvious from the body language of a number of the members of the jury that they began to resent the interruptions by the defence team. They simply couldn't get enough of Konofski's remarks. As a result, he added effectively to the prosecution's case. He explained how he had paid protection money to the Mafia to keep his trucking contracts and that he was sure the Mafia were behind the blowing up of his truck and the killing of his driver – "Who else?" he said, appealing to the Jury, who all nodded, sagely.

The defence was slick and polished. They produced several witnesses, most of them public officials, who testified, nervously, that the defendants were reputable and honourable men who simply did their best for the local community. However, their nervousness was obvious and palpable and despite their official positions, they made poor witnesses, invariably treading a fine line between perjury and the threat of reprisal.

The major defence argument, however, was that the evidence was entirely circumstantial.

"There is not one shred of hard evidence that my clients were in any way responsible for the murder of Mr Jackson or of any other murder. The tape evidence merely shows that the defendants were annoyed at Mr Jackson; it doesn't prove that they were responsible for his death."

They also focussed on the evidence given by Konofski. "He was obviously a man driven by anger and revenge," stressed the lead attorney. "His so-called evidence is nothing more that an attempt to get back at my clients. His evidence is completely without foundation."

The defence lawyers returned to these arguments over and over again. They constituted the entire case for the defence in their summing up.

The judge advised the jury to reflect on the main points:

"Was it reasonable to assume that the defendants were responsible for Mr Jackson's death? And secondly, is it proven beyond reasonable doubt that the defendants carried out his murder." He also added, "The evidence provided by Mr Konofski must be treated with some degree of caution. I am instructing you not to disregard his evidence, but to ignore those elements of his testimony that were personal rather than factual."

Of course the Jury couldn't simply ignore Konofski's remarks. In fact they talked of little else in the jury room. It was if they too shared in Konofski's desire to punish the Mafia.

It took the jury took less than two hours to reach a verdict.

"Guilty … guilty of murder your Honour."

The judge turned to the defendants and read the sentence. "You have each been found guilty of murder. I have taken on board the arguments of the defence and therefore find the crime to be murder in the second degree. You will each be imprisoned for 15 years and without the possibility of parole."

Darryl Keogh felt the eyes of the defendants staring at him as they were led away. He breathed a huge sigh of relief.

Ingrid and Bill met with the District Attorney in his office immediately after the verdict was given.

"An excellent result," she said, addressing the DA.

"We are, of course delighted," he replied, as if speaking for the entire New Jersey populace. "The Police Chief has pursued these two over a number of years. We've been close to making arrests several times, but it's always broken down through lack of evidence."

"Nobody willing to testify," Bill remarked. The DA grunted as if acknowledging the obvious. "They're kingpins in the New Jersey underworld. It'll bring down their Mafia family and that usually means we can clean up some of the major rackets these guys have been running – and you guys can remove them from the FBI's list," commented the DA. He paused and looked intently at Ingrid.

"You may know this already, but the Police Chief, and the Mayor, are pretty annoyed they weren't kept informed by the Bureau."

"We are aware that we have some fences to mend. But it was imperative that we handled what we knew would be a difficult case entirely on our own," she replied.

"That's my gripe with the FBI, you always want it kept close and in my book, that often means you are acting outside the law," replied the DA.

Bill's lazy eye began to twitch. Ingrid was concerned he might say something they would later regret.

"There's one thing in particular that bothered me about this case," he continued. "The body, Joe Jackson's body – it was …"

Ingrid jumped in before the DA could complete his sentence.

"That's why we had a murder trial," she said, as if steering the discussion to a conclusion.

The DA nodded.

He was sure that Ingrid gave a hint of a smile as she closed his office door.